Fire from the Andes

FIRE FROM THE ANDES

Short Fiction by Women from Bolivia, Ecuador, and Peru

Edited and Translated by Susan E. Benner and Kathy S. Leonard

Foreword by Marjorie Agosín

University of New Mexico Press Albuquerque

First edition

For permission to publish or reproduce the material which appears in this anthology, acknowledgment is made to the following sources:

"The Legacy" by Carmen Luz Gorriti, translated by Kathy S. Leonard, first appeared in *The Antigonish Review* 101 (1995): 113–16.

"The Señorita Didn't Teach Me" by Bethzabé Guevara, translated by Kathy S. Leonard, first appeared in *Critical Matrix: Princeton Journal of Women, Gender, and Culture* 9.1 (1995): 107–20.

"Mery Yagual (Secretary)" by Mónica Ortiz Salas, translated by Kathy S. Leonard, first appeared in *Feminist Studies* 21.1 (spring 1995): 103–13.

"Bibliography of Short Story Collections by or Including Women Authors from Bolivia, Ecuador, and Peru," compiled by Kathy S. Leonard, first appeared in an earlier and much reduced version in *Critical Matrix: Princeton Journal of Women, Gender, and Culture* 9.1 (1995): 117–120.

"Prayer to the Goddesses," by Virginia Ayllón Soria, translated by Kathy S. Leonard, first appeared in *Calyx: A Journal of Art and Literature by Women* 17.3 (1997).

"Before It's Time," by Fabiola Solis de King, translated by Kathy S. Leonard, first appeared in *Xavier Review* 17.1 (1997): 23–27.

"Between Clouds and Lizards," by Gaby Cevasco, translated by Kathy S. Leonard, first appeared in *The Antigonish Review* 108 (Winter 1997): 105–7.

Library of Congress Cataloging-in-Publication Data

Fire from the Andes : short fiction by women from Bolivia, Ecuador, and Peru / edited and translated by Susan E. Benner and Kathy S. Leonard : foreword by Marjorie Agosín. — 1st ed.
p. cm.
Includes bibliographical references (p.).
ISBN 0-8263-1824-X. — ISBN 0-8263-1825-8 (pbk.)
1. Bolivian fiction—Women authors—Translations into English. 2. Short stories. Bolivian—Translations into English. 3. Bolivian fiction—20th century—Translations into English. 4. Ecuadorian fiction—Women authors—Translations into English. 5. Short stories, Ecuadorian—Translations into English. 6. Ecuadorian fiction—20th century—Translations into English. 7. Peruvian fiction—Women authors—Translations into English. 8. Short stories, Peruvian—Translations into English. 9. Peruvian fiction—20th century—Translations into English. I. Benner, Susan E. (Susan Elizabeth), 1957– . II. Leonard, Kathy S., 1952– .
PQ7816.F57 1997
863'.01089287'098—DC21

97-4746
CIP

CONTENTS

Foreword by Marjorie Agosín

When Kathy Leonard and Susan Benner invited me to write the foreword for this anthology dedicated to the dissemination of work by women authors from Bolivia, Ecuador, and Peru, I felt great enthusiasm, but at the same time, I also felt great fear. I felt enthusiastic at the possibility of collaborating in the effort to make the silenced voices of Latin American authors known, voices often destined for oblivion. The fear I felt stemmed from the realization that the feminist literary criticism of the past several decades has not given visibility to the women writers from these three countries. This oversight has occurred even while the dissemination of work produced in the 1970s and 1980s by women writers from the Southern Cone has proliferated, buoyed by their inclusion in anthologies, conferences, and courses dealing with Latin and Central America. Unfortunately, despite these occurrences, Bolivia, Ecuador, and Peru have remained somewhat anonymous, and their literature largely unknown.

We should ask ourselves why there is so much silence surrounding the women who write in these countries. In responding to this question, I am forced to speculate. During the 1930s, Latin American women's poetry enjoyed a singular period of prosperity in the cultural history of Latin America. We have the great authors of postmodernist poetry: writers such as Gabriela Mistral from Chile, Alfonsina Storni from Argentina, and Juana de Ibarbourou and Delmira Agustini from Uruguay. These four extraordinary women and their writing are perhaps the founders of the literature written by women in Latin America. Through their writing, readers have become familiar with women authors native to various South American regions. In the last several decades, however, greater awareness has been accorded to those women writers who come from countries strategically important for Europe and the United States. This is the case of Chile and Argentina, whose literature became known in the era of "the dirty wars" due to the participation of the United States in that conflict, as well as to the testimonies of the numerous exiles from those countries. Among the more well known authors from these countries are Luisa Valenzuela from Argentina, who is one of the most widely translated Latin American authors, and Isabel Allende from Chile. On the other hand, although numerous women writers from Bolivia, Ecuador, and Peru are actively writing, they have not yet entered the international literary marketplace. Indeed, one could say, broadly speaking, that the literature by women from these three countries is only now emerging, principally motivated by a powerful vision of social justice and an alliance with marginalized members of society: the indigenous groups, the destitute, the voiceless, and, of course, women.

Every anthology is by its very nature arbitrary, but therein lies its merit. The editors responsible for this selection have brought to this volume an ensemble of voices whose common denominator is the quality of the writing, not a false sense of regionalism or geography. Readers who long to find in each story a native or indigenous voice, or the stereotypical magical realism that has stigmatized Latin American literature, will be disappointed. These are not dominant elements in this current selection. Touches of surrealism and the fantastic do appear, similar to those used by great Argentine masters such as Jorge Luís Borges and Julio Cortázar, but the voices we find united here are far more similar to each other than to commercial literary figures. They are original, unique and innovative, rebellious, challenging—but they are also marked with a sign of sadness.

A general reading of the stories collected in this anthology shows that they possess a certain common characteristic: a strongly interior view of women's experiences and circumstances. This is to say that they are stories about looks, about gestures, about the experience of dwelling within and feeling as a woman does. I say "dwelling" because many of the stories use the room itself as a metaphor. It is not, however, a room used for creating, but rather a room where one merely survives. The stories unfold in dark houses, in closed rooms, in buses populated by thousands of people, where the narrating voice desperately attempts to relate the story to itself, to make itself "heard" in the cloistered space that the situation of women has delineated. We do not see in these texts the stories of openly courageous women, but rather stories of women plunged into an atavistic silence, women attempting to weave their stories, tying them together by the use of words and images, binding them to the cultural fabric that is as much a part of feminine mythology as are the narrations of Penelope and Scheherazade. These may not be courageous women, but they are women doing battle, thanks to the power of words.

Kathy Leonard and Susan Benner have compiled a valuable and important volume by rescuing these voices that have been hidden in the shadows. The complex and sophisticated images in these stories have been translated with great care and elegance. More than anything else, this anthology will be the beginning of the recovery and dissemination of the work by women writers from three countries that have been overlooked. We can only hope that their work will continue to be translated and included with the voices of other women writers from the Americas, whose work is now appearing at an accelerated pace.

Perhaps the most outstanding merit of these works is that they do not imitate; they cannot be compared with the familiar sagas of Isabel Allende, nor with the lost heroines of someone like María Luisa Bombal. These stories are original, motivated by a detailed elaboration of the language, which is rendered with care, elegance, and extreme beauty. Each of these stories is a unique discovery that allows us to penetrate the history of the weavers of the other America.

Introduction

Until very recently, the Latin American literature available to readers in English, or in Spanish for that matter, included works written primarily by male authors, many of whom came into the limelight during the "boom" of the 1960s and subsequently enjoyed great commercial success. Unfortunately, this time of increased exposure for Latin American writers largely ignored the region's women authors, who have remained hidden for many of the same reasons that women writers have remained in the shadows around the world. Relegated to rigid social roles as wives and mothers, few women throughout history have had the time, opportunity, or, in many cases, the courage to write, for writing has generally not been considered an acceptable activity for women. To write has been an act of defiance, an act of rebellion, an act that requires considerable strength of character. At the same time, women have often been denied the opportunity for education, relegating them to an illiterate or semiliterate state. These conditions have been largely universal and are well recognized, but in Latin America, a culture with strong traditional values, a very powerful Catholic Church, exacting social expectations, and severe poverty for a large part of the population, these limitations have been particularly forceful.

And yet, despite these obstacles, women in Latin America, like women everywhere, *have* written. In stolen moments while seated at the kitchen table, late at night while their children slept, in old age when the demands of family and society had diminished, women have written their hearts out and presented the world through their eyes, creating an ever-growing corpus of literature.

Since the mid-1980s, women writers from Latin America have experienced something of their own "boom," being published in numerous anthologies in English focusing specifically on women's writing, a reflection of the interest that English-speaking readers are showing in this work. Between 1990 and 1996 alone, more than twelve such anthologies were published in the United States.[1] It is now very common to find translated works by such authors as Marjorie Agosín and Diamela Eltit from Chile, Rosario Ferré from

Puerto Rico, Luisa Valenzuela from Argentina, Clarice Lispector from Brazil, Claribel Alegría from El Salvador, and Rosario Castellanos from Mexico, all of whom are now considered prominent writers. This welcome turn of events (since, traditionally, Latin American women writers have fared rather poorly in translation) has been encouraged by the academic, scholarly, and small presses that have begun to actively promote and publish women's work, including the University of Nebraska Press, which has a Latin American Women Writers series; the University of Texas Press, which publishes women's writing in their Texas Pan-American series; and the University of New Mexico Press, which also publishes primary and critical works about Latin American women writers.

Despite this recent widespread awareness and popularity of Latin American literature, several countries continue to be underrepresented, in particular, Ecuador, Bolivia, and Peru. Not a single anthology dedicated to the short story in translation by women writers from these countries has been published, and the region's women authors are rarely represented in other general anthologies of Latin American work. Nevertheless, it is extremely important that writing from these three countries be collected and disseminated because experiences in the Andean regions often differ dramatically from those in other areas. Through this collection we hope to acquaint the English-speaking world with the realities and perspectives of contemporary women from these countries, to bring their voices to a wider audience, and to share something of the scope and depth, the traditions and innovations, and the great delight of contemporary literature by women from these "forgotten" countries.

Acquiring the works in this anthology was not an easy process. One of the most difficult tasks initially was simply finding short stories by women authors from these countries, although Ecuador presented fewer problems than did Peru and Bolivia. Casa de la Cultura Ecuatoriana, which has branches in various Ecuadorian cities, has produced most of the anthologies that include women's writing, and this work was readily available. A newer addition to Ecuador's publishing scene is Abrapalabra Editores, which has published many titles by women authors and continues to do so. In Peru, an important source for women's writing has been Centro de la Mujer Peruana "Flora Tristán," an organization that holds annual literary contests for Peruvian women writers and then publishes the award-winning entries in book form. Several of our stories—specifically, "The Legacy" by Carmen Luz Goritti, "The Señorita Didn't Teach Me" by Bethzabé Guevara, and "The Red Line" by Catalina Lohmann—came from this source. Bolivia presented us with our greatest challenge. Not only did we have difficulty locating Bolivian women's short stories, but we also found very few published critical studies of such work. Although Bolivian literature has recently begun to receive more attention, few of the country's women writers have been included in anthologies, nor have many garnered critical attention outside of their own country.[2]

During the search process, several reasons for the difficulty in obtaining work by Bolivian women writers became clear. It is not that Bolivian women are not writing; on the contrary, many of them are actively writing and winning prestigious national awards. Publication, however, is difficult, and authors complain that they themselves must often finance the publication and promotion of their books, something that is prohibitively expensive for most Bolivians. Their country is one of the poorest and most isolated of the Latin American republics, with a literacy rate of only 75 percent, a factor that obviously influences the amount and type of materials published. With many people unable to read, and others unable to afford books, the lack of published materials is not surprising.

Ultimately, after many months of searching, we were able to acquire a multitude of stories from Bolivia, Ecuador, and Peru, but only after four visits to South America, hundreds of interlibrary-loan requests, a summer at Cornell University pouring over its library holdings in Andean literature, and countless intercontinental phone calls, letters, and faxes.

One of our main purposes in preparing this anthology was to make "new" work available to English-speaking audiences, so we chose to include only the work of living authors who were still writing as this anthology was being prepared. We are fortunate to be able to include the work of several of Latin America's most outstanding writers, as well as the work of other excellent authors who are just beginning to publish. Although many of the authors represented are well known in their respective countries, they will be largely unfamiliar to most English-speaking readers.

The final choice of works to include was difficult, and several factors influenced our decisions. Above all, we sought stories of high literary quality representing a wide range of themes and styles. We wished to include some works that help to illustrate the realities, struggles, and situations faced by women in these countries, as well as stories that reflect the general social and cultural realities of the Andean region. Yet, at the same time, we have purposely included stories that do not necessarily deal with themes of women and society, but which do reflect the range of creativity, innovation, and ideas of contemporary women writers from the area. We both read and discussed all the stories, and although we did not always agree on which stories to include, we finally decided that our differences of opinion and taste were a positive factor, allowing us to select a diverse group of stories that would ultimately appeal to a diverse audience. All in all, we believe that this extremely labor-intensive project has yielded twenty-four exceptional stories that represent a variety of literary styles and themes reflecting Latin American women's perceptions.

As with any such collection, a reader well versed in the literature of these countries will be able to find omissions. There are many other excellent and important writers from each of these countries who have not been included for a variety of reasons, including the length of their work, repetition of a theme, or a poor fit with selected stories. Among those writers not included who are beginning to find their voice and gain recognition are Bolivia's Gaby Vallejo, Velia Calvimontes, and Roxana Selum; Ecuador's Gilda Holst, Lucrecia Maldonado, Yanna Hadatty, and Natasha Salguero; and Peru's Carla Sagástegui, Viviana Mellet, and Mariella Sala. The excellent work of these writers must, unfortunately, be left for future anthologies.

Western civilization should be perceived as a reflection of a variety of voices of human experience, and we hope that this anthology will be an important contribution to the growing body of work available to readers of English who have previously been unaware of, or have been unable to appreciate, the voices of Latin American women due to the unavailability of such work.

We believe that this anthology will be of interest to general readers as well as to scholars of Latin American literature (men as well as women) who are interested in expanding their knowledge or using these literary works as research tools. The anthology will also be of interest to professors and students in courses dealing with Latin American literature in translation, comparative literature, ethnic studies, and women's studies, all of which are being promoted and developed at U.S. universities. In keeping with this intent, we have provided a more lengthy biography for each author than is traditionally found in anthologies, and we have also included a complete, up-to-date bibliography of primary and secondary sources for each author. In addition, an extensive bibliography lists sources that include short stories by other women authors from Bolivia, Ecuador, and Peru, and it is hoped that this information will promote further study and wider reading of these women's work.

NOTES TO THE PREFACE

1. For a complete guide to short fiction by Latin American women published in translation since 1945, see Kathy Leonard's *Index to Translated Short Fiction by Latin American Women Authors*, Greenwood Press.

2. Alice Weldon's dissertation (University of Maryland, 1996) "In Reference to the National Revolution of Bolivia: Three Novels by Women," is one of the few works dealing with Bolivian women authors. It details the work of Yolanda Bedregal (*Bajo el oscuro sol*), Giancarla de Quiroga (*La flor de "La Candelaria"*), and Gaby Vallejo de Bolívar (*Hijo de opa*).

Acknowledgments

This anthology would not have been possible without the help of many people and sources, and we would like to recognize them.

Susan Benner wishes to express her deepest gratitude to all of her family in Ecuador, and especially to María Agusta Calle Andrade, Juan Meriguet, Alexandra Borja, Fernando Calle, and Marta Sánchez Andrade, all of whose help was crucial to this project. Deepest thanks to Daniel Calle Andrade for his support and for sharing his country and his heart. She would also like to thank Iván Egüez for his generous assistance and interest in this undertaking, and to everyone at Abrapalabra Editores in Quito for their help.

She is also very grateful to the numerous people who generously opened their homes and hearts to her during her travels throughout the region researching this project: Yvonne Macasi León, Mery León, María Cecilia Menz, Rosa María Castillo, and Daniel Infante. And special thanks to Mónica Menz and José Iturrios for editorial assistance, tape transcriptions, advice, and friendship.

Kathy Leonard would like to gratefully acknowledge support from the following sources for their help in making her contributions to this anthology possible: Iowa State University, for the granting of a Faculty Improvement Leave, which provided uninterrupted release time to complete work on this project; and the Cornell/Pittsburgh Consortium for a Research Fellowship/Visiting Scholar appointment to Cornell University, which allowed access to the extensive collection of Andean literature housed in Olin Library. She also offers a very special thank-you to Michael Porter for his patience and support throughout this entire process, and whose absolute ignorance of Spanish proved to be not only surprisingly helpful, but also an essential factor in his abilities as a reader and editor of all the translations and other materials.

We both would like to thank the staff at Inter-Library Loan at Iowa State University for their courteous and efficient handling of hundreds of requests, and Mariella Sala and the staff of Centro de la Mujer Peruana "Flora Tristán" for permission to translate and publish several of the stories included here, as well as for help and suggestions for acquiring other work by Peruvian authors. We are also grateful to Oscar Rivera-Rodás for his help with contacts in Bolivia in the initial stages of this project, to Michael Handelsman for his early work with Ecuadorian women authors, and to David and Charlotte Bruner for their advice and encouragement. Finally, we offer our most sincere gratitude to our editor at the University of New Mexico Press, Dana Asbury, for believing in this project, and to the authors whose work appears in this anthology, for their enthusiasm and cooperation throughout the entire process.

As this anthology is the product of a collaborative effort, we have listed our names as editors in alphabetical order, as is customary.

BOLIVIA

Virginia Ayllón Soria

Born in Bolivia in 1958, Virginia Ayllón studied literature and sociology at the Universidad Mayor de San Andrés. Although she considers herself a literary critic and essayist, her preferred form of writing is the narrative. She writes a regular column for the magazine *Sopocachi*, has published several articles in newspapers and magazines in Bolivia, and is coauthor of two bibliographic works, one concerning Bolivian women from 1986 to 1992, and the other dealing with the history of Bolivian cities.

Ayllón's most recent publication, *Búsquedas*, a collection of short stories and poetry, is an effort that reflects her search for self. The book's thematic content revolves around women, because, says Ayllón, "I am a woman. I am convinced that because women's existence in society varies so dramatically from men's, that the literature we produce is very different from what men produce: neither inferior nor superior, simply different. I grew up reading women's literature, especially narrative, and it has greatly influenced me."

Ayllón's stories often reflect urban life and the daily dramas that unfold in the cities, with particular attention paid to women. Her story "Prayer to the Goddesses" deals with the situation of poor women living in large Bolivian cities. Although the protagonist's ethnicity is not identified, she is most likely a *chola*, a woman of mixed heritage, judging by her laments to indigenous goddesses. A woman of very humble circumstances who must work at whatever is available to her, she believes she has complied with all of society's rules, and she is unable to comprehend why she has been completely abandoned by all the higher powers she was taught to believe should protect her.

Violence against women, with its many manifestations, is the central theme of Ayllón's story, which portrays a system that cannot protect or provide for its weaker members, who are abused not only by their own government, but also by the men who are closest to them. The protagonist of the story breaks with the usual silence surrounding women of her circumstances, but her cries for help are in vain: she is forced into the ultimate form of subjugation in order to survive. Ayllón says that one of her principal motivations for writing this story was "To rescue some of the goddesses—hidden by a patriarchal religion—goddesses which still exist within the indigenous cultures of my country. The parallel with Greek and Roman goddesses was made in order to patent what the patriarchy has stolen from us: our female deities. What differentiates this story from others which have the same plot is precisely the presence of these goddesses, the majority of whom are unknown."

Ayllón has worked in a variety of capacities researching the condition of Bolivian women. She currently works as a researcher in La Paz, investigating the plight of women prisoners and violence against women. She has recently completed a project investigating the presentation of women subjects in the narratives of Bolivian women authors. Portions of this study have been published in a feminist supplement titled *Equidad*.

1. All quotes in author's biographies come from personal interviews or correspondence with the authors.

PRAYER TO THE GODDESSES

Virginia Ayllón Soria

> Zeus expelled the matriarchal goddesses and the Titans
> from Olympus, and to maintain his authority, he used force.

There's nothing else left, my dear *señoras*. Listen to my plea. Don't abandon me. For so long I've prayed to God, to Jehovah, to Saint Martin, and to the Señor of the Column, but nothing, nothing happens. Everything stays the same; not a cent for food, there's nothing to protect me from the cold (who hid them, then, Mother Isis, lady of bread; Mama Curaj, Mother Kallawaya of the ekekos). My babies have been abandoned, and that devil José beats me whenever he feels like it. And me, begging and begging for the gods to help me, but nothing happens.

Of course, I didn't just pray and pray, I also did my part; those Gods know how I did my part! (And surely you, the Erinias sisters, who steer the helm of necessity, you knew it.) First I went off to sell oranges for three meager *pesos*, then I scalped tickets outside the Universe Theater, where, to make things worse, the police caught me and stole all the money I had earned. (Who hid you from me, Goddess Demeter? The legislator?) Then I worked as a washerwoman going from house to house in rich neighborhoods so they could tell me "no" over and over again, or where they let me wash mountains of clothing in exchange for so-called food; then I worked as a maid where the mistress hit me and the children looked at me strange and the master touched me strange or entered my room at night to do strange things.

But I've already done it all, I even collected trash to see if I could find something to eat. And I put in my prayers, day and night, clasping my hands together to keep them from stealing, sealing off my mouth and my rage to keep from drinking and drinking not knowing where I'll end up. I go to church every Sunday, and I take the children, too, doing everything that the Bible says to do, that the Priest and the sisters say to do, but nothing happens. José keeps beating me, making me have babies, telling me I'm ugly and stupid, good for nothing, coming home drunk and mistreating my babies and turning everything upside down. My father and brothers playing dumb. Sure, by stealing they can just barely get by and when they feel like it, they throw it in my face that life is like that for a woman, so I should just resign myself to it.

My blessed mother always brought you offerings, Mother Pachamama, (and to you, too, Goddess Gea, Heras or Era, mothers of everything), she prayed to you for me, too, don't abandon me now. Maybe, dear Virgin of Copacabana, maybe having been baptized in your church hasn't helped me at all. Weren't you supposed to always take care of me? If even my godmother has forgotten about me, don't you leave me, too. Pulimama, Goddess Kallayway with the beautiful veiled brown face, you who protect the innocent and the good, help me.

I haven't lost all hope, I take inspiration from you, Goddess Kallaway Pacharaqarey, matron of the dawn, matron of hope and beautiful clothes, of change, of transformation, of complexity, of constant rebirth.

If those gods have abandoned me, all of you, women like me who know how one suffers in this world, you know that we are born into misfortune, don't reject me.

You know that we women draw strength from wherever we can so we can go on living, you know we don't abandon our dreams even when everything conspires to crush us. You know, my mothers, that bringing children into the world gives us the strength to go on and on, like Cuña, the Chirguana goddess who continued the proliferation of her race after her people were destroyed.

That's why, my mothers: Tiiti, goddess of snow, Waire, goddess of hurricanes, Yazi, goddess of the moon, Aqarapi, goddess of the rain and the wind, Achalya, queen of love and sex, Quesintuu and Umantuu, beautiful sirens of Titkaka, don't leave me now, now when I begin to walk the sinuous path of surrender and attempt to sell the only property left to me.

Translated by Kathy S. Leonard

Yolanda Bedregal

Proclaimed "Yolanda of Bolivia" in 1948 by "Gesta Barbara," and "Yolanda of America" by the Argentine Society of Writers, Yolanda Bedregal is a poet, novelist, short story writer, and sculptor.

Bedregal was born into an artistic and intellectual family in La Paz in 1916, and her parents, Juan Francisco Bedregal and Carmen Iturri, greatly influenced the trajectory her life would later take. She studied fine arts at the University of San Andrés, later becoming a professor at the same university, teaching courses in aesthetics and art history. In 1936, she traveled to the United States as the first Bolivian woman to receive a scholarship to study at Barnard College.

Bedregal's literary career began when she was very young, even before she knew how to write. "I started by making up little verses, and then later, during my adolescence, I wrote 'little books' in my school notebooks; not even my father suspected. For one of his birthdays, I left a notebook beneath his pillow, with what would later become *Naufragio*." *Naufragio*, her first book, was published in 1936 without her knowledge when she was studying in the United States. "When I was studying in New York, I received the book, already edited and in print; it was a very moving experience for me. I never would have confessed to my father that I wrote, because once, in a conversation with his friends, the most important intellectuals of the time, I heard him say that he didn't care if his sons were writers, but a woman writer in the family, never!"

Despite this initial lack of encouragement on the part of her father, Bedregal continued to write and quickly became one of Bolivia's most important authors. In her long literary career, she has published more than sixteen books, over fifty articles dealing with the history of art, written for children, as well as articles dealing with pedagogy, religion, myths, folklore, and Aymara and Quechua folk art. Many of her short stories and poems have been translated into various languages and included in journals and anthologies in the United States and Europe.

Bedregal has received numerous awards for her writing and activities dealing with the dissemination of literature in her country: the *Premio Nacional de Poesía*, the *Premio Nacional del Ministerio de Cultura, Honor al Mérito*, the *Premio Nacional de Novela "Erich Guttentag"* for her novel *Bajo el oscuro sol*, and most recently the "*Condecoración Franz Tamayo en el grado de Gran Cruz*," awarded by the *Prefectura del Departamento de La Laz, Bolivia*, in 1995. She has also represented her country in various international congresses and was designated as the Bolivian ambassador to Spain.

Critics have described Bedregal's work as atemporal, containing traces of mysticism and surrealism, especially in her poetry. These elements are also present in "The Traveler," a story which Bedregal says is based on an actual event. "During a trip, I had a fortuitous meeting with a painter who showed me a painting which seemed to be my portrait. The story contains real events to which I added fantasy." The story reveals the musings of a dead woman, who reflects on the inexplicable nature of events that took place in her life, and then witnesses the strange circumstances of her own death. Rather than experiencing death in the traditional sense, the narrator finds herself replaced by "another" who resembles her, who occupies the space she left behind.

Yolanda Bedregal currently lives in La Paz, Bolivia, with her daughter Rosángela, and continues to be active in literary organizations.

THE TRAVELER

Yolanda Bedregal

I died on the eighth of June, the last date entered in my diary, but my agony has lasted longer. Anyway, my death is still fresh, like a freshly fallen fruit. I watched my funeral with the consternation or indifference of the curious who witnessed it. I protested; I tried to explain that I was alive, but no one took notice of me. They pushed me aside, they crowded together, forcing me to levitate so I wouldn't be crushed. I insisted until the last moment. They carried me to the cemetery in a box. They threw dirt over me. I'm not dead, however. Any certificate of death is false.

I exist. I am, and I can relate in minute detail what happened to me, what I did and what I felt during those days. On the thirteenth of this month I'll be twenty-eight years old. I travel frequently with the theater company, and I also write librettos for them (I don't know if I do it as a diversion, as a compulsion, or to compensate for my dislike of speaking). I have had to deal with people of sensibility and people who were brutes. I shared with all of them, I understand them all equally well. I don't know which group I belong to.

Not long ago, we left the Old Continent to tour South America. During that time I was invited to a conference for writers in Brazil. I went unnoticed there; a number of delegates spoke with erudition, but none of them mentioned what I believed to be fundamental: the importance of ethics in writing. My notes remained in their folder. I was inhibited by the fear of words, the undisguisable vanity of the speakers, the suspicion of finding myself alone. I never stood behind the podium. I was left with a sin of omission on my consciousness, and also with the feeling of freedom for not involving anyone in my doubts; by being detached from everyone, but affectionately detached.

At the end of the conference, part of the program included an excursion to Brasilia. Since my watch never works properly, I missed the plane that was carrying the group to São Paulo. I therefore remained at the hotel; later I went out to wander around, either walking or riding the cable car. While looking at the group of diverse passengers, I experienced something (perhaps the result of my professional transformation where I interpret characters and episodes which are anachronistic), I saw them being progressively transformed, or in reverse, like a movie being projected backwards. The large, coarse man who was holding a roll of wires was converted into a little boy embracing his multicolored ball covered with little ducks; the voluptuous, talkative mulatta became emaciated, old, and sad; the impeccable young man who was seated, playing with a gold pen on his elegant briefcase, was converted into a shady individual manipulating a suspicious-looking instrument into someone else's strongbox; the plain girl wearing a white smock turned into a seductive woman. And so on, in turn, a series of transformations, until we reached the final stop in the suburbs. When I was getting off, I nearly bumped into a couple locked in an embrace under the protection of a luxurious tree . . . and felt a sudden nostalgia when moving away from them. . . . To be the tree or to be the woman in love who was being kissed. Being alone in a crowd awakens within me feelings of love, of community, of death. . . . I wandered until dark, expectant, disoriented. When I passed by a discrete cafe, its appearance tempted me.

While I was being waited on, I scanned the art exposition on the mezzanine. A painting with strange hues of gray and cadmium powerfully caught my attention. It was me! Or was it my reflection in the glass? Bah! This modern art. . . . I continued to examine it.

At that moment, someone sat down next to me and a firm hand was placed over the back of mine, making it a prisoner. Without subterfuges, a persuasive masculine voice said: "Do you like it?"

"Like it? I don't know. I find it . . ." I was going to answer, but should I answer so directly to a stranger, I wondered.

"You must come to my studio, it's nearby, you've been there."

I told him that he had the wrong person, that I was only passing through. But I allowed myself to be led. All we had to do was cross the little terrace with flower pots, then cross the road. On the corner next to the cigarette stand there was a stairway that led to a passageway. He went ahead and pushed open the last door. "Come in. I'll show it to you right away." What was he going to show me, this pale man with beautiful green eyes whom I was obeying?

The spacious room, with a recessed skylight, smelled like turpentine and oil. There was a sofa, two or three tables, a bookcase, earthenware pots, frames, and wooden bowls. A suggestive atmosphere, mysterious.

He opened a corner curtain and dragged over an easel, choosing the best light for the painting that he immediately produced. In the background of the scene were a bridge and a street light, barely outlined, and a yellow figure of normal size. He was attentive to my long and silent stare. "What do you think of it?"

"Strange. It looks like me," I responded.

"Looks like, no. It is you," he insisted.

"We've never seen each other before," I objected.

"I have. I saw you once, just like in this canvas. When I was just about to finish it, you got up and left. A little while ago, some impulse pushed me to go to the café, and that's where I found myself. Do you understand why I was so brusque? Forgive me. Unexplainable things happen to me."

At my request, he related a simple example. He has a habit of taking notes, and before leaving his country, while he was standing on the dock, he had sketched a sleeping child holding a red teddy bear. When he was getting off the boat, the first thing he saw on the dock was the same child in the same position, except that, having been run over by a motorcycle, the child lay there dead, his chest and little arms covered with blood.

"Coincidences," I said. "So many children, so many ports in the world."

"For a painter's eyes, there are never two things alike. Light, form, color, attitude, and essence are unique, unmistakable."

I made him notice that, as an actress myself, everyday situations or any person, when isolated within the frame of a scene, appear more exclusive. (The truth is, what had happened in the café and this painting . . . made me doubtful.)

I asked him if he had used a model of my type for the painting. He denied this. "The canvas was destined to be used in another project, but when I took up my palette," he explained, "without hesitating in my brush strokes, the portrait turned out to be exact. Only here, on the bridge, Mephistopheles, who was accompanying you, escaped from me, and I was just about to paint him."

A vivid memory from six months ago assaulted me; I was in my dressing room, concentrating on rehearsing my part in front of the dressing table, when a devil appeared before me. I jumped with fright! But it was an actor, reflected in the mirror, who was dressed to give the last speech of *Faust*. I sent him away, angry. I was wearing the yellow dishabille, as usual.

"Artists are incomprehensible beings," I thought.

"Don't think that I live with beings that are invented by me; they exist in reality. (Pointing) Those blue horses with palm tree wings, those bulls with serpent feet, the roosters with the moon's fire on their crests that you see on the canvas, they really exist."

His attitude changed, he threw aside the color-stained rag that he was squeezing. "Excuse me. I haven't even introduced myself; Anton Bruck, at your service."

Perplexed, words escaped me. The circumstances were not such that I could assume he was making a joke. Anton Bruck, my brother's name, as it was engraved on his tombstone. Overcoming my bewilderment, I smiled at him: "We have the same surname, my name is Marion Bruck."

"What a happy coincidence, my real name is difficult to pronounce, so I changed it. It wouldn't have made a difference if I had taken the name of Tot, Mack, Flix, something short, without pretensions, easy to forget, remember, or confuse."

We were silent for long minutes. We sat down and he offered me an orange; we removed the fruit bowl from the table, he moved a painting closer. "These oranges are more delicious than those that come from the market, they give off an aroma of orange blossoms. I've tasted their juice from the ripening seeds, before they fully mature. I've touched their sap on the branch where they were hanging. Can you smell it? Eat some."

I confess that his incoherences didn't surprise me because I often keep my own quiet, out of cowardice, or I relate them innocently to someone I don't know. I asked him if he fed dead still lifes to his friends.

"That's what they call them, but they're alive. No. I mean, yes. I feed my friends . . . whom I don't have. Perhaps you, at this moment, and never again," he emphasized the last sentence, underlining it with a premonitory tone while looking at me strangely.

I extended my hand; the fruit jumped off the painting and accommodated its dome of frozen sun in my palm.

Why am I relating this story since it has no relation to my false death? Perhaps because of the naturalness with which everyday miracles occur.

Let's return to the beginning. I died on June eighth. Our company's tour continued to Paraguay, Argentina, and Bolivia. In Bolivia, a group similar to ours was waiting; they sent us to private homes for lodging. I was sent to a family educated in the European tradition; we only gathered pleasantly for breakfast. One night, after our performance, my colleagues accompanied me to my lodging located on a peaceful street that ran perpendicular to a main road. I waited until the car had turned the corner as we waved good-bye to one another.

I was getting ready to open the main door when I noticed that I had forgotten my scarf with the key tied to the fringe. I ran, trying to catch the car, but it was already far away. Should I ring the bell? Better not to wake my hosts. I would go to a hotel and leave them a note for tomorrow.

I retraced my steps. In front of the door was a shape. I stopped. Mine? I compared my clothing, my hat, my suitcase.

The woman who was standing there deposited her luggage on the ground, she took off a glove, she felt for the lock; she pushed the left door and carefully pulled on the other one, just as they had advised me to do so as not to make noise. I imagined the closing of the partition on the second floor. From the sidewalk on the opposite side of the street I saw the light come on in the room. Mine. She, the other one, put her coat on a hanger, just as I had done. She hung it on the handle of the window; she left her hat on the dresser, removed her hairpins and shook back her loosened hair. She disappeared for a moment. I then saw her silhouette wearing a bathrobe. From the shadows cast by the lamp, I could tell that she was seated at the desk where every night I would write in my diary. It was the seventeenth of June, and I don't know if that date was written by her or by me.

Meanwhile, in the middle of the street, whipped by the winter plateau winds, I was freezing. A cat jumped over the wall behind me, landing with a riverlike whisper on the pavement. A woman wearing a black cloak passed, dragging a bundle of branches that seemed to be lifted by skeletal hands. The street brightened with intermittent flashes. Loose bundles of wires swung in the air, behind them rose a snow-covered mountain, and I remained immobile, below a sky riddled with pins. The overall impression was like that of a desolate etching. The woman with the branches returned for the third time and she passed through me, as if I were air, without harming me. The illuminated window. . . . She probably continued to write. The night seemed to rejuvenate itself. I don't think I cried, but my face was covered with a cold frost that seeped into my pores and into my blood, and even into my bones. At that moment, she appeared on the balcony, her hands on her cheeks in my usual gesture. She seemed to be watching me intensely. She closed the curtains and turned off the light.

At that precise moment, an ambulance stopped on the street. "To the morgue!" I heard them order. A white coat descended, its floating sleeves grabbed me softly and placed me on the stretcher. Some beautiful green eyes and that same voice . . . "friends . . . perhaps you, at this moment, and never again. . . ."

Translated by Kathy S. Leonard

Erika Bruzonic

A native of La Paz, Erika Bruzonic was born there in 1962. Her father's family immigrated to Bolivia from Galicia in Spain, and her mother's family were Slovenians from Yugoslavia. Bruzonic claims that her punctuality, organization, and sense of duty come from her Slovenian roots, and her stubbornness from her Galician genes.

A linguist by profession, Bruzonic studied languages, linguistics, and translation in France from 1979 to 1987. She now directs the Bilingual Publication and Computation Center at the bilingual Calvert High School in La Paz, and in her "spare" time she studies law at the Universidad de San Andrés in La Paz. In addition, she works as a journalist, writing articles on culture for *Presencia* and *La Razón,* two of the most important newspapers in La Paz, and she is a frequent contributor and columnist for several literary journals.

Bruzonic is fascinated by the individual in all her complexity and all her contradictions. As individuals we are shaped and influenced by the culture and society in which we live, and yet as individuals we respond to those influences in very different and, for Bruzonic, fascinating ways. It is this mystery of individual character and how each person reacts differently to outward and inward experiences that she explores in her writing.

Bruzonic's stories are sometimes enigmatic and purposefully confusing, and sometimes stark, clearly drawn portraits. They often deal with tragedy and the darker side of human character, yet contain a touch of wry humor easily missed if the reader is not wary. Bruzonic prefers not to be confined by a setting limited to La Paz or Bolivia, a constraint she feels would stagnate her writing. Instead, her stories take place in various parts of the world: Argentina, Costa Rica, the former Yugoslavia, unnamed Caribbean islands, and in the case of this story, a place closer to home, Peru.

"Inheritance" is largely a personal history of Bruzonic's family, and like its fictional character, she grew up surrounded by women because, in her family, "the men don't last." She was raised by her mother after her parents divorced shortly after she was born, and she was brought up with the idea that women are all-powerful, that they can and must do everything. At times she is criticized as being "cruel" to the men in her stories, or for killing them off or making them into caricatures. She insists, however, that this is not intentional, nor does she wish to devalue men. Rather, she is merely writing from the point of view of her own family history, in which men were always transitory and minor characters. Unlike her fictional character in "Inheritance," Bruzonic is happily married to her first husband, who is still very much alive, and she is determined that she will break the curse that has dogged her family for generations.

> In literature, women, when they write, tend to confess things they have done and men tend to invent things they've never actually lived. The great adventures, Homer, for example, the epic novel, have been written by men, something which they would have liked to have lived. And the great stories of human relations have been written by women who have dared to actually live them and not just create them in their imagination. Women are more real because they write what they know. Men are more ideal because they write what they imagine.

INHERITANCE

Erika Bruzonic

She is descended from a hardy lot. From Nazaria on one side, the mother of ten or eleven children (her grandmother among them). Nazaria, the wife of two husbands; the first died leaving her still young and energetic, going about with her skirt gathered up in her arm showing just a few centimeters of her black boots—all that a young lady could show—as she ran the hacienda in God knows what spot of Cuzco, no one ever specified where. Nazaria, they told her, at thirty something, was a mature woman, and being one, she set out to find a father for her children, as well as a husband for herself. But she never forgot about her first one, in whose honor she built a small altar in one of the rooms of the huge house on her estate.

But Nazaria wasn't the first. Before Nazaria, on the most important side of the family, there was Matilde, her great-great-grandmother, who never drank water, only beer, and who told her children that from her they would inherit the water from the tap in order to quench their thirst and the paving stones from the street to walk upon. Also widowed young, she searched for another husband, found him, and was widowed for a second time. Tired of the whole process of loss—search—discovery—loss, she concentrated on her grandchildren, especially her granddaughters, whose faces she washed with oatmeal so that they would have lovely skin to help them catch one or two husbands.

Isabel, Matilde's daughter (and her great-grandmother), married a man she didn't even know, her mother having arranged for him to see Isabel for his approval at one of the choir practices at the Church of the Daughters of Mary. The approval given, six children were born from that union, among them her grandmother, Helena, the first girl born after four boys. "My little miss daughter," as her father called her. The great-grandfather died of Heaven knows what, but the widowed Isabel, a connoisseur of good food despite her diabetes, and an eater of hot spiced cat—yes, cat—found a Peruvian, "a smart dresser, a gentleman" in the words of a popular song of the time, and fearlessly married him, adding four more children to her brood.

Following in these women's footsteps, her grandmother Helena, the first daughter from the first marriage, eloped with a Slovenian immigrant, the son of Nazaria. They had four children and lived a happy life perhaps, or perhaps a not so happy one—no one ever gave her any details about that grandfather who was always enveloped in mystery, having died before his time in an accident in his adopted land, Cuzco. She knew even less about the second man in Helena's life, only that he had also died, leaving Helena alone and resentful, unable now to become pregnant and drink wine right out of the tap on the barrel due to her "cravings" and then collapse, always capricious, for a siesta beneath the dining room table, as she had done in her first marriage.

Her mother, named Milada, preferred being chubby to toasting her tender skin in the sun. The first daughter of Helena, born after two boys, she had the same luck as the grandmother, the great-grandmothers, and the great-great-grandmother. Milada's first husband (her father) passed on via divorce, that minor death so in vogue in this century and, in many cases, a great relief. Mario, the second husband, died of old age after a well-spent life, at least at Milada's side.

She carries in her Nazaria's strength and vigor, although there are no longer any haciendas to tend nor altars to create. But new challenges await: taxes to pay and rights to assert. However, she has Nazaria's effervescent energy, and from Matilde she has inherited her love of beer, and she carries the dignity of these women in her bones. Without having known more than two of the five, she knows for certain that they are all her and that she carries within her a part of each of them. And it is for that reason that she does not want anyone to continue after her: "Because enough is enough," she says, "enough of being a depository for old peculiarities and inevitable legacies." Perhaps because the power is in her hands, she has managed not to leave to anyone that which, little by little, they have left to her. But the rest is inevitable.

And so, knowing that she cannot avoid it, and in fact, knowing that she would not want to, she waits. Her first husband has already gone.

Translated by Susan Benner

Giancarla de Quiroga

Giancarla Zabalaga de Quiroga was born in Rome to an Italian mother and a Bolivian father, and moved to Bolivia when she was seventeen. She was deeply influenced by her Italian grandmother and her Bolivian grandfather, who would recount true stories of the past, stories which often seemed more fascinating than fiction. These grandparents helped develop her imagination and encouraged her ability to create stories of her own.

Quiroga began writing poems in Italian as an adolescent, and after arriving in Bolivia and learning Spanish, she began to write short stories. A friend encouraged her to enter a contest in which she won an honorable mention, and inspired by this success, she began to write more and continued to win recognition. She published her first collection of short stories, from which "Of Anguish and Illusions" is taken, in 1989, and her first novel, *La flor de "La Candelaria,"* in 1990. That novel was awarded an honorable mention in the prestigious XI Concurso de Novela "Erich Guttentag" in Bolivia, and in 1993 she won first prize in the national literary contest held under the auspices of one of Bolivia's most important newspapers, *Presencia*.

Quiroga studied philosophy at the Universidad Católica Boliviana and for many years has been on the faculty of the sociology department of the Universidad Mayor de San Simón in Cochabamba, where she has done extensive research on the condition of women in her country. Her understanding of the situations facing women is clear in much of her writing. Many of her stories are centered around women from many different walks of life—young, old, sophisticated and urbane, innocent and ignorant, rich or poor—who find themselves confronting an often harsh world that penalizes them for being female. Yet her characters, male and female, in facing the circumstances in which they find themselves, frequently come to sharp, stark realizations about the world and themselves, and often triumph through strength of character.

Giancarla de Quiroga's stories move between the mundane and the fantastic, with an ironic wit and an ability to expose the absurdity of many of society's conventions and of the frail human ego. In "Of Anguish and Illusions," as in many other stories, she presents with wry humor a panorama of eccentric characters whose foibles and eccentricities mirror numerous facets of the human condition, while making a powerful statement about creating a just and egalitarian world.

Quiroga is working on a novel, which, in contrast to her previous one, takes place in the present, and whose central protagonist is a young man. Through this novel she hopes to reflect the problems that affect today's youth. She lives in Cochabamba with her husband and three children, and in addition to her work on the faculty of the Universidad Mayor de San Simón, she also serves as Director of Inter-Institutional Coordination for the City of Cochabamba.

> I write for those who hope to find in literature other facets of human existence, especially for those solitary beings, women and men, who in reading hope to find a form of communication, or simply the pleasure of the text.
>
> Some, through their writing, look to create a form of transcendence, a kind of mortality, a way not to die completely; others seek resonance, that is, that the reader identify with what the author has written; García Márquez says that he writes so that "my friends love me." I feel happy if my readers are entertained, distracted, and if at the same time, they are able to capture the messages which, unconsciously, appear in my stories, so that we all might live together in a more satisfying and humane way.

OF ANGUISH AND ILLUSIONS

Giancarla de Quiroga

It's just chance, pure coincidence," Misericordia Gómez commented as she scrutinized the almanac, but her determination betrayed a hidden fear.

"Just a damned coincidence!" Alamaquio Escóbar, the retired schoolmaster replied angrily. "Just in time to spoil the party!"

"I think it's God's punishment. . . . Things were much better in the old days," Doña Purísima Arenas declared with a touch of nostalgia, and she began to recall distant deaths of family members:

"My mother died in childbirth, and so she went straight to heaven; my brother died in love, of a broken heart, in the spring; my father of pneumonia, in August; my grandfather died of old age, one day in winter; my grandson of a military coup. . . . May God keep them in His glory!"

Everyone had reached the same conclusion: death no longer arrived as a surprise or as the logical end of a prolonged agony. People died on their birthdays, only on that day, for no apparent reason, with a gesture of surprise that exposed their hearts, their heads, or their pocketbooks. Furthermore, people said the deaths coincided with the exact hour of the person's birth, unknown by some and which others attempted to erase from memory so as not to remain prisoners of permanent anxiety. But Death arrived inexorably and punctually, converting the birthday parties of skeptics into wakes, replacing the candles on the cake with funeral candles, substituting condolences for best wishes and mixing funeral crowns with birthday bouquets.

The poor did not fall victim to this coincidence, perhaps because they ignored their birthdays, because they died a little every day anyway, because no one paid any attention to their disappearances, or for some other unexplainable reason that nobody bothered to investigate. Children also did not die on their birthdays, thanks, perhaps, to their innocence.

People talked of nothing else in their homes, on the streets, or in their meetings; many suspected that such happenings had something to do with those perverse nuclear experiments or with the imminent end of the world, proclaimed in the town's plazas by furious, long-haired men from distant places.

The opposition assured everyone that it was a question of some sinister government plot that hoped to do away with all dissidents, yet the members of the party in power died in just the same manner. The authorities, who prepared the municipal elections, hoped to free themselves of such a fate thanks to their service to the party, but upon reaching their birthdays, they had to resign themselves to sympathy telegrams from the president and military honors at their burials.

In the café, people commented on this nightmare, hazarding diverse interpretations, but without referring directly to death, instead alluding to "the coincidence." One thing was certain: all those who died, died on their birthdays, but not everyone who reached a birthday necessarily died on that day.

The measures carried out by the officials consisted of immobilizing the hands of the clock on the bell tower with barbed wire, and there was an agreement on the part of the press to remain silent about the matter and to replace the date on the masthead with the names of the saints of each day, but only the most unpopular ones, the ones that no one would be named after, so as not to spread panic.

Private measures were reduced to naive schemes such as destroying clocks and burning calendars. Some people paid astronomical sums to notary publics to have the dates altered on their birth certificates, pretending that in this way they could fool Death, which nevertheless ignored all their tricks and arrived, implacable and punctual, on the precise day.

For this reason, people decided to suspend birthday parties, feigning forgetfulness, and everyone let out a sigh of relief if they survived the ill-fated day; nevertheless, when they awoke the next morning to learn of various deaths of friends and relatives which coincided with the anniversary of their birth, an obsessive fear began to gnaw away at them that it would be their deadly turn next year. In the midst of this collective anxiety, those survivors who were born in a leap year went about happily making four-year plans, becoming a kind of privileged caste and forming their own syndicate.

The infamous coincidence provoked very disparate reactions: there were those who recovered their childhood faith and began once more to frequent the church, which they had not entered since the day of their first communion. In apocalyptic tones, the parish priest, Friar Adolfo Benito, exhorted the stray flock that packed the church during the novena, the triduum, and the mass, to prepare themselves to die a Christian death, interpreting the mortal coincidence as an unequivocal sign of infinite divine generosity that granted a set period for an opportune repentance.

The well-to-do calmed their panic by building luxurious mausoleums, acquiring caskets with silver handles and engravings alluding to their business activities, and attending rehearsals of the funeral choir formed by dozens of angelic voices. Their morbid obsession reached such extremes as dictating their own obituary and assuring the presence of carefully selected orators who would recite the eulogy of their extraordinary virtues during their splendid funerals.

Some neglected their business affairs and urgently spent all of their fortunes, while others dedicated themselves to drink so that Death would surprise them as they were sleeping, or at least when they were sufficiently drunk so as not to know what was going on. Still others, despite the fear of leaving orphaned and abandoned posthumous descendants, gave themselves over to frenetic reproductive practices in order to mock Death by prolonging themselves in their children.

Having decided to live his forbidden dreams, Estalín Monsalvo took off on a trip to the Caribbean Islands in the company of his mistress and returned just in time, one month before the anniversary of his birth, to be pardoned by his wife and die a Christian death in her legal arms.

Lola Caracol, employed in the oldest of professions, wanted to celebrate her forty years of life frolicking in her bed so that posterity would remember that she had died as she had lived. She waited in vain for the fatal outcome to arrive, drinking champagne with her regular and occasional clients alike, but at the precise moment, the tension was so overwhelming that she became paralyzed and had to abandon her trade.

Doña Deidamia Luceros, known as the "virgin widow," longed to die in order to be reunited with her husband, whom fate had snatched away the day of their wedding some seventy years before. On her birthday she bathed in scented herbs, donned her wedding dress, placed the wax crown of citrus blossoms on her white head, laid herself down in her virginal coffin, and passed on to a better life with a placid expression on her face and infinite hopes.

The anguished wait for misfortune's hazardous arrival produced in some a desire to live intensely, sunk others in resigned apathy, and, in a few cases, awakened suicidal tendencies. Efemérides Ramos, for example, sick with unrequited love, declared before the mirror one day two months before his birthday, "I'm not pleasing death, I want to die when I choose!" and he shot himself with the rifle he used for hunting alligators. After his demise, everyone learned the truth: he hadn't been born when he thought, but rather two months beforehand. He wasn't born at seven months gestation as his mother had claimed, and the day he chose to end his life coincided exactly with the true date of his birth.

Against all advice, Don Washington Mamani, the rich miner, resolved not to forgo the festivities that he usually celebrated each year: "I want to die happy!" he declared to his guests, who attended the party dressed in black, whether for the formality of the occasion or to be conveniently dressed for the imminent mourning, no one could say for sure. The host offered up a magnificent banquet. He sacrificed a Christmas turkey early, roasted a whole herd of Dutch cows, turned young suckling pigs into fricassee, and topped it all off with rivers of foaming beer, aged wines, and *chicha* corn liquor well-fermented from the corn being carefully chewed and spit by young Indian maidens. Such extravagance had no precedent, and one guest, completely overcome, exclaimed, "Don Washico, you're throwing everything out the window!" This comment did not fall on deaf ears, and the host took it literally when he made the wise discovery that he couldn't take it all with him when he died. So, having no deserving heirs, and before the eyes of his greedy nephews who had been waiting impatiently to enjoy their inheritance, he began to toss everything he had into the street: food, money, furniture, silverware, and everything that could fit through the wide window in his living room. The guests suspected that the terror of death had gone to his head, but after vain attempts to dissuade him from such intentions, they all joined in, flinging all the household goods and wares out the window, hoping in this way to ward off bad luck.

Meanwhile, a crowd had begun to gather in the street. The neighbors and the city's poor, having become aware of the occurrences, began, amidst tremendous din and greedy struggles, to parcel out amongst themselves the booty that had fallen from the sky. In the process of these proprietary disputes, there were forty severe contusions and dozens of injuries, not counting the old man who lost his dentures, which were never found again.

Since they couldn't get the bulky furniture and the grand piano out, even through the balcony, some kind soul opened the doors of the mansion, which was immediately invaded by hundreds of beggars who finished up the pillaging with the blessing of the self-same owner of the house. The twelve strokes of midnight from a surviving clock found him collapsed and exhausted in his empty house, but triumphant, having won the battle against death.

No one knew if the feared demise did not occur because his hour hadn't arrived yet, thanks to his ostentatious lavishness of the evening, or if it were merely a happy coincidence. But many in the town followed his example, celebrating their birthdays in a spirit of desperate festiveness that they finished off by literally throwing it all out the window.

Upon celebrating his sixtieth birthday, Don Urkupiño Sánchez, the owner of hundreds of *coca* plantations, did the proper thing, and he became so enthusiastic that he hurled the family jewels through the window, ignoring the pleas and threats of his wife. Faced with the *fait accompli*, she reacted with such aggression that she bit his hand, upon which Sánchez, at the height of his worldly detachment, tossed her out the window. Luckily it was only a single-story house and his consort was received in the arms of a hungry mob who tore off her earrings and pearls and her velvet suit and left her in nothing but her slip in the middle of the street, sobbing inconsolably and fervently wishing for her spouse's immediate death, which, nevertheless, did not occur.

The townspeople divided themselves into two groups: some asserted that total detachment from material goods was what saved people's lives, since no one had died yet who had adopted the unusual ritual, now a daily occurrence. Others considered such behavior indecent wastefulness and a dangerous action that threatened the established order, and asserted that instead, anonymous charity and silent pious practices without exaggeration or morbid exhibitions were equally as capable of holding off the lethal coincidence, which, at any rate, should be awaited with dignity.

Among the former was Simón I. Morales, a loyal genealogy aficionado who had amassed a fortune endowing people with more noble and decent ancestries. On the anniversary of his birth, he decided to evade the curse by throwing out the window not only his riches, but also the family trees and portraits of colonial relatives; the beggars received these with open arms, recognized them as legitimate ancestors, and began immediately to weave imaginary family memories.

A pair of eternal lovers had postponed their wedding for twenty years due to economic reasons, but faced with the threat of impending misfortune, they decided to marry before their birthdays, planning to finance the ceremony and their future life with what luck would send them thanks to the terrified generosity of rich landowners. However, the mature and impatient lovers didn't get so much as a cooking pot or their wedding rings, and instead of the marital bed that would harbor their unbridled passions, all that fell from the window were a claw-foot bathtub and a heavy chamber pot made of silver from Potosí.

After a year of this nightmare, of wild, uncontrolled celebrations and delirious scenes in the houses, plazas, and streets of the town, there was no longer any doubt about the best survival strategy: only those who threw everything out the window were able to evade death's ambush, while those who did not do so died for no apparent reason.

Meanwhile, the poor, beneficiaries of all this forced generosity, saw their impossible dreams become reality, and after having legitimately accumulated the fortunes of others, they became rich and greedy and began to die on the day of their birthdays. Thus, they too resolved to celebrate their birthdays with the anti-death ceremony. In their recently acquired houses full of diverse styles of furniture, of colonial portraits and abstract art, of Persian rugs and silk sheets with someone else's monogram, they reproduced the scenes recently acted out by the former rich, who now lived in misery. The latter, overcoming their innate repulsion, found themselves obliged to stand beneath the windows of the *nouveau riche,* and upon occasion, if lucky, they were able to recover something of their possessions: a piece of silverware, a portrait of an uncle who was a bishop, their wedding bands, or a cot or two.

In the café, people stopped commenting on the fatal coincidence and, smiling ironically, spoke only of their obligated altruism and the collective generosity, thanks to which everyone's fortunes, upon changing hands and surnames so many times, were distributed painlessly and equitably.

One evening Josefino Amor, a teacher by profession and a poet by vocation, realized between drinks that when the day arrived in which the newly rich and the newly poor had their stomachs half-full and their houses half-empty, Death would stop visiting people on the anniversary of their birth and would return to its usual condition of surprise, taking into account only those dates and times that were written in the book of destiny.

Translated by Susan Benner

Elsa Dorado de Revilla Valenzuela

Elsa Dorado de Revilla Valenzuela's childhood years were intense and mysterious, linked to the stories, real and imagined, about Bolivia's mines. In her father's study she found and read books such as *El manual del minero* (The Miner's Manual), *El arte de los metales* (Metallic Arts), and anything else she could find that related to mining in Bolivia. This obsession carried over into her literary production, the majority of which deals in some way with this subject, an interest that few other Bolivian authors, and certainly few women authors, have shown.

Dorado de Revilla Valenzuela has ample material to draw from for her literature. She spent ten years living in the Quechisla mining camp in southern Bolivia, where her husband was working as the legal counsel for the Corporación Minera de Bolivia (COMIBOL). It was during this time that Dorado de Revilla Valenzuela wrote the short stories in the collection titled *Filón de ensueño*, which was published in 1977. "The Parrot," along with the other stories in this collection, shows a marked preoccupation with the daily events surrounding Bolivian miners, men as well as women, who work under the most precarious conditions, aware that their lives depend on uncontrollable factors, human as well as natural.

Dorado de Revilla Valenzuela says her interest in portraying the miners' lives was heightened when she viewed firsthand their indescribable sacrifice, how wives shared their husbands' danger, the fight for survival, and the emotion of the discovery of a new vein, its subsequent drilling and flooding, and the celebrations that followed. But it was perhaps the mines themselves, with their mystery, greed, and fertility, that motivated Dorado de Revilla Valenzuela to document the events suffered by the stoic miners and their loyal companions. In these stories, the author attempts to capture events that form part of the daily life of those who inhabit a mining camp, but events which are not always interpreted with the magnitude of their realism. Dorado de Revilla Valenzuela's stories are bitterly realistic; she has no need to add fantasy to what life doles out to these people, courageous yet impassive, simple folk who inhabit the bowels of the earth as well as the frozen peaks of the mountains, and who, no matter what might befall them, continue to believe in God without question or rebellion. With these stories, Dorado de Revilla Valenzuela demonstrates her sincere love of the earth, of the desolate Bolivian plateaus, and most of all, of her people.

Dorado de Revilla Valenzuela's second collection of short stories, *Las bacterias no hacen huelga* (Bacteria Don't Go On Strike) was published in 1994. She began writing these stories in 1980 when she was living in Bonn, Germany, where her husband represented COMIBOL and acted as an advisor to the Bolivian embassy. During the four years that the couple resided in Germany, Dorado de Revilla took courses dealing with mining technology, specifically the use of bacteria in depleted mines. This information influenced her second book of short stories, an indictment of advanced technology, which in various ways places humans second, removing them from their position as supreme beings.

Elsa Dorado de Revilla Valenzuela currently lives with her husband Dr. Hugo Revilla Valenzuela in La Paz, where she is president of the civic organization called Centro de Acción Orureña.

THE PARROT

Elsa Dorado de Revilla Valenzuela

The night is calm and clear. The stars light up, weaving luminous garlands; the moon casts its light softly over the mining camp. It's a night so full of brilliance that the hills are clearly outlined as if they were sentinels, ever watchful over the passing of time.

Chorolque Mountain, with an elevation of 11,000 feet, exhibits its shape, its solitary granite formation capped with snow, like an imaginary sphinx profiled in a clearing—obscured from the Andean night. From its rounded pedestal rise five visible faces: Acero Cruz, Chimborazo, Sagrario, Santa Bárbara, and Mina 7—Mine 7. It appears generous and arrogant, that ancient and legendary monarch of the ancient *Chicha* people. From the heights of its age-old dignity, it proudly contemplates the Cotagaita and Tupiza valleys, adorned with its subjects' heroic coat of arms and the many colors of its woods which contrast with the reddish clay columns of the Palala Gorge, resembling suspended cathedrals in the clear blue diaphanous sky.

How many generations of miners have perished in its interior? Picks, drills, and dynamite have pierced it thousands of times, subtly eroding pieces of its core. However, Chorolque, far from yielding, appears colossal, strong, and fertile, and impassively kills those who harm it. The insatiable monster, which continually exhibits in the ironic smile of the *tío*, the devil which resides in the mines, an anxiousness to drink from the inexhaustible source of miners' blood, the red fertilizer that nourishes the motherlode.

Spring wrings out the last drops of snow that doze in the foothills of the colossus, and by way of the steep path that leads to the depths of the tin mine, a group of miners sets out for their jobs to begin their work day. The lights from stationary lamps reflect off their goggles like strange glowworms, uneasy among the fantastic shapes formed along on the road that leads through the difficult terrain to the cavern in mine number seven.

Francisco Huayta, one more in the crowded line of stoic miners, laboriously climbs the craggy hill, feeling the fluttering of a cool breeze against his forehead. His painful travel becomes hurried now and again in search of the coveted card to mark the beginning of his forced labor, his check-in for the day's work. However, upon turning a bend in the road, he is amazed as he stands facing the majestic Chorolque, bathed by the whitish splendor of the moon, which capriciously gives it the appearance of a beautiful female breast, covered with some unidentifiable primitive lace, subtle, exciting. That strange revelation brings to Francisco's memory the image of a woman . . . a beautiful breast, stirring his thoughts, which hammer in his temples and make him awaken to the tremendous reality of his love for María, his stepdaughter.

When had this crazy adventure begun? He didn't know because he was unable to determine the exact moment. For him, María had been, up to a short time ago, a little girl. It seemed like only yesterday when she was playing with her rag doll, and it felt impossible seeing her now transformed into a captivating young woman. In his mind, that tragic picture painted by the unmistakable reality of the mine grew; his friend, Sixto Dávalos, crushed by an *aysu*, a slide, and his failing voice asking him to care for his wife and daughter. Francisco had promised to fulfill that wish.

In his simple and superstitious reasoning, Francisco believed that a curse had made him fall in love with Andrea, the widow of his dead friend. However, he had felt that he really did love her, and he had made her his wife. "Could it be?" he asked himself. "Could that possibly be true what they say about the curse? That the curse has made me fall in love, this time with María?"

The truth boiled in his mind: María, with the vigor of a seventeen-year-old, who suddenly had been revealed to him as a beautiful woman. He remembered how one night when he returned from work, he entered the room that served as the family's bedroom. They were sound asleep, and in the unconsciousness of dreams, María had flung the blankets off, leaving her body uncovered, her breasts erect, white and swollen, her disheveled hair forming a frame around her face, which in the drowsiness of sleep looked enticingly beautiful. He remembered how he had felt a fervent desire awaken within him as he stood near that young body, knowing she was forbidden to him, and with great effort he averted his eyes. Still, he felt the beginning of a heavy burden of painful emotions, which he hid to avoid the suspicions of his wife.

Buried in his thoughts, Francisco arrived at the entrance to the mine, and as if looking for solace for his troubles, he entered with a determined step, losing himself in the labyrinth of shadows and grotesque shapes silhouetted on the live rock.

The wail of the siren announces one o'clock in the afternoon in the Chorolque camp. In the sheer and arid terrain, the sun's rays scorch the wild and sparse vegetation, whose stunted bushes entwine their sharp branches, like lances, braced for an attack. Everything is dry, hostile, dusty; crouching, with their bodies bent and their hats covering their eyes, the *palliris*, the women miners, work at the foot of the mountain, their sledgehammers in hand, crushing piles of rocks, turning them into fragments bearing traces of minerals. The excessive pounding creates a strange melody, a counterpoint, a hard rhythm of painstaking skill in an exhausting struggle. Since the incessant pounding numbs the arms and weakens the lungs of the workers, only the strongest and the youngest can tolerate this work. Andrea, Francisco Huayta's wife, was a palliri until a short time ago, but her age and lack of resistance forced them to change her to the job of lookout in the area of rock slides, facing the foot of the mountain at Mine 7, a job commonly known in the simple language of the Chorolque miners as "the Parrot."

Andrea, at her observation post, looking out over the mountain, allows her thoughts to wander; her job is important, tricky, because the lives of the more than twenty palliris working at the foot of the mountain depend on her good eyesight. From the summit her eyes move toward the sky, becoming distracted by the fantasy-like shapes formed by the clouds . . . one of them looks like a small horse, another like a child's face . . . and so, between watching the sky and the summit, the afternoon passes by. A great restlessness invades the soul of the Parrot; for some time she has suspected something, and day after day her suspicions have been confirmed; she sees that Francisco is falling in love with her daughter María. She discovered it in his passionate looks that follow María and in the flirtatiousness with which her daughter accepts his silent tribute. A quiet rage overpowers the woman, and briefly taking her eyes off the mountain, she looks resentfully at her daughter, who, together with the other women miners, works as a palliri. Before, María was her pride and joy, but now she looks at her bitterly, jealously. Her youthful figure stands out in the group; María doesn't bend over to work. Her upright body is outlined, elegant, vibrant, her erect breasts swollen. . . . The Parrot returns her eyes to the mountain and thinks painfully that for her, death will not come from above, that she won't be crushed by a boulder, but rather by the ungratefulness of those she most loves in the world. Suddenly, a fine cloud of dust that begins to rise from around the mountain and a few timidly rolling stones announce the danger. She puts her hand over her eyes like a visor to see better, and she realizes that some huge rocks are about to slide. She yells with all her strength: "Landslide!" and her voice booms into the sunstruck afternoon. More than a warning before the avalanche of boulders, it is the anguished cry of a woman who sees her joy disintegrating. The palliris run to protect themselves from the slide; in a few seconds, a deafening noise precedes a dense cloud of dust near the job site.

Inside the mine, the lights on the lanterns seem about to go out. Their dim glimmers vaguely outline the emaciated shapes of the workers against the outcroppings of rock. Prometheus multiplied, chained to a job by need, a job that with time, effort, and the daily struggle quickly transforms even the youngest and strongest into decrepit old men.

Francisco Huayta was working the drill, boring into the hard core of the earth, forcing from his mind the premonition that he would die inside the mine. Like a bird of light his thoughts flew to the surface in search of sun and happiness. María was the reason for his happiness and his anguish; if any sense of loyalty bound him to Andrea, desire and passion pushed him toward his stepdaughter. He knew little about life; the only school he had known was the mine, his only mentors the old workers, who, during their minutes of rest, spoke to him about the world, about men, about the science of good and bad. But they had never taught him about passion, the feeling that now alienated him and engulfed him in the depths of anxiety.

Francisco, in his rudimentary understanding, sensed that life was not composed solely of work and harshness, the companionship of a woman, a salary of thin bread, and death; some other force that moves the world must exist: love . . . and it wasn't love that tied him to Andrea. First there was the obligation to his dying friend that forced him to join his life to the widow's, then, it was habit. Older than he, the woman was aging more rapidly and his desire had waned along with the appearance of her first gray hairs. True love was just recently awakening within Francisco, with a force that frightened him. His entire being cried out to life for the right to be happy, but he saw that the current situation was impossible. His hands tightened with impotence on the drill, his pain turned into a furious rage, and he violently attacked the vein, tearing away huge chunks of rock that piled up at the feet of the miner.

Around noontime, the work in the mine continues. A transparent ray of sunlight lights up a golden spot on the silver head of Chorolque; an unending stream of miners enters and leaves the depths of the colossus. Like a noisy swarm, the palliris continue their hammering. Facing them, Andrea, the Parrot at her lookout, fixes her eyes on the mountain, immobile, as if she lives only to yell "Landslide!" More depressed than usual, she is indifferent to all that surrounds her. The night before she surprised her husband holding María's hand, an act of intimacy that wounded her deeply. Like a hunted animal, she must choose between the love for her offspring and her feelings as a woman. Suddenly, her breathing becomes strained; she has made a decision: she will fight for her man. If death wrenched her first husband from her, it won't be life that steals Francisco. The lives of the women who work at the foot of the mountain are in her hands, among them, her daughter's. Silence on her part, at the precise moment, would mean death for the palliris. Furtively, she situates herself next to a trolley that has been turned upside down and is leaning against the side of the mountain. It will make a wonderful hiding place at the right moment. The hours pass slowly for the

Parrot; drops of sweat dot her forehead and hands. Frightened by the step she will take, but ready for anything, she looks at the workers with pity. They will be the innocent victims of her drama; it won't be her voice with the shout of "Landslide!" that alerts them, but rather death, which will speak to them with words of stone and blood. Black clouds cover the sun; the afternoon is already beginning to fade, a soft breeze can be felt. The Parrot has noticed that tiny stones surround the mountain. Holding her breath and drowning her screams in her throat, she watches the transformation of the mountain; except for the palliris, no other people are nearby. Suddenly, when the first boulder breaks loose and begins its threatening descent, Andrea runs to take shelter in her hiding place. The women become aware of the slide and run, terrified. An enormous boulder crashes into a rocky outcropping formed by mineral deposits and, without warning, bounces, smashing the trolley where the Parrot is hiding. The impact mortally crushes the woman in her refuge, pinning her with the weight of the boulder. Wild-eyed and bleeding profusely, Andrea realizes with horror, in the throes of death, that she has been the only victim of her infamy. Before closing her eyes forever, she looks up and hurls a curse at Chorolque, which stands erect and indifferent to the human drama, proffering its peaks to the heavens.

Translated by Kathy S. Leonard

Marcela Gutiérrez

Marcela Gutiérrez was born in La Paz in 1954. Her father was a soccer player, and her mother was a Bolivian diplomat in Lima for several years. From this mixture of perspectives and experiences sprang a writer with a sharp sense of humor and an ability to write with compassion for, and understanding of, people from many different walks of life.

Gutiérrez has worked as a journalist for many years, writing for *Presencia* and *La Hora*, two of the major newspapers in La Paz, and later co-directing the Bolivian literary journal *Siesta Nacional*. Although she did not begin writing creative works until the 1980s, her poems and short stories were soon published in *Presencia Literaria* (the newspaper's literary supplement) and other literary journals in La Paz and Cochabamba, and she quickly gained a reputation as a writer. In 1995 she was invited to take part in the Primer Encuentro de Escritores Chileno-Boliviano (First Chilean-Bolivian Writers' Conference) in Santiago, Chile.

For Gutiérrez, writing is an arduous task. She says that she writes her poetry under extreme emotional pressure: anguish, passion, depression, or a sense of impotence in the face of reality, and she writes them as a form of exorcism. In contrast, she sees her works of fiction as more controlled exercises in writing; nevertheless, she always seems to find herself exhausted, sick, and suffering from heart palpitations when she finishes writing a book.

Gutiérrez's stories show keen perception for the people and situations around her, often revealed in her narratives by interior monologues, personal diaries, or revealing conversations. Recurring themes in her writing include the situation of women in her society as well as that of youth, and the tensions between genders and generations. Many of her stories examine sexuality, particularly women's sexuality, and the struggle between the passions and pleasure of the body, and the sense of guilt and confusion created by society's strictures and taboos. Her stories are sometimes intense and tender explorations of a character's most inner thoughts and feelings. At other times she writes with an ironic and irreverent sense of humor, clearly exhibited in "The Feathered Serpent," where God himself cannot escape judgment, whether by the judge or Gutiérrez's barbed pen.

Gutiérrez continues to work as a journalist in La Paz and has recently finished two books: a book of poems and a book of short stories that explore the often absurd and bizarre reality of daily life in La Paz.

THE FEATHERED SERPENT

Marcela Gutiérrez

Plaintiff: My name is Lilith, and having been driven to legal recourse, I hereby make this accusation and recount the events as they occurred on the morning of November 17 of this year, when I was violently evicted, had my belongings taken from me, and was spirited away in an elegant Mercedes Benz along an unknown route. When we arrived at the final destination, I was beaten and blindfolded and left that way for some time, given only bread and water and kept in a wooden box, four feet by four feet. Under these circumstances I lost all sense of time until a week ago, when, eluding my tormentors, I was able to flee my prison, Sir, and bring myself before this court and before your person, in order to make my accusation against Mr. and Mrs. Kau, seated here, as having been the masterminds behind my kidnapping and detention, and against the three men seated here dressed in white, named Ariel, Ezekiel, and Uriel, for having carried out this crime, Your Honor.

Defendant #1: I have been called before this court, Your Honor, and I will begin with my name. I am Eve Kau, housewife, and you have asked me to recount the events that occurred after the day I left the operating room in the Great Mansion. Well, when I opened my eyes, I found a brand new husband lying next to me wearing a bandage around his ribs.

The Lord greeted me with a wide smile and ordered me to serve my companion with love and dedication and to be his wife for all my life, and I obeyed, and have acted in this manner since that moment, and our life has gone by happily and peacefully until the plaintiff, present here, through deception and scheming, convinced the Lord to drive us away, and since then we have suffered all kinds of deprivation.

Plaintiff: All be quiet and pay close attention to what I have to say. You, Your Honor, have ordered me to discuss the expulsion of Adam and Eve Kau from the Great Mansion, of which, according to the proceedings that their lawyer has deposited in your hands, I have been accused of being the perpetrator.

When the subject seated in front of me was given to me as my companion, for as everyone knows, Adam was my companion first, life went along quietly and monotonously in that marvelous garden. And there's no other place in the world that can compare. From the entrance carpeted with grass and lined with sweetly scented flowers, you can see the Great Mansion, so spectacular with its marble pillars. The burnished red copper door has a solid-gold door knocker, and above that, written on a large plaque also made of precious metal, is the name of the owner. In the evenings the breeze makes its presence known as it stirs the willow trees, which have grown to amazing proportions due to the influence of the fertile waters. The vegetation grows abundantly all year. That green forest along the banks of the river is a feast for the eyes of everyone who sees it. And it was in that gorgeous place where we both lived, along with the perfect beings, who are the bodyguards of the Lord and who threw me out of my home.

But you, Your Honor, order me not to change the subject, so let us return to the tale. As I said, I was the first companion of Mr. Adam Kau, and although my appearance has changed, as you know, Your Honor, I used to be very beautiful back then. But he was a very boring sort, too quiet for my tastes, and I tired of him.

We used to wander through the endless gardens singing songs of praise to the owner of the house, accompanied by the perfect beings who served as the chorus singing hallelujah in their soprano voices. Around six in the evening, at the sounding of Michael's trumpet, who at that time belonged to the royal guard, we would all retire for the night to sleep.

Defendant #1: When we were kicked out of the Great Mansion, far from the protection of the Lord, dark clouds formed over our heads, bringing with them the darkest night imaginable. The wind froze our bones and tangled our hair. A brilliant light appeared suddenly in the sky and for the first time we experienced lightning and the fury of the storm. Lost, we wandered a long, long way until we found a hollowing in the rock, which served as a shelter. Clinging to each other, my husband and I came to know cold for the first time, and we exchanged the leaves we used to cover our genitals for more substantial clothes made of leather.

Defendant #2: I am called before the court and first I will give my name, Your Honor. Adam Kau, no profession, at your service, Sir, and at the service of everyone else here, after that of my Lord, Almighty.

My first wife, Lilith, was always a flirt. As her husband, I tried to ignore this, and when we would go out on our evening walks, it was evident that she was interested in Gabriel, the marksman, who amused himself shooting salvos into the air in honor of the Lord. Lilith was constantly making eyes at him and sighing whenever she would pass by close to him. But I didn't worry about it since he didn't seem to know what was going on. Gabriel, the marksman, would look surprised and disappear, jumping lightly away, beating his silky, blonde wings.

Not having received any response, Lilith dropped her romantic advances toward Gabriel and started to take note of Lucifer, who was the most handsome of all. I, like a good husband, rebuked her every day of the Lord, and every night when we went to bed, I made her pray to the Lord to take away those terrible thoughts so she would appear more pleasing in the eyes of the owner of the Great Mansion.

Plaintiff: Please understand, Your Honor, that my married life with Adam Kau was terribly boring. As the companion of a man as strange as he, how could I not take interest in the perfect beings?

If I became interested in Lucifer, it was because of Adam, since all he wanted to do was pray every night—the only thing we did was pray and pray, night after night, and I began to feel desires to be desired by . . . how can I say it, by someone more impudent and daring.

So I have charges of adultery and abandonment of my home against me? Well, I was only looking for a better time, as I already explained. The first time that Lucifer held me, he was so rough that I swooned; it was different than with my husband, who almost never wanted to do anything with me because he was afraid of the owner of the house, who knows everything and misses nothing. So Lucifer and I started doing it as much as four or five times a day, on the river bank, in the river, beneath the trees, in the trees. . . . What can I say. . . . And when he suggested we escape, I didn't stop to think. I grabbed as many leaves as I could and fled with him, far away from the Great Mansion.

Defendant #2: When Lilith abandoned me, I was filled with sadness and I ran to the Lord and asked Him for another companion, Your Honor, because I needed, as you know, someone I could pray with every night. So I went running to stand before the Lord. This took place at the beginning of last year, one springlike morning with the birds chirping overhead while I thought and thought about my situation. . . .

I had suspected for a long time that my wife was having an affair with Lucifer, because I'd seen their initials, surrounded by a heart, carved into the trunk of one of the apple trees. And furthermore, she was obsessive about how she was dressed, constantly changing her leaves. But despite this, I felt as if someone had stabbed me in the heart when she left, and so I went to the owner of the house and asked Him for another wife, one less wild than my first one.

And, prompt and heedful of my wishes as always, He took me to the operating room in the Great Mansion, where He gave me sodium pentothal and I dreamed sweet dreams. When I woke up, I found Eve at my side. I was almost paralyzed with joy when I went to embrace her, but an intense pain in my ribs made me lie back down again. The Lord smiled; He rubbed His hands together and said, "That won't last." "No," I told him, "I feel like I'm missing something, a bone . . . I don't know. . . ."

Plaintiff: When Lucifer and I left the Great Mansion, we felt like two schoolchildren released for recess. We ran as far as our legs would carry us. I'm sure he was thinking the same thing I was: now we could screw as much as we wanted. He was running ahead of me; several minutes had passed, and we collapsed, exhausted. I looked at my companion's back and saw that his white wings were beginning to take on a dark gray color, and instead of being two beautiful sails, they were bit by bit turning into pointed wings. Terrified, I lowered my eyes, and then I saw the end of his back. . . . He wanted to say something, but only a grunt came out. I was scared. I thought, "He's changed. I'm going back to the Great Mansion and fall in love with someone else—and this time I'll be more careful about whom I choose."

Crestfallen and depressed, I returned, slithering, to the Great Mansion and took refuge in one of the huge bushes that grow along the left side of the river, and not, as the story claims, in an apple tree. And that is where I lived peacefully, without bothering anyone, until I was surprised by these men present here, Mr. Ariel, Mr. Ezekiel, and Mr. Uriel.

Defendant #1: It was my naivete which made me fall into the trap set by the plaintiff, Your Honor. We were free to do as we pleased in the Great Mansion, and we could eat whatever we desired and drink from the crystal clear waters of the river. The owner of the house had told us that fruit was good for us, and so Adam preferred the pear tree and I preferred that of the pacay. But the owner wouldn't allow us to go near the bush where Lilith lived. We were prohibited from touching that bush and we never bothered to wonder why, since after all, there wasn't any fruit growing there, just some strange, five-pointed leaves. But then one day Lilith insisted on giving me a stick made of the dried leaves from the heart of that plant where she lived, and, lighting it, she herself put the end of the stick in her mouth and breathed in the smoke. She told me it was a trick for distracting my husband, and that if I tried it, I would see everything in three dimensions and who knows what else, Your Honor. She insisted so much that finally I did it, and suddenly I was seized with an overwhelming sense of tranquility and I started to laugh uncontrollably. Adam came over then to see why I was laughing so hard, and I insisted that he try this wonderful herb that put you in such a good mood. So he tried it, and he too started to laugh so hard that the perfect beings came over, watching us in astonishment. Since it didn't seem wrong to us, we kept asking Lilith for more and more smoke, which she generously gave us. When we were rolling on the floor in pain from having laughed so much, it was she herself, Your Honor, who slithered away to tell the owner of the house so that He'd get mad and punish us for our disobedience. That, Your Honor, was how, in the middle of all the confusion, the owner of the house appeared with a sign which said: "Cannabis, leaves prohibited: stay away" and then He kicked us out.

Defendant #2: What my companion Eve said earlier is all true, Your Honor. I think that she and I have suffered the most damage in this, and in no way are we the masterminds of the serpent's, my first companion's, kidnapping. She has no proof we were involved. Furthermore, she herself has stated that it was the perfect beings who yanked her out of her bush, gagged her, and took her away in a Mercedes Benz.

Defendant #3: My name is Ezekiel, angel by profession and ex-marksman of the royal guard, and I am now called before the court in order to testify on behalf of my colleagues Ariel and Uriel and describe everything as it happened. I swear on the Bible to tell the truth, the whole truth, and nothing but the truth, so help me God, the Almighty, the Magnanimous, Owner of the House, and of every living being and everything else.

It happened that on July fourth, Adam was celebrating his son Cain's first birthday; we were invited, myself and my friends Ariel and Uriel, and around about eleven at night, when he had had a bit to drink, Adam began to grow bitter thinking about how he, who used to be pleasing in the eyes of the Lord, had been expelled from the Great Mansion. How was it possible that Lilith, the traitor, still lived there in that wonderful place! And he begged us to give her a good scare and teach her a lesson.

That is all I have to say in honor of the truth, for whatever purpose the Good Lord, the Almighty, the Owner of the House, sees fit.

Judge: The jury having deliberated for several hours over the issue in question, I now have here the verdict. Will the following people please rise: the accused couple Adam and Eve Kau and the other defendants, Ariel, Uriel, and Ezekiel; Madame Lilith may remain coiled up while hearing the verdict of the jury:

Adam and Eve Kau are found innocent of all charges, as there is no proof whatsoever of their involvement.

The gentlemen Ariel, Ezekiel, and Uriel are found guilty of being the perpetrators of the serpent's kidnapping, which they have confessed to, and they are hereby condemned to imprisonment for forty days and forty nights. These same gentlemen are hereby accused of having lied under oath in trying to implicate Adam and Eve Kau as the masterminds behind the kidnapping of the injured party. Furthermore, for trying to aid and abet the true guilty party, who is the owner of the Great Mansion, they are condemned to another forty days and forty nights of prison. Yes, it's all clear by simple deduction, since when Adam underwent surgical intervention in the Great Mansion, in that same operating room, the owner of the house made threats against the serpent. For this, He is hereby indicted to stand before this court and respond to these charges, and furthermore, to the charge of having used His magic for His own benefit.

Besides being sentenced to detention, I also sentence Mr. Ariel, Mr. Ezekiel, and Mr. Uriel to pay a fine of forty crates of red apples and forty crates of green apples to Ms. Lilith, for personal injuries suffered.

I have spoken.

Given, this twenty-eighth day of December of the present year.

Translated by Susan Benner

Beatriz Kuramoto

The word "Bolivia" usually conjures up images of high Andean mountains and the steep, cobblestoned streets of colonial La Paz. Yet the majority of Bolivia's territory is actually tropical. Santa Cruz, located in Bolivia's tropical region, is today the country's largest city, but for many years it was a kind of frontier town, an isolated backwater lost in Amazonian forests. It was in that city that Beatriz Kuramoto was born in 1954, the child of an Argentine mother and a Japanese father. It was a family where art, music, history, and reading were highly valued and encouraged, and Beatriz grew up feeling isolated and out of place in the provincial and closed society around her.

She dreamed of studying archeology but found herself pushed into dentistry by her family's economic necessity. Thus, at the age of sixteen she left home to study in São Paulo, Brazil. There she discovered a whole new world of theater, movies, and art—and also experienced for the first time the darker side of urban society with its cruelty, corruption, and greed. These experiences had a profound impact on her, and the tension between the idealistic view she had of the world and the world she encountered on the streets of São Paulo often surfaces in her writing.

After graduating, Kuramoto returned to Santa Cruz, where she now lives and practices dentistry. But she has forged for herself the space to write and create as well. Kuramoto is also deeply committed to the development of literature and culture in Santa Cruz and has taken this task on as a personal crusade. She is the founder and current president of the Writers' Society of Santa Cruz, and regularly conducts a series of writing workshops. She also writes frequent articles in local newspapers, through which she hopes to make people more aware of literature, arts, and new ideas.

Kuramoto's stories tend to be enigmatic and complex. They are full of insinuations without clear-cut answers, and endings which remain open to the reader's own interpretation. Her characters are generally complicated and full of conflicts, seldom likable but always capable of exciting the reader's interest. Her narratives are challenging and at times perplexing, and the story presented here reflects these tendencies. Time shifts between present and past with no clear demarcation, and voices mix so that one is sometimes unsure which character has spoken. This story reads something like a film script, with its clearly drawn and shifting scenes presented in a cinematic montage.

Kuramoto is currently working on several projects at once (her usual *modus operandi*, she claims wryly): a book of fantasy and terror stories for children, a book of love stories, and a novel that is still very hazy but which touches upon the theme of homosexuality.

> Because a woman at times has to be a mother, a wife, a professional, she has to separate out a space after all of that in order to write. She has to find a space after the children are asleep, when her husband stops bothering her. . . . For that reason, I think that women tend to dedicate themselves to poetry more. It seems to me that narrative requires larger chunks of time and greater concentration. So women have to learn to adapt themselves more than men when they write.

THE AGREEMENT

Beatriz Kuramoto

The man is tense, his passing feet sending the road spinning as they raise the dust, shaking off their inertia as they travel along the route. The mules used to be his guides in the beginning, later the memory of the path stayed in his mind as if they were still leading him; pure habit.

And on the edge of morning, the creatures of the night seem to be whispering their good-byes, filling the air with soothing murmurs. He is the only one who breaks the monotony of the moment as he makes the trip back, sweating, sad, with a look full of doubts and the deliberate desire to arrive as soon as possible.

It happened yesterday. Nothing would change his daily habits, but the stranger arrived just as he was preparing his daily *mate*. The newcomer left his dappled horse shaded beneath the tamarind tree and, without any greeting, sat down in front of him. In a hoarse voice he asked:

"Well . . . Have you told the girl yet?"

"Not yet, Señor. Look, I'm thinking she's still very young, and she hasn't even learned how to keep house yet."

Together they watched her swaying walk as she headed toward the kitchen.

The pang had begun to grow in his chest, a strange, new sensation, which bit by bit was beginning to undo his courage. Silently he offered the stranger something to eat. He began to sweat as he cut off a piece of beef jerky and put it in his mouth, and he knew it wasn't due to the warmth of the afternoon nor to the work of sucking the thick *mate* up through the fine silver straw.

For a moment he remembered how everything had been different once, before the day he returned after a long trip to hear his wife tell him:

"This is Filomena, your daughter."

Devastated, he never accepted her. When the child's mother died, he began the unjust job of rejecting the little girl.

Quiet and reserved, Filomena grew up without complaining. What lay hidden in her heart or mind when he surprised her watching him intently from a distance during the tired hours in the heat of the afternoon?

He never asked her.

One day he decided that she should go, and so he went to talk with Finsen. Finsen, the gringo with money, needed a woman companion.

Solitude is bad counsel in these mountains, he had told him, the day the gringo met Filomena and decided he wanted her for himself.

That day he had returned happily with a new team of oxen, which he hurried to release in the corral. It was the first time that she asked:

"Papá, who gave you those oxen?"

"I bought them," he said, with a certain air of arrogance while he watched her reaction. She looked at him as if she didn't understand.

"I bought them from Finsen," he added.

She said nothing, but he thought he saw her face fill with uneasiness. Later, as if she suddenly understood what was happening, her eyes flooded with tears, which wavered on the edge of falling. Her silent plea filled the still empty spaces of his soul and settled deep within him. Perhaps for the first time he began to feel that something struggled inside of him, overwhelming his misery and giving birth to an implacable anguish on the surface.

During the siesta, all that could be heard was the rhythmic sound of the *mate* being strained through the silver straw.

When the pain and guilt were at the point of becoming a solid mass in his chest, he said:

"No, what I mean to say is that she's not going, Señor."

"What? Don't give me your stories, I came for what is mine," the stranger said indignantly, and furious, he demanded an explanation.

"Perhaps you want more money? Well you know damn well that we had an agreement, and I'm not giving you one more cent!" His eyes glowed catlike, and his face turned red; then the man noticed that the stranger was trembling and it frightened him, yet despite everything he heard himself say:

"You can take the oxen team, I told you there's no sale here."

"Listen idiot, you should know you can't play around with me," Finsen growled as he dropped the *mate* and moved his hand ominously toward his belt.

"Don't move or I'll bury you," the man said in a calm, deliberate voice, and before he could defend himself, the stranger felt something sharp penetrating deep inside him. By the time he realized what was happening, the sun had spattered him with drops of supplication.

The man's fear disappeared when the flies began to arrive, harassing them both.

Silently, Filomena participated in the scene and in the funeral. When the moon hid beneath a black cloud, the man disappeared with the dappled horse.

Now he can just begin to make out the roof of the house among the blackberry bushes, and he is surprised to see the skittish smoke rising from the morning fire.

He realizes that the sun is beginning to rise, but he doesn't enjoy it, for the anguish still eats away at him. Being accustomed to living in sadness, he expects only bad news.

She waits for him with the door half-open:

"Your coffee is ready, Papá," she says, and then, as if remembering something she adds, "Today I'll help you work the farm, if you like."

And in that instant, everything is suddenly perfectly clear.

Translated by Susan Benner

Beatriz Loayza Millán

Beatriz Loayza Millán, a native of Bolivia, was born in La Paz in 1953. She studied at the Universidad Mayor de San Andrés and completed a thesis on the work of Bolivian writer Armando Chirveches. She has also completed courses in diplomacy at the Ministerio de Relaciones Exteriores de Bolivia, and she has worked in the Bolivian embassy in Lima, Peru, and also as a professor of literature at the Colegio "Saint Andrew" in La Paz.

Loayza Millán has published numerous poems and short stories in Bolivian magazines and newspapers, specifically *Presencia*, *Aquí*, and *El Zorro Antonio*. She began winning awards for her work at a very early age, earning an intercollegiate prize while still in high school. She later won awards for her writing dealing with legends and traditions. More recently, she received first prize in a literary contest sponsored by La Carrera Humanidades for poetry, and her short story "The Mirror" received the prestigious Premio Givré in Argentina, a prize recognizing young Latin American writers.

Loayza Millán says of her writing, "It's a form of catharsis, a liberation of the senses which allows me to gain complete harmony with the universe. When a writer faces a blank page, she is like a goddess who has the ability to create or destroy worlds, as she sees fit."

Loayza Millán's story "The Mirror," which pays homage to the work of the great Argentine writer Jorge Luís Borges, was motivated by a search for identity in a space and time completely removed from reality. Loayza Millán feels that women can find themselves in other realities outside of their everyday lives, that they can become the protagonists of dreamlike games created by their minds, and that they have the ability to free themselves from prejudices and social restrictions at the very moment they cross over the threshold of the unknown. For Loayza Millán, "The Mirror" represents a cry for freedom by a woman who feels herself trapped inside a mirror. When she comes face to face with "the other" on the opposite side of the mirror, she has also come face to face with her lost freedom. The protagonist of this story is a woman who is finally able to find herself, to then fly off to some formerly prohibited space, to "some distant Babylon."

Loayza Millán currently lives in La Paz, where she works as a professor of Spanish for foreigners residing in Bolivia.

THE MIRROR

Beatriz Loayza Millán

Everything I relate here actually happened, under strange circumstances and in a space where various factors came together to create a privileged point of connection. The day when all these events developed, or rather, the night when they developed, was the twenty-third of June. While people were amusing themselves by lighting bonfires and dancing around them, I took advantage of the magic of that special night to attempt to confirm certain theories (mine, of course) about mirrors.

The day before, I had received a call from my friend Espósito Aramaya Posadas, a very knowledgeable antique store owner who was also the author of an essay titled "Mirrors and Ghosts in Potosí During the Seventeenth Century," which still has not been published. This is due in large part to my friend's determination to complete his research with some data that was very difficult to obtain, since the majority of the testimonies that make up the central corpus of his work have been orally transmitted from parents to children. Because of this, very little written documentation exists.

I could feel the nervous repressed anxiety in my friend's voice when he made an appointment for me the next evening at eleven o'clock at the home of his aunt, Angelines Posadas, who had died in Buenos Aires only a month earlier. His Aunt Angelines had been one of the most fascinating women of her time, not only because of her beauty, but also because of her keen wit and her way with words. When I met her, she was a venerable old woman with light eyes and parchment-like skin, and it was she and none other who awoke within me a curiosity for the mystery of mirrors. During her continual and prolonged visits to her cousin Eunice, who resided in Buenos Aires, Angelines had fallen in love with someone "very special" who had never noticed her, but who succeeded in impressing her in such a way that she spent the rest of her days venerating and admiring him through his books and his writing. She visited the main bookstores in the city every week to determine if some new books by "Jorge Luís" had arrived. (Aunt Angelines constantly repeated that from the moment she met Jorge Luís, she spent her life searching for "the aleph" where her dreams would join with his). When she found one, she would read it avidly and lovingly, and later place it, in a kind of sacred ritual, in the secret refuge her loneliness had assigned to her.

I arrived punctually at the appointment, having easily found the house thanks to the notes I had written in a small notebook. The house was an old English Victorian from the last century, and had an uncared for and neglected appearance (its owner had spent most of the last few years out of the country). No sooner had I rung the bell when the door opened slowly and Espósito stuck his flushed face out, inviting me to enter with mysterious gestures. We passed through a small salon whose only window lacked curtains and drapes. Through all the room's furnishings, two small armchairs could be seen, upholstered in green velveteen, as well as a round table on which stood an empty and unattractive flower vase. But what really drew my attention was a large mirror with a gilt frame which hung on the wall, its magnificent beauty contrasting with the simple room and its furnishings. For a moment I looked at myself in it and had the strange sensation that it was not me who was looking back, but rather that my own image (freed in some way) contemplated me with a mixture of impudence and irony.

Espósito explained to me that the reason for his call was precisely because of the mirror. His Aunt Angelines had recommended before she died that it remain in the possession of her "favorite nephew," since she was sure that in his hands it would be kept intact, just as it had been for some three hundred years, in the possession of her family. In a soft voice, my friend related some facts and legends about the mirror, since he was familiar with my great fondness for antique mirrors and their history. He then left me in the company of "the most fascinating mirror in the world," departing rapidly and disappearing into the night.

A tenuous ray of light entered the bare window and reflected off the burnished surface of the mirror. There were no lamps in the room, and the only light that hung from the ceiling did not work. This caused a soft semidarkness to envelop the space, allowing objects to be seen, but in a very unusual manner. The shadows caused the pieces of furniture to take on an unreal quality, giving them an animated appearance, ready to begin a macabre dance at any moment.

Mirrors and Aunt Angelines. I remember how impressed I was when she showed me some notes she had managed to take on one occasion when "he" had referred to the mirrors. Some names: Cipriano de Valera, León Bloy, Saint Paul; isolated phrases: " . . . at the moment we cannot see God except as in a mirror, and under dark images: but then we will see him face to face . . . the pleasures of this world would be the torments of hell, seen backwards in a mirror . . . there is no human being on earth capable of denying who she is, with certainty . . . no one knows what they have come to do in this world; what their actions mean, their feelings and ideas, nor what their true name is, his immortal Name in the register of the light. . . ."

I placed one of the chairs in front of the mirror and sat down, ready to spend the night there in hopes of witnessing something worthwhile. I don't know how long I remained in the same position with my eyes fixed on my own image, without moving, my back very straight and my knees held together. I think I fell asleep for a short period of time. What is certain is that suddenly I heard a voice coming from the depths of the mirror, softly calling me.

I rose quickly with a single jump and asked, very frightened: "Who is it? Who's calling me?"

Then I saw her, it was her, the other one, the one on the opposite side of the mirror. She was looking at me with her bright catlike eyes; her half-opened lips showed a row of very white teeth that seemed phosphorescent in the moonlight. Her loose flowing hair framed the paleness of her angular face.

"Don't be afraid," she told me. "How can you be afraid of yourself?"

"I'm not afraid of me, I'm afraid of you. You are the hidden face of the moon, the hidden part which should never appear," I told her trembling.

"Yes, it's true, I am the 'other,' but you and I are joined. You refuse to recognize my existence and that is why you fear me. You have kept me hidden for many years. We have met several times in your dreams and you have awakened crying. . . ."

"Go away! Please, go away!" I screamed at her in anguish. "I don't want to see you. I don't want to remember that you exist!"

Her catlike eyes seemed to light up, her cheeks became flushed, and pointing at me with her finger, she began to laugh loudly. Her laugh ricocheted off my brain; it was daring, sarcastic, and strident. I wanted to escape but I could not; I was paralyzed in front of the mirror; I wanted to look elsewhere so I wouldn't see her, but my eyes remained locked on hers. An irresistible attraction drew me toward her. I realized that her image attracted and repelled me at the same time. Her voice reminded me of my own delirious voice heard in dream worlds; her laugh was like the silence of my stifled laugh in the labyrinth of my nightmares; I hated her and I loved her. I feared her but I didn't want to separate myself from her. I was fascinated by her feline movements, which made her seem daring and insolent, her hands bloodthirsty for capturing the world and not letting go of it: her graceful figure, the thickened area from which her brazen hips emerged; her moistened lips; her orchid-like skin, torn by the jaguar in the first jungle. . . .

I have returned to the Victorian house where the mirror is still located. I don't like to stop in front of it for very long because the image of the puritanical old maid reflected in its burnished surface disgusts me. I have come only because I wished to see it for the last time, for it's possible that I shall never again return. I have managed to capture the world between my hands and I want to enjoy it in some distant Babylon.

Translated by Kathy S. Leonard

Blanca Elena Paz

Blanca Elena Paz was born in Santa Cruz, Bolivia, where she completed her early education. She later studied in São Paulo, Brazil, as well as in Argentina, where she received a degree in nursing. She also holds degrees in veterinary medicine and zoology.

Paz has spent considerable time living abroad. From 1990 to 1995, her longest stay outside of Bolivia, Paz was in Spain, where she directed workshops in children's and adult literature and participated in conferences dealing with Bolivian and Latin American literature.

Paz began to write poetry at an early age, shortly after she discovered she could read at age four. Although she continued to write for herself for many years, it was not until 1985, when she entered a short story contest and won a prize, that she became serious about her writing. She says of her work, "I write faced with the impossibility of containing that powerful impulse. I have never been a great speaker, and yet, I have so much to say, based on what I have heard, dreamed, invented, and thought."

Paz has much material to draw from for the development of her short stories, material that manifests itself cruelly in her story "The Light." In 1971, Paz's father was executed in Santa Cruz, Bolivia, during a coup. In 1974, her boyfriend was "disappeared" from Cochabamba. Then, during the years Paz was studying in Argentina, the country was experiencing what are commonly known as "the dirty wars," a period of great political upheaval between 1976 and 1982 when some 30,000 Argentines "disappeared." She cannot forget that she still owes the neighborhood baker money for bread she bought in 1976. He disappeared forever, along with his wife, both kidnapped from the street in broad daylight. She cannot forget a nursing classmate who was abducted at eight o'clock one October morning by three hooded men, dragged from the hospital in La Plata, leaving behind her physiology book, a thermometer, and her stethoscope.

"The Light," originally published in *Taller del Cuento Nuevo* in Bolivia in 1986, addresses this time of tremendous terror felt by the citizens of Argentina. It was not uncommon for hooded soldiers to target the homes and places of work where "subversives" or others involved in political activity could be found. This kidnapping or "disappearance" of an individual typically led to their incarceration in some undisclosed location where they were often tortured or killed. The military invariably denied that the prisoner was in their hands, making it impossible for families to locate their relatives.

The protagonist and her husband in "The Light," although not involved in politics, realize that they are not safe, although they may wish to pretend otherwise. Doctors were especially vulnerable, not only because many were sympathetic to the subversives and could offer support in the way of medical aid, but also because they were often used by the military in torture sessions to gauge a prisoner's physical limits. It was the doctor's job to indicate to the torturer how much punishment could be inflicted on a prisoner without actually killing him or her. The writing of this story has been a form of catharsis for Paz. "I wrote this story because the characters who are not present, except between the lines, demand it and deserve it. And by doing so, I felt that I also released part of the pain I carry inside."

Paz has received several awards for her short stories as well as for her poetry in literary competitions organized by South American universities. She currently lives in Santa Cruz, where she continues to direct literary workshops. In 1995 she published a volume of short stories titled *Teorema*.

THE LIGHT

Blanca Elena Paz

You're worried. Your husband has changed during the past few months. It's not that he has stopped loving you. On the contrary, he has never treated you so tenderly; it's only that at moments he becomes so distant, as if he were in another place. Now that you think about it, he began to change after the day that woman was looking for him, that pregnant woman. He was just about to turn the shift over to the doctor who was going to replace him, when she showed up; she cried, she got down on her knees. And, well, you know how your husband is; he allowed himself to be persuaded. It was a gunshot wound. He removed the bullet, he sutured the wound, and he didn't record the incident in the appropriate log. Later, although he didn't tell you, you sensed that the woman had sought him out again. Yes, it was after that when your husband began to change. Sometimes he comes home so tired that he doesn't want to do anything but sleep. And you can't sleep unless you read first. You turn on the night light, you let him sleep, and you read.

Since the curfew was imposed, the nights have become long and tedious. The television is unbearable: it broadcasts westerns and military communiques, so you turn it off. Well, at least you have that right: if they can censor you, you can censor them. What you wouldn't give to quit suffering from this damned insomnia. In the middle of the night, when the hands on the clock advance toward dawn, the city is inhabited by a mysterious and ominous concert. Trucks patrol, brakes squeal, there's machine-gun fire, and the sound of advancing boots. You already know, although you won't allow yourself to mention it, what is happening in the street. You have asked yourself if your husband has something to do with that drama. But no, because he was never involved in politics, although it's possible that now he has begun to change. You yourself are changing. Sleep. Sleep. It's better to think about nothing and to sleep. Turn off the light, sleep, and don't listen to the sound of footsteps on the street. On your street. You would like to get up and look through the missing slat on the blinds to see what's happening. No, it's better not to, because the echoing of boots is too near. Is it at the house next door? You think about the doctor's placard on the front of your house, as if that placard makes your house inviolable. Yes, it's better to turn out the light and pretend not to know what's happening. After all . . . you . . . what can you do? You can't change the world. You extend your arms because you have realized that the thunder of boots is coming toward your house. Did you leave the door open? No, but you can hear how it is opening. Your left hand reaches out toward your husband's body. With your right hand you search for the light switch. Someone, on the other side of the door to your bedroom, turns the doorknob. And you turn off, finally, the light, because you realize, too late, that the only refuge left to you is the darkness.

Translated by Kathy S. Leonard

ECUADOR

Mónica Bravo

Mónica Bravo is part of a new generation of young writers in Ecuador who are beginning to make their voices heard, and who are giving new life and fresh perspectives to a long literary tradition. Although she has only recently begun to be published, she has quickly gained notice for her beautifully written stories.

Despite a strong interest in literature since she was an adolescent, Bravo did not begin writing for many years. However, a musician by trade, she won a scholarship to study music in Argentina, where she participated in workshops that explored many aspects of creativity. She was forced to write as part of the workshops and, in the process, discovered a calling. Upon returning to Ecuador, she enrolled in a writing workshop, from which the story presented here eventually emerged. She entered this work in the prestigious Segunda Bienal del Cuento Ecuatoriano "Pablo Palacio" short story contest, in which it received an honorable mention and was published in the collection of notable stories from the competition. She has continued to write, and several of her stories have been published in a recent anthology. She is now working on a collection of short stories that will be published as a volume of her own work.

Mónica Bravo was born in 1962 in Quito, where she has lived most of her life, and where most of her stories occur. But her mother was from the coast of Ecuador, and her family frequently traveled there when she was a child to visit her grandmother. She states that she prefers to write about places she knows well—places she has explored, discovered, experienced, and come to know in all their complexity. Her writing reveals a sharp perception and a keen eye for details. Her stories beautifully capture the sights, sounds, and feel of a place, and her readers find themselves transported to another world, often a world of magical realism where strange things happen beneath a veneer of familiarity and normalcy. Her stories are also notable for the development of their complex characters and her ability to take the reader into the hearts and minds of her protagonists.

"Wings for Dominga," the story presented here, is no exception. It came to Bravo in a dream, and she awoke the next day to sit and write it from beginning to end, finding it all waiting there in her subconscious. It takes place in an unnamed town on the coast of Ecuador, and she is sure the roots of the story lie in her childhood visits to her grandmother. Like the protagonist, Dominga, her grandmother was a person who remembered everything she had ever heard, seen, or read, and who loved to tell stories and recount events (although, unlike Dominga, she did not knit). It is a story that celebrates the ability of a woman to triumph over infirmity and death through the strength of her character, the power of her memory, and her love for life.

> Through the experience that I've had in writing and through reading things written by both men and women, I've come to believe that we have different themes, that at times we have different ways of perceiving life, and since we have different ways of perceiving life, I think that perception is also transmitted in different ways. I'm not saying that there are women's themes and men's themes, but let's say that there are different sensibilities . . . and due to that, different ways of confronting artistic creation.

WINGS FOR DOMINGA

Mónica Bravo

She knew that she would die as soon as she finished. After the accident that left her chained to a wheelchair, Doña Dominga dedicated herself completely to her knitting. She made caps, sweaters, mufflers, socks, booties, doilies, puppets—in other words, hundreds of garments that nobody would ever use due to the endemic heat. Years later it occurred to her to knit her own shroud, for she had always been surrounded by rituals, and she wanted her own death to be yet another.

From among all the various colors possible, she chose yellow and turquoise as the background, since they were the colors of the Virgin of Carmen, and she was very devoted to her dear saint; she owed her for the many favors she had been granted. One day while she was working on her knitting, images of when she was a child came to her, and she began to remember circumstances and details that had occurred more than sixty years before. Her skillful hands continued working the yarn, but her eyes became lost in time. Suddenly, a gust of strong July wind jolted her from her thoughts and brought her back to the sharp contours of her darkened room. The figures of the saints sitting on their home altar watched her impassively, and a slight movement of the flame from the candles indicated that a current of air had entered from the wooden blinds. When she turned to continue her knitting and purling, she saw to her surprise that her own hands, guided by some hidden power, had shaped into her knitting, in turquoise and yellow figures, scenes from her memories. Having a tendency toward the mystical, Doña Dominga took this as a divine revelation and decided she should create her own shroud into which she would knit the story of her life.

And so the yarn began to multiply in her house. She had them bring her baskets into which she separated the wool by color and texture, and settled these all around her. Then, between knits and purls, she began to create new stitches from the mixture.

Four months of work found her knitting the memory of when her father removed her first tooth, tying one end of a string to the bathroom door. How she cried at the moment he slammed the door shut! And then there was the time she almost drowned in the duck pond when she leaned down to get a drink of water, and the huge gander pecked her nose so hard that it had been slightly crooked ever since. But what she most enjoyed knitting was her memory of the first time she saw the ocean, an immense quantity of white, because of the foam, and blue, because of its depth. She stood motionless, awed, in her checkered dress and her new sandals. It took so much yellow to knit that January sun.

Doña Dominga was enjoying the re-creation of her memories so much that, bit by bit, she forgot the reason for her knitting. Then one afternoon while she was trying to knit the figure of a *mamay* flower, the first flower that her husband had ever given her, she heard the sound of someone climbing the wooden stairs, which echoed dully with each step on the hollow boards. She wasn't particularly worried, since some of her grandchildren, or perhaps one of the maids, were bound to be outside. It had rained all week, and the sour scent of stagnant water rose from the muddy street below; now, with the humid heat, the bugs and mosquitoes had appeared.

The footsteps didn't stop in the living room and continued through the dining room at a slow, tired pace, until they reached the very door of her room. She didn't look up from the tiny stem she was knitting until they stopped their progress directly in front of her wheelchair, blocking the light that slipped in through the cracks in the blinds.

The woman was dressed in an elegant but worn black suit, which covered her tall, thin body. On her hands she wore fine leather gloves, and on her feet, muddy boots that had left mud all along the waxed floors. A veil discreetly covered her face, so that Doña Dominga didn't realize at first whom she faced. Just the same, she invited her to have a seat in the wicker armchair in front of her, and offered her milk and cookies.

For a long time no one spoke. Pieces of yarn and wool fuzz floated in the close air of the high-walled room. The old woman turned to continue her task of knitting the birth of her first child when suddenly, from the dying light of the late afternoon, the woman spoke in a hoarse but ceremonious voice:

"I have come early because I had to take care of some business in the neighboring village and had to walk quite far to find it, so I thought it would be best to take advantage of the opportunity and come for you now rather than later. After all, with the life you lead, what do a few months less matter?"

Doña Dominga wasn't alarmed, since she was certain that nothing could happen to her until she finished her shroud, and she calmly told the woman:

"I haven't knit even half my life yet. I still have to include my eight children and forty-three grandchildren, not to mention the great-grandchildren. Nor have I knit the time when, due to the flood, I got to fly in an airplane and I could rise above the clouds. And I haven't yet recorded the day I almost died after being run over by that donkey cart, when my husband and I went out to see *Blood and Sand*, the first movie ever shown in the village. It's been twenty-five years since then, but I'll never forget it, since I could never walk again after that."

The woman looked at her with a certain tenderness and, settling herself more comfortably in the chair, replied, "All right, Dominga, I'll let you finish the story you wish to tell, but I suggest you hurry, since before morning breaks, we must be elsewhere. While you do so, I'm going to rest a bit. I need to regain my strength in order to carry you."

Night fell surprisingly early for Dominga, and a chill ran down her curved spine. She didn't go to eat beside the balcony of the dining room as she usually did, and instead had the servants bring her supper to her room. Nobody remarked on the strange presence sitting there because the woman was hidden in a dark corner. Knits and purls, purls and knits mixed together in the passing minutes, which Doña Dominga believed to be her last. Her hands never stopped creating images, the number of which increased by the minute; the more she could remember, the longer she could hold off death.

And so the hundreds of stories she had read, the ones she could remember from the movie theater the few times she had gone, those her mother had told her, and the ones she had heard on the radio, all came to her. The man whose life was spared in the Roman arena because years before he had taken the thorn from the paw of a lion; the agony of Camille; the fireworks, the silk, and the paper of the Chinese sages; Porfirio Cadena and his glass eye; the follies of Bertoldo, Bertoldino, and Cacaseno; the hanging gardens of Babylon and the Colossus of Rhodes; the bewitching song of the sirens; the Queen of Hearts and the giant rabbit from Alice's adventures; the cicadas flying through the light from the movie projector; the wedding at Canaan; the adventures of her uncle while harvesting rubber in the jungles of the province of Esmeraldas; fifty of Scheherazade's thousand and one tales; the afternoons spent at the river; the miracles of Saint Marianita of Jesus; Father Almeida's binges; the hundred thousand devils who built the Cathedral of San Francisco; the love of Don Quixote for Dulcinea; the struggle of her godmother Pepa bringing her piano up the mountains on the back of a donkey; the death of Juliet next to her Romeo; the circles made by the mule turning the sugar mill; starch breads, honey cakes, and ladyfingers with moonshine for her grandmother's saints; comic books of her favorite cartoon character, Peneca . . . everything she transformed into the flowing yarn.

From time to time the mysterious woman, looking fixedly at Doña Dominga, asked her how much longer she would have to wait, and Dominga answered leisurely, "I'm only up to the birth of my fourth child."

Turning around in the chair and giving a big yawn, the woman leaned her head wearily on her hand.

The night passed slowly, growing warmer and warmer. The stranger, overcome by the heat and lethargy, nodded off now and then, but would immediately reposition herself in a posture more fitting of her distinction and her role. Improvising a fan from the obituary page of the *Voice of the Province* helped her endure the oppressiveness of the room. At one point she gently scolded Dominga, who calmly reported that she had just started grandchild number thirty-six. The light from the candle amplified the shadows on the wall, which took on dancing forms due to the instability of the flame.

It was almost dawn when the strange woman could no longer fight her own tiredness and fell soundly asleep. The air was cooler now, and so she was able to settle herself more comfortably, stretching out full length in the chair. A snore escaped from her half-opened mouth, which one would never have expected from such a somber woman.

Doña Dominga quickly finished; she had included all of her forty-three grandchildren and even her great-grandchildren. She hadn't forgotten her husband's funeral and the almost three hundred people who had attended it. To all of these figures she added the image of the Virgin of Carmen and the Lord of Good Hope, of Saint Anthony and Saint Rita next to the Archangel Michael. She couldn't forget the *patrón* of the village of San Cayetano, and of course Pope John XXIII. She framed them all with rosettes and jacaranda trees, with angels and cherubs hovering nearby eating scallops and mangoes, while the baby Jesus lay cradled in the manger.

And finally, Doña Dominga knit herself in her wheelchair, the chair that had deprived her of so many things in her life.

Worn out from the effort, she stopped her knitting, and her eyes then lit upon the sleeping woman whose presence she only now remembered. A sudden curiosity to know her led Dominga, slowly rolling the wheels of her wheelchair, toward the sleeping form. Noticing that the woman was in the deepest stage of sleep, Dominga didn't worry about waking her. Seeing her up close, she was seized with sudden astonishment: there was an extraordinary similarity between the two women. She could even have said that it was herself reflected in a mirror. In the wrinkled face now unveiled, a grimace etched at the corners of her mouth spoke of a past of dissatisfaction and resignation. At that moment Doña Dominga felt she could see her life reflected in that face.

A knot in her throat paralyzed her for several seconds, but abruptly she noticed that two small butterfly wings had been added to the image of herself that she had just finished knitting. She understood then that her story wouldn't end there—there was something more.

Filled with unaccustomed strength and decisiveness, she hurriedly, but with much effort, dressed Death in her shroud. She purposely didn't finish off the last stitches, and left a long string of yarn in order to keep it from unraveling. But the stranger slept soundly, unaware of the old woman's deeds. Doña Dominga felt a tingling in her legs, and realized she could now move them.

The day broke with the scent of fresh cacao, which took her back to her childhood. She stood up, unafraid, and remembered how to walk. She had to return to the ocean. She put on the light green suit, which she had never used, and readied herself to descend the worn-out stairs.

Then, quietly, she crossed the dirt patio that opened onto the plaza, leaving behind her Death, dead and wrapped in her shroud.

Translated by Susan Benner

Aminta Buenaño

Aminta Buenaño was born in 1958 in the small village of Santa Lucía on the Ecuadorian coast, where her childhood was spent among the sea salt, sand, and fields. Her childhood continues to influence her writing, as can be seen in the story presented here. She began to dream of being a writer at age eleven after reading *A Thousand and One Tales of the Arabian Nights,* a book which so fascinated and delighted her that she prayed to become a writer so that she could move people and make them happy, just as these stories had done for her.

Buenaño studied literature and Spanish at the Universidad Católica Santiago de Guayaquil and also received a degree in communication from the Universidad de Guayaquil. She later traveled to Spain, where she studied pedagogy at the Instituto Nacional de Pedagogía Terapéutica in Madrid, and in 1989 she traveled to the then Soviet Union, where she studied cultural communication at the Patricio Lumumba People's University in Moscow.

Buenaño's first incursions into writing were in poetry and, like so many Latin American writers before her, journalism. She has worked as a journalist for many years, writing frequently about politics and culture. Her first book, a collection of poetry, was published by her high school when she was eighteen, and she published her first collection of short stories in 1985. Her writing, both journalistic and creative, has been highly praised in her country, and she has won various prizes for her stories and articles. A number of her stories have been anthologized, and her work has been translated into French and Italian. She has also been a leading figure in cultural and literary circles in Ecuador, and she was the director of the feminist journal *La Maga* for several years.

For Buenaño, the language a writer uses is as important as the story to be told. Her writing is most notably characterized by her extremely poetic and fluid language and her ability to create very vivid and vibrant images. These attributes are clearly present in the work presented here, filled with startling, intense images laden with symbolism, and language crafted so poetically that her words seem to sing. In writing this story, Buenaño says, "I was intensely concerned with the language, which for me is a vital part of good literature. The language tries to describe, in the most poetic and alive way, the natural elements. For me, language without poetry is not literature."

"The Strange Invasion That Rose From the Sea" is based on a dream the author had after spending several days at the ocean side, once again immersed in the wild power of the sea. It is filled with the nostalgia and longing she still feels for her roots, and is also a powerful metaphor for the numerous and often overwhelming forces in Ecuador that drive people to migrate from the country to the city, drawn by often false illusions and the phantom of "progress."

Buenaño recently received the honor of being named the National Cultural Director in Ecuador. She lives in the city of Guayaquil, where she teaches literature and continues to write, and she is at work on a new novel.

I'm a woman whose childhood was spent in the country, touching the earth, feeling the rainwater under my bare feet, breathing in the scent of smoke and the freshly-planted fields; I think it is because of this that "The Strange Invasion That Rose from the Sea" re-creates these obsessions—that is, those that respond to scents, textures, landscapes, and a sacred worship for everything which is fluid, transparent, and eternal as water.

THE STRANGE INVASION THAT ROSE FROM THE SEA

Aminta Buenaño

The sea awoke drifting, sad, and bloated like a dead fish. The autumnal sky, lackluster and faded, threatened to topple over onto the ashen quiet of the beach, and only the ghostly cries of a fan of sea gulls broke the silence at intervals as they aimed the open scissors of their beaks, with obsessive though useless enthusiasm, over the crests and troughs of a green and desolate sea, as if waiting for it to suddenly open its translucent throat and vomit up the unforgettable spell of its most bizarre and delicious fish, or the most cherished treasures from its remote and untouchable depths.

The beach stretched out, vast and deserted like a lunar valley, but the sky devoured it, covering it with a sense of terror, and a humid cloud of intense sadness seemed to rise from the sea to cover the beach and stain it with November. Nothing was going to come from the water, neither a flower nor a fish. No matter how stubbornly the fishermen flung forth their hopes, their nets were pulled in empty time and time again. It was as if some silent resentment compelled the ocean to maintain a sustained, bitter grudge against these inveterate thieves of her most fragrant pearls.

For hundreds of miles around, the only person who was aware of something strange in the air was Fortunato, the younger; Fortunato, with his myopic eyes and his clumsy tongue, bent over from his shyness, had learned the bubbling and stubborn language of the sea, knew how to decipher its multiple tongues, its torrential angers, its drowsy calms that were like terrifying time bombs. And he suspected now with a certainty that came more from wisdom and experience than from intuition or magic that something disturbing hovered in the atmosphere ready to destroy the routine, as if the universal cataclysm constantly predicted by that Basque priest was going to occur right then and there.

Fortunato remembered how the priest's thick, bushy beard, like that of a Spanish colonizer lost in a time warp, had suddenly been attacked, in an unfortunate welcome, by the fierce advance of an aggressive army of vengeful lice. The pests declared war without truce, and with such determination that despite the counterattack of soap, salt, and home remedies, the priest was forced to accept the humiliating surrender of having his beard shaved off and burned in an embarrassing retreat. The people of the town were startled to discover his childlike face, previously hidden by the beard, and an inquiring, almost tender look about him that bewildered the fishermen and made them ask themselves who this strange man was who had suddenly appeared out of nowhere like some kind of apparition; for this young priest, who had arrived in the village wearing faded blue jeans and a knapsack and whistling the melancholy tune "Imagine" by John Lennon, seemed more like an ancient Roman gladiator than a humble servant of God. And his sermons, instead of producing calm and contrition in the hearts of his flock, made their hearts boil and brought bubbling up to their lips all the wrongs they had suffered, their accusations and their protests. After each mass the fishermen and their wives left speaking of taking the sea by storm and declaring a strike, of turning their boats into flaming pyres so that no one would be tempted to return to work, although it might be more out of habit than out of betrayal. And they talked of capturing those abusive landowners who returned after interminable weekends in the Bahamas or Bermuda, each time even more boring and inflexible. They would take justice into their own hands once and for all and tie those scoundrels between two runaway horses until the only thing left to remember them by would be the dust and the blood.

The elders of the community watched the astonishment and confusion, and they couldn't find any way to decide whether what the priest said was real or if they were merely dreaming.

Fortunato stubbornly believed in God and his minions when the Basque cleric with his wild eyes and politician's voice insisted in his five o'clock sermon that faith could move mountains. Fortunato was filled with amazement, and over and over he questioned the priest, who emphatically confirmed this to be true. For seven days and seven nights Fortunato prayed ardently that his mother's ring would appear, the one she kept to pay off the debts she owed to Don Apolinario, the local moneylender, and which, in one of her many moments of dreaminess, she had lost. At the end of the seventh day, Fortunato felt he had been made a fool and headed off to confront the priest. Fortunately for the cleric, however, he had already left the village due to one of those unexpected decisions of the archdiocese which ordered him to return immediately, without any time for farewells or speeches. All he left behind as a kind of memento was a copy of *The Communist Manifesto*. Despairing of priests and faith, Fortunato could only lament that the Basque cleric no longer had his beard, as he dreamed now of humiliating the priest once and for all by yanking out his beard in fistfuls as if plucking off the petals of a daisy. From that day on he kept God at a distrustful distance, convinced that He was an unreachable being, a demagogue who, like the government, only remembered the poor at election time.

But on this day, anything could happen in this strange and incomprehensible sea, Fortunato thought. For example, a fierce band of green reptile men could land on the beach, equipped with a dense cloud of airplanes and bullets. Or a band of playful, white dolphins could be bloodily sacrificed, condemned to terror by an interstellar war between countries that hadn't the slightest scruples about affixing to their docile bodies a sophisticated apparatus capable of picking up sounds and relaying them to the far side of the moon, or mines that would explode upon sensing the slightest rumble of enemy motors, or long-range missiles that would convert the foamy, clear water into a thick, bloody soup. Or perhaps what would appear would be the dreaded landing of a band of ancient Dutch pirates whom he would join in dangerous and exciting adventures, and who would seek refuge among the enormous cliffs of volcanic rock where the sea sighed every night and the concentric magnet of its enigmatic, bellowing waves would, like a thief lying in wait, surprise suicidal wanderers, urging them on to make their just sacrifice, which would feed the cosmogonic spell of its fatal beauty. Or perhaps some new mystery, one of those which had steadily been rising from the sea, bit by bit, would abruptly explode like a flower bud breaking into bloom.

But whatever it might be, it didn't matter, he could wait. He had spent his entire adolescence waiting, watching from the broad window where the cold, whistling wind from the beach slipped in like a snake, watching the rise and fall of the tides, the curling and bubbling of the waves when the moon took possession of their monstrous, crystalline bodies, their uneasy calms like that of a sleeping panther, their cries of agony and ecstasy; he had learned so much that now his uneasiness grew minute by minute, expecting the unexpected with a secret hope that rooted him tightly to the lands of adventure.

Besides, he was sure that his father wouldn't go to work that day; he would sit in the doorway with that meekness inherited from centuries of waiting and resignation, his back bent over the casting net, patiently looking for the most hidden hole, the most imperceptible tear, which would justify his obligatory lethargy. And so, like a ritual, he would begin a story, any story, as if simply killing time, talking and listening to himself in impossible dialogues while Fortunato the younger's mother, large and dark, would mechanically open the windows to let out the smoke from the tortillas that always suffocated her, even when she wasn't cooking, moving as if all of her actions were preprogrammed and she were merely a puppet of some playful and slightly mad genie. They would do all of this without noticing Fortunato the younger, without knowing that he existed, because they had forgotten about him before he was born. When his father spoke to him, it was as if he only wanted to hear himself speak, to listen to his own words, to verify his own good judgment, and his mother, although sweet and solicitous, looked after him with the same silent regularity of a gardener with his plants. He always felt out of place and alone, even when the woman with the red stockings and darkly painted eyes smiled at him, showing the bloody gem of her gums, even when Floresmilo led him to the granary and began to tell him the twisted roots of all of his misfortunes while kneeling against his thighs and attempting to weep on his shoulder, even when he caught the first sardines of the season and they quivered naked and dazed in his warm hands. He always felt as if he were a mirror in which people saw only themselves without appreciating the texture of the glass or the frame, without seeing the mirror at all.

Only the blonde girl who arose from the sea with her enormous breasts, like those of a cow who has just given birth, with her sweet, childlike voice, told him that he was an idiot, a fool, but very clever, and that while he seemed to possess only three of the five senses, it was clear that his cunning allowed him to multiply those three by three. She didn't say anything else, but lifted her satisfied mouth to his inexperienced lips and showed him how to kiss until he was covered with goose bumps, confessing that these were the kisses of the sea. That day he returned from the beach blue and happy, but his parents seemed not to notice. His mother, blowing into the fire to rekindle it, handed him a rag for a towel and continued to remember with painful insistence her dead son who had lived for the brief span of only two months, but who in her mind had reached the age, size, and habits of Fortunato. His father abruptly interrupted his storytelling in order to comment, frowning, that the sudden changes in the weather were driving the fish away from the area.

From that day on, Fortunato began to observe other strange things, but no one else seemed to notice them. The sea would reach a crisis, unexpected spasms like an epileptic climax would break its apparent calm, and then, one of *them* would appear.

The first, the one with the blue cap and the mysterious smile, was wearing a striped T-shirt and nothing else. He strolled by the women with mocking arrogance, indecently exhibiting his enormous body covered with a dizzying array of tattoos, his tight, hairy buttocks, his powerful arms like anchors, and his dark member, big as that of a horse, which hung there insolently with the open impertinence of a child and on which appeared the tattoo of a boa constrictor and the word "champion" written vertically. To Fortunato it seemed incredible that the women weren't aware of his presence, or that Don Prudencio's daughter didn't seem the slightest bit disturbed when, in an act of terrible lechery, the man lasciviously dared to suck on her innocent, tiny, blue, prepubescent nipples, or fondle her pink buttocks, or when he ran his hook into her from end to end. Next, the woman with the wolf eyes slipped out from the sea. She was the one who kidnapped children, and after several days she would terrorize swimmers by returning her victims to the beach in the undertow, leaving them there, bloated like balloons and bug-eyed from asphyxia. Then it was the bearded warrior with thick armor and riding a white horse, who emerged from the sea with the imperial nobility of one who has returned in victory from across a great desert. He created a commotion on the beach and founded a city there, whose name carried the scent of God and sounded like the tinkling of bells. Later, dreamy, nostalgic shadows wandered by, protected by the mist on the beach, telling stories of their misfortunes and recounting in great detail the day and the hour of their ruin, as if reliving the fatal moment were a way to ward off that unexpected and absurd death. On another day, a fragile maiden whose long eyelashes trembled beneath the pressing weight of drops of brine and whose glance was filled with hidden mysteries, leaped out of the water with the boldness of a flying fish. She sat in front of Fortunato's window and with short, subtle gestures, began to cut her interminably long hair. Then she removed all her clothes from her thin body and buried herself in the sand, like someone folding a suit, as if her deepest, most longed-for aspiration were to sink her delicate bones into solid ground beneath a burning sun.

Perhaps all of this would have given Fortunato a heart attack if he had not realized that these were only signs of something greater and inevitable yet to come. He waited, reviving his own dreams of a naval war with its torpedo submarines, of the fleeting passage of an army of white dolphins, of the fierce assault of the pirates, anything that would break the thread of waiting.

At the break of day he heard a brutal sound, like a bloodcurdling scream, and saw not just a few, but a multitude of strange and greedy men and women arise from the sea. Some were missing an arm or a leg, others had disfigured faces ravaged by sharks and sea salt, and only shreds of skin still clung to their yellowed bones. Others appeared intact and somber, as if the sea had recognized the delicate dignity of their destinies and had feared to defile them. Others leapt out belligerent and aggressive, and screaming, they took possession of the beach.

Fortunato cowered in the sand; he wanted to grab his father's weapons—a heavy club and a razor, but the surprise and the brutality of the attack kept him pinned to the ground. He waited. Startled, he realized that the invaders were going into people's houses, taking possession of their fires, lying in their beds, playing on the beach, walking along the streets and kicking at the dogs as if their silent attack of rage kept them from understanding that the village was already inhabited and that everything had its owner and its place.

Wide-eyed from bewilderment, he realized once again that no one was aware of the presence of these ferocious underwater people, and that everyone acted as if the rain, the smoke, and the salt were the same as ever, as if life were simply repeating the tedium of its daily routine. The only difference was that it suddenly occurred to the young people of the village to leave for the city, which called to them with the bright spell of its neon lights, its transparent skyscrapers, and its gigantic factories. The women of the town, looking into the future, began rapidly weaving new destinies for their children, and the men, roused by their wives, grabbed what few belongings they had, hoisted their bundles of children, and without a backwards glance, settled themselves into the back of any truck heading toward the city.

Only the oldest of the elders, worn down by the sadness of too many good-byes and the weariness of their bones, explained that they had to stay behind since someone had to keep their dead relatives company. Who else would put flowers on their graves, who else would talk to them, who else would appease their fears with the traditional prayers for the dead? Who, I ask you, who? Only Juana, the crippled old woman who still painted her lips a brilliant crimson, folded up her rheumatic legs and knelt down in the back of a pickup truck with a moth-eaten trunk and her seventeen dogs.

Everyone left. Nobody dared to stay; they all found some excuse, some reason that drove them on like a whip on their backs. No one wanted to admit that they were thrown out by a bad-smelling phantom people who arose from the sea and took over their houses, their lands, and their nets, who seized their very past and the vital power of their nostalgia.

I was the only one who cried out to the four winds until I tore my throat apart and a knot of terror and tears stopped me from haranguing everyone to resist, to build forts, to fill the canons with gun powder, to look for supplies, to arm the men and stubbornly challenge these invaders entrenched with the enormous power of the nostalgia they had stolen away from us. We should fight to the death until the last ghoul is beaten and pushed back into the sea, and then everything would be better than before because we would have found ourselves after so many centuries of being lost.

But no one wanted to listen to me, and by the time I realized that, Fortunato the elder and the vague shadow that was Fortunato the younger had already tied a rope around my neck and were dragging me toward the road where the last truck was waiting to leave.

Straining to lift myself, I was able to see the town far off in the distance sinking into oblivion, disloyally turned over to the voracity of phantoms, at the foot of the naked cliffs. I watched it retreat into the distance until a thick cloud as big a mausoleum finally killed it for me.

Translated by Susan Benner

María del Carmen Garcés

One of Ecuador's new, talented writers, María del Carmen Garcés is a woman with strong passions and a burning desire to experience the world. Born in 1958 in the small town of Latacunga in the central Andes of Ecuador, she grew up in the nearby town of Ambato, but at 18, she left to spend her senior year of high school in the United States. That experience triggered a lifelong passion for travel and for learning languages. She has traveled the length and breadth of Latin America at various points in her life and ventured across a large part of Europe. Besides the United States, she has lived in several other countries, including Argentina, Bolivia, Chile, and France. All of these experiences have marked her deeply and are a source of inspiration she draws upon in her writing.

Garcés has worked as a translator and as the editor of several national and international news bulletins, as well as a guide for trekking expeditions. From 1983 to 1988 she lived in Bolivia, where in addition to her work as an editor and translator, she dedicated herself to another passion, researching the life and history of Ernesto "Che" Guevara. From this research she has published three volumes about his time in Bolivia, and she has written a third, as yet unpublished, book on the subject.

As a young girl, Garcés began writing "the typical adolescent diaries and a poem or two," but she did not begin writing fiction until the early 1990s. In 1992, she joined a writer's workshop in Quito, which proved to be a decisive experience. Several of her stories that grew out of the workshop were published in an anthology of the group's writers, and a year later she published a collection of her own short stories, from which the story presented here is taken. Her writing has met with wide critical acclaim in Ecuador, and one of her stories recently won an honorable mention in the Tercera Bienal del Cuento Ecuatoriano.

Garcés is a keen observer of the lives that surround her, and her writing displays a deep sensitivity to the human condition, an understanding of the inner workings of the human soul, and an ability to see the world through the eyes of others. Her stories are peopled with characters from all walks of life—men and women, young and old—as they face the often harsh realities of the world around them and struggle to find ways to survive, ways to find meaning in their existence. She writes, she says, about events that have actually occurred, people who really exist, and situations that she has experienced or seen. For her, writing has become an important form of personal expression: "I write to express myself spiritually, as a person, as a woman. It is also a way to share experiences, feelings, ideas, dreams, loneliness . . . , which in one way or another are a part of being a woman in our countries."

"The Blue Handkerchief" grew out of several experiences: it was partly inspired by a man she knew from whom she developed the male character of the story, and partly by a conversation she had with a woman she met once in Chile, who told her, "We all have our blue handkerchief in life, without which it would be impossible to live." In this story, Garcés wishes to portray the cold and lonely reality of single, older women in Latin America who are often forgotten in a society that has no role or place for them.

Since 1995 Garcés has lived in Argentina with her daughter and Argentine husband in an isolated, quiet spot near the Chilean border, which she says is perfect for writing. She is finishing another book of short stories and plans to start a book of poetry soon, as well as continuing her research about Che Guevara.

> My writing has been influenced by many things: the experiences that one accumulates throughout one's life, some very difficult, painful, which mark you. Other influences from the world that surrounds me: the Andean winds, people's suffering, women and their tragic destinies. What I've read. . . . In short, the history of Latin America. And of course, my travels, different languages, which open one up to new horizons and new cultures.

THE BLUE HANDKERCHIEF

María del Carmen Garcés

She came up with the idea of the blue handkerchief because the thought of dying without ever having known a night of love tormented her even more than the terror of ending up in abject poverty; the economic crisis had left so many retired people in the street that she lived in fear, and every time she thought about it, she got up to turn off the lights in the house.

But the other was impossible to accept: to go out every afternoon to clean the sidewalk and meet with the other single women in the neighborhood. No, her life would not end like this—raking dry leaves in the fall, cleaning the sidewalk in winter, and pruning the trees in the garden in the spring. She couldn't remember when she had become tied to that treadmill. And yet, the first sign of rebellion appeared in an unexpected way one summer morning when she grabbed her knitting needles and threw them into the garbage. All of her sisters and nieces already had more than enough sweaters to protect them through the coming winters of who knows how many years. And she was definitely tired of inventing new stitches and color combinations.

She had also left behind her period of sculpting in clay; she couldn't keep on showing off the Greek-style sculptures she had made with her own hands to any and all visitors who passed through her house. All that effort just to hear the same old comments about her innate talent in sculpture?

"And of course," she said to herself, "if you take into account the life I've led, all these reactions are normal, even understandable. But this thing with the blue handkerchief is more than strange—it's embarrassing."

Perhaps it was all due to the fact that despite her sixty-four years, she still hoped to find him again and live happily. And the blue handkerchief was the only thing that brought her closer to him.

One night, when her loneliness lay heavily on her heart, she took out the blue handkerchief from the bureau drawer and put it on the bed. She used it to form a human silhouette, of a man, which she eyed tenderly and with whom she began to chat.

"Ansaldo," she said softly, "finally you've returned! You can't imagine how I've waited for this moment. Close your eyes and listen to me. Don't watch while I take off my clothes; you know I've never undressed in front of a man before, and I'm embarrassed. Don't open your eyes, I beg you. Finally you are here with me, my dear! I was so afraid I would die without ever seeing you again! There. Wait a second while I put on my nightgown. Don't go opening your eyes yet."

When she told him that he could now look, she was lying at his side. She was wearing her impeccably white nightgown and had drawn the covers all the way up to her lower lip.

She talked with him for awhile about little things. She told him about the bug she had found in the garden and the new shoots on the everlasting plant. "Ansaldo, Ansaldo," she repeated over and over until she slowly fell asleep with the clear sensation of a hand resting on her waist. She slept without resorting to pills—and without sighs. And she dreamed.

She dreamed that years ago, when she had turned forty-six and had begun to recover from the pain caused by the death of her mother, she had met a man. A construction worker and something of a wanderer, he arrived at her house recommended by the brick mason. Her nieces were still small, and she thought that the best Christmas gift for them would be a brick wading pool. That way she would be less lonely, she thought.

That day they talked about prices, measurements, materials, and time periods. They agreed upon a daily wage plus food and wine ("the good kind"). The evening flew by in arranging schedules and discussing the best design. Ansaldo left promising to begin Monday at eight.

"Oh no! Eight o'clock!" she exclaimed in reproach, startled.

It was the first time in years that she had slept so late. She leapt out of bed, and while yelling to the man selling bread that she would be down to open the door right away, that he wait just a moment, she folded the blue handkerchief and hurriedly put it away in the bottom drawer of the bureau.

After she collected the bread she had a shower and her time at the mirror. It was then that she made the realization. Her eyes, how her eyes shone! She hummed a song as she made breakfast and even her voice sounded new. When was the last time that she had found herself singing? She couldn't remember.

For several nights she followed the same routine with the blue handkerchief, and her dreams repeated in amazing detail the chronology of the construction of the pool. There was the *mate* at ten and up to twenty minutes, no more, spent conversing, because she couldn't go too far. She couldn't let some laborer think she liked to talk with him, no. She did it out of consideration. He was reliable and hard-working, and she thought he deserved some well-prepared *mate* and a twenty-minute rest.

Her dreams then relived the moments at lunch. Because although her mother had admonished her until her dying day that she always remember the family's origins and that she keep the proper distances, it seemed to her that these were no longer the times in which workers should be made to eat in the kitchen. And besides, Ansaldo made such delightful conversation. He knew a great deal about music and he liked to recite poetry; he told her about Van Gogh and his letters to his brother lamenting the fact that he had no other company but the cockroaches scampering about on the floor in the dining room. He knew everything about the life and death of Che Guevara, and he loved to talk about him. "An Argentine," he remarked, and finished his stories asserting, "We always seem to manage to kill off the best of us, señora. Think of Socrates, Christ, Che. . . ." At this point in the dream she searched for the blue handkerchief and clutched it to her heart. She woke up sobbing.

She had a terrible morning. She didn't sing, and the man who delivered the bread didn't praise the freshness of her face. She returned to the position she had adopted during her periods of severe depression, with her arms crossed, her head erect, and her eyes fixed on the blank television. She only got up to bring in the milk at ten, to take out the garbage at eleven, and when the vegetable seller came at one. They all realized it wasn't a good day to talk with the señora. The rest of the afternoon she stayed seated with her eyes fixed on the blank television screen until the chiming of a distant clock announced that it was twelve o'clock midnight. She didn't want to go to sleep.

"Don't look at me," she said to the blue handkerchief in the early hours of the morning. "Hold me, if you like, by the waist. But don't look at me."

Curled up on his imaginary chest and lacing her legs in through his, she fell asleep, and dreamed:

The pool was finally finished. That day Ansaldo didn't wear his work clothes. He came dressed in white. His eyes sparkled like those of a happy child. He knocked on the door (she never understood why he didn't use the doorbell), and when she opened it, she found a bouquet of blue flowers (the only ones she ever received in her life).

"I need to talk to you," he said.

She led him into the parlor reserved for important visitors. He sat down before she could ask him to, and in a trembling voice he confessed his love:

"If we were younger I would propose marriage, but you can see how it is; I don't know how to tell you something so simple, what can I say, that I love you, that life is very sad, and, I don't know, that one needs company, no? How I would take care of you! We need each other. You are. . . ."

In her dream Ansaldo's voice sounded clear and sharp. His eyes shown with intensity. She forced herself to record in her mind the image of him saying that he loved her. She knew it was the last of the dreams, that the horrible routine would take charge of erasing those beautiful moments from her memory, that once again life would be nothing more than the fear of inflation, the bills, the taxes, and the mechanical act of turning off the lights left on in her house.

Until one night, after exactly three years, she would take the blue handkerchief out from the bottom drawer of the bureau and hire Ansaldo to construct the seventh pool.

Translated by Susan Benner

Nela Martínez

One of Ecuador's most important political figures, as well as a prolific writer, Nela Martínez has spent a lifetime fighting tirelessly for the rights of women, workers, indigenous peoples, and the poor and downtrodden. She was born in 1914 in the province of Cañar, famous for the stubbornness and determination of its people, characteristics she clearly exhibits herself.

Martínez was born into a family of wealthy, conservative, Catholic landowners, but at an early age her powerful intellect and sense of justice and equality led her to a lifelong commitment to militancy and political struggle. She soon became a central figure in leftist political activities in Ecuador and remains one of the country's most important progressive voices. Throughout her life she has been involved in numerous demonstrations, led many movements, and founded various organizations for justice and human rights, and in 1938 she helped found the first women's movement in her country, the Women's Alliance of Ecuador. Over the years she has been imprisoned and persecuted, but never silenced.

Writing has always been integral to Martínez's life and work, and she has written innumerable articles about culture and politics for a wide range of newspapers and journals, often under a pseudonym, since she was at times not allowed to publish in her own country. In the 1960s she founded and directed the country's first feminist journal, *Nuestra Palabra*. She has also continued throughout her life to write numerous narratives and short stories, which have been published in newspapers, journals, and occasional publications, but she has unfortunately never kept track of her published works.

Martínez is a writer with realist tendencies who seeks to reflect the stark realities of her country, but who does so with great skill and technical mastery. The situation of indigenous peoples and race relations in her country are frequent themes of her works. She also writes about the abuse of power by dictatorial governments; the situation of workers, women, and the disenfranchised; and human rights abuses.

"La Machorra," the story presented here, deals with a number of these issues, including class and racial prejudice, as well as issues of patriarchy and gender. It paints a stark picture of the complex race relations of the Andean region where prejudice and scorn towards "Indian" people is overwhelming and almost universal. The majority of indigenous people live in poverty, subjected to extreme discrimination, abysmal education, and political powerlessness. Yet most people of this region carry a significant amount of indigenous blood in their veins, and thus there is a denial and self-loathing in this complex interplay of prejudices, which is clearly illustrated in "La Machorra." The story's central character heaps scorn and disdain on those she considers more Indian than herself, while denying her own indigenous roots. This intense societal prejudice, both external and internalized, together with a patriarchal society that sees women, particularly women of working classes, as sexual objects, eventually drives her towards madness as the story builds towards its inevitable ending.

Today Martínez remains as active as ever in political and social movements in her country and around the world. She continues to write and is working on several projects. She is in the process of finishing a collection of short stories dealing with political torture, and she has recently started a short novel about a great aunt who was a guerrilla fighter.

> For me, writing is a simple necessity; it's not a career, a profession. It's something I combine with life, with the struggles, with the things that have occurred in this life and for the need to express things that I think, that I have, that I perceive and that I think need to be said. . . . It's a way of expressing history, definitely.

LA MACHORRA

Nela Martínez

She stumbled slowly up the steep slope of the mountain. Among the brush and brambles, her wild, uncombed hair, the color of dry straw, was like a clump of tundra grass whipped by the wind.

"Go to sleep my son, go to sleep now . . . ," she sang in her raspy voice. "I'll take care of you, I'll love you, I'll keep you warm and cozy, so go to sleep now."

She rocked her bundle of rags rhythmically, gently. A transient sun, distant and cold, still lit up the highest peaks.

"We've got to keep going. Just wait—up there we'll wrap ourselves up warm and tight, go to sleep now."

She climbed slowly, so as not to wake the baby, protecting him with her frayed shawl from the wind gusting over them like angry ocean waves. Her bare feet were scraped and bloodied as she walked through rocks and thorns that she neither saw nor felt, aware only of the rhythm of her arms, which formed a gently moving cradle to rock her child to sleep.

The profile of the mountain, stretching westward, walling in the river that dropped towards the coast, stood out sharp and clear between the reds and golds flaming in the west. The children had named it "The Monster" because it looked so much like a giant. She climbed it steadily, following the last rays of the sun, but the illusive light rose higher by the minute.

"We can't go on, there's no road. Even the goats haven't been up this high."

And as the glow in the west turned ashen among the mists of the high plateau, she sought another warmth, that of the earth. Leaning against the mountain crag as if it were human, warm and receptive, she allowed herself the illusion of being protected. She set down the weight from her back and from her heart onto the gritty loneliness of the Andean plateau, and she began shouting, as if talking to an old friend, pouring out everything she had kept inside for so long.

"Now you're finally quiet. I'm going to tell you my whole story. But this damned wind won't let me talk. Can you hear me? Okay, louder, louder!"

Caught by the wailing wind of the bleak mesa, her shrieks were but an echo of the greater voice that rose from the sleeping valleys, growing in a wild dizziness of air to become a dense mass, finally breaking loudly against the immutable rocks.

"I'm the child of white parents, like you. Mama Dolores herded cows for the master when he came up to find her on the mountain. It would have been better if I'd never been born. Mama Dolores married the *huasicama* from the hacienda, that Indian who watched over the grounds. Aye, then there were two to beat me. . . .

"They used to call me '*chaupi* white,' an Indian pretending to be white, with eyes like a cat, daughter of the *sacha runa*, the wild beast-man of the mountains, half beast, half Indian. Ha, ha, ha, I laughed when I had to care for those *huahuas*, my mother's Indian children. I was a lady, I should have been the mistress of those *longos*, and I had to carry them, care for them, feed them. But I was fond of them. They were warm and soft like baby birds. When they were hungry and cried, I put them to my chest to nurse, though my breasts were like small hard apples and gave no milk. But the *longuitos* would quiet down until their mother came back from work. Then Mama Dolores would take the children from me and push me out into the cold to see to the animals, to get water from the gorge, to help Papa Lino tend the fields. Once, when he was drunk, he tried to take advantage of me. But no, no, no. I fought him, I bit him and I ran, I ran away down the mountain to the village. Because I'm white, you understand? And my child couldn't be some piggish Indian *longo*. He has to be a baby pigeon, white and gold like the Baby Jesus, so that he'll be beautiful and respected and loved, like this little child that I have, like you, my baby. I waited for you so long. . . . If you only knew how hard it was to find work":

"Indian *huambra*, what did you say you can do?"

"Well, if you just had some kind of skill, but you're worthless!"

"No, I don't need any more servants. There are plenty of servants around."

"You've got a face that spells trouble."

"Ah, you're probably a *shua*, a thief."

"That's what it was like, door to door, day by day, for weeks. You should see how your mama suffered. I slept on porches, on the steps of the church, wherever the darkness caught me. I was starving. How my stomach ached from eating wild berries and roots I scrounged from fence rows. Once they offered me work. They wanted me to take care of Domitila Toapanta's crippled son. But she was just an Indian, even if she was an Indian with servants, with her Indian son without legs. Oh sure, they had money. They had shining necklaces and earrings, but nothing could change their color. Indians, just Indians with money. And I don't work for Indians, not that, not for all the money in the world."

"Okay, well, stay here and take care of the children, but I won't pay you anything until you learn to work. If you at least had a father or a mother who were selling you. I wouldn't pay much for a *huambra* Indian girl like you, but at least I'd feel more comfortable."

"Finally I got work with a white family. Rosita accepted me on one condition: if I ever complained about anything, she'd put me back out on the street. I learned what they taught me, but even more I learned how to keep my crying inside, how to suffer in silence. They shaved my head to get rid of the lice, they made me wash in freezing cold water at five in the morning, they whipped me every day, because yes, because no, because I did something, because I didn't do something. I had to work with the children on my back. How heavy they were, those fat, over-stuffed kids! Almost as big as me!"

"What's the matter? You're frowning. I pay you so the boy has his own mule, you know that. If you're not happy, then get out of here!"

"Where could I go? I ended up saying 'No, no, please Ma'am, I'll get stronger. Just wait, I'll work harder.'

"And that's how it went. Time went by and the children got bigger, they went to grade school, to high school, to the city. They'd come back during vacation. How I loved those vacations! We'd all go out to the hacienda. I was the white people's maid and I was white, so the Indians addressed me with respect. I ordered them around and they'd obey me. How nice it is to have someone obey you! The mestizos licked their lips when they saw me. They tried to pinch me when they got the chance. I'd spit in their faces—disgusting trash!

"Young Teodoro had hands as soft as silk. He used to call to me with his sweet voice. . . . We'd meet in the barn and bury ourselves in the straw from the thresher, letting it be our bed, our blanket. I was happy, it's true, even if I didn't sleep a single minute all night. He was like water for the burning thirst inside of me. I wanted more, always more, and—men are like that when you love them—he got tired of me. As happy as I was, even if he hurt me, even if he bit me, even if he kicked me. Nothing could satisfy me, nothing. A child, a son like Teodoro, that's what I wanted.

"They threw me out. He said I was trash and they left me with what little I had in the middle of the street. How I suffered! And I kept on looking for you. I worked in white people's houses and I didn't ask them for anything except that they give me a baby. They all kicked me out. People began to call me 'La Machorra,' the barren woman. They said I was like the mules that can't reproduce and the whole town started to insult me. Wives would curse me. I stopped working all together. I just looked for a man and I'd follow him as long as he was white. I started to pray all the time. I'd do penance. All the prayers I'd learned in Teodoro's house that I used to say before going to sleep came back to me. I'd repeat them over and over, I'd repeat them even if I was in the arms of some man. Some of them would get up and slap me and leave. But I kept praying, asking God for a baby, a baby to take away this thirst, a baby to bring me peace. I dreamed of walking past all those men who had scorned me, all those women who had insulted me, with my baby in my arms, and of shouting: 'Look at this beautiful baby La Machorra has now! Turns out she had the insides of a mare, not a mule!'

"Aye, how I prayed, how I begged, how many promises I made: God, if you'll give me a baby I'll never go with another man ever again! I went on pilgrimages, I walked on my knees and kissed the ground after the lepers passed by on their way to the hospital. And nothing. You didn't show up, you little rascal, you didn't show up. I looked for pilgrims to help me produce this miracle, as long as they were white. But none of them soothed this fire inside me, none of them left me pregnant, none of them gave me the one thing I asked for: a baby.

"But then one day, you know what happened? It was during Carnival, when everyone throws water on each other. It was during Carnival when people cool themselves and burn themselves at the same time. Ice water on the outside, fire-water on the inside, like my neighbor used to say. Dead drunk, all the *chullos* from the village, all those snotty boys who thought themselves better than everyone else, they all attacked me in my room. It was a battalion of boys. I couldn't choose: mestizos and blue bloods, all gathered together to rape me. They crucified me on the floor and took turns for hours. They emptied themselves in me like the stallions of the hacienda on the mares in heat. And as each one got up he'd spit on me."

"Now I gave you that damned baby, you bitch."

"I thought I would die. It was like being beaten and having your guts yanked out so they could laugh at you. When I could finally loosen the rag they'd gagged me with, I screamed and screamed. God himself could have heard me, or my father who's the master of the hacienda or my mama Dolores from the mountains. But nobody heard me, nobody came. I screamed so much I lost my voice, I couldn't move, I was left half-dead in the middle of the night. Ah, but when I woke up, I thanked God. Because you were there at my side, you sweet little thing, newborn and shivering from the cold like the Baby Jesus. I wrapped you up in my only new dress, the one I'd never even worn. I wrapped you up warmly and started a huge fire. I burned the boards from my trunk, the Saint Anthony statue, the saint's shelf. I wanted to tear down the doors of my room to throw onto the blaze, as big as the fires on the eve of the feast of Saint Peter, but I didn't have the strength. And then the neighbors came, and the cops and the landlord."

"She's gone crazy! La Machorra's gone crazy!"

"They beat me with sticks like they do to the dogs that get rabies. But I got away. I saved you and now nobody can take you away from me, sweetheart, my love, light of my life, you beautiful baby like Baby Jesus. Sweet dreams, my son, now we can sleep."

She rolled up into a ball next to the rock wall, crouching beneath its shadow, still afraid.

"I'm not crazy, it's a lie. I'm your mother."

She pulled out her emaciated breast to feed the infant, whom she had placed very carefully on her knees. She opened her dull, glassy eyes wide, wide as she could, to scrutinize the coming night.

Suddenly she heard the sound of barking off in the distance. The dogs were tracking closer and closer by the minute. The sound of galloping horses resonated through the rocks, like a rising river, enveloping her, drowning her in fear. The rough dirt road lay only a few yards from her hiding place. She hadn't seen it as she had climbed aimlessly, destroying her feet.

"Who can it be? They're still after me. The things a poor woman has to suffer to save her baby. I know, all those people in the village are jealous, especially all those awful women who stoned me. They're jealous because my child is a miracle, so beautiful, so blond, so . . ."

Her words dropped to a hoarse whisper when suddenly one of the dogs racing nearby caught her scent and leaped for her just as the horsemen arrived. They had been hunting on the plateau, but stopped their horses when they saw her. Somebody called off the dog. Another yelled, "Look who it is, La Machorra. They told me she'd gone crazy."

"Raving lunatic. Be careful," someone else advised.

The woman, who had escaped to the very edge of the summit, turned her head as she heard that voice, that voice which jolted her heart, awakening her memories of vacation days long ago, warm and distant. A stout man wrapped in a wool poncho, he walked toward her, laughing, encouraging the pack of hounds:

"Go on, git her, git her. . . ."

It was Teodoro, his riding whip in hand.

"Machorra, you whore. You've slept with the whole town. I hope the dogs eat you!"

Rage rose inside of him, setting him on fire, making him drunk like too much liquor. What did he care about some no-account whore. Still, it hurt his male pride, seeing her up close. He remembered the agile, passionate young girl he had initiated.

"Git her, Sultan. Git her. . . ."

His whip whistled through the air. La Machorra ran, enveloped by the cries of the men, the baying of the hounds, the howling of the wind across the plateau. She fled with her baby, fled from Teodoro's burning eyes, fled, downhill like the first time, when she was just a young girl as fast as the deer.

His laugh, pursuing her, pushing her toward the abyss, drowned out the sound of her falling body hitting the ground.

The next day, when the villagers searched the banks of the river, the body they found was a formless, red mass, but they could still make out her arm, curved protectively, firmly grasping the pillow wrapped in rags, to which she had sung:

"Go to sleep, my son, go to sleep now. . . ."

And the waves washing up on the rocks of the riverbank seemed to chant in chorus:

"Go to sleep, my son, go to sleep now. . . ."

Translated by Susan Benner

Mónica Ortiz Salas

Born in 1967 in Quito, Mónica Ortiz Salas was educated in a Catholic bilingual school, where her interest in literature first began. Through the analysis of classic and modern American and British novels, she learned to appreciate literature, which, she says, allowed her to begin to write her own short stories in 1990.

Ortiz Salas prefers to write about the feelings and interior lives of her protagonists rather than their actions or the physical world. She expresses a preference for writing about women and identity, what it means to be a woman, as well as dealing with such traditional juxtapositions as feminism/tradition, working woman/housewife, and teenagers/middle-aged women: "Every woman, just as every man, must look for her own identity rather than trying to live by the recipes handed down by someone else."

"Mery Yagual (Secretary)" was the first story Ortiz Salas wrote as an adult. She based the story on her experiences in the bilingual school, where some of her classmates anglicized their names: Sandra became Sandy, Isabel became Elizabeth, and, of course, María became Mary. Ortiz Salas named her protagonist "Mery," changing the "a" to "e" to more closely approximate in Spanish the pronunciation of the English name. The protagonist's complete first name of María de las Mercedes would be equivalent to "Mary of Mercies." Ortiz Salas has fused within her protagonist a variety of neurotic characteristics that she has observed in many women, including herself, characteristics that give shape to Mery Yagual's personality.

Although the conflict in this story is presented as a one-woman drama, Ortiz Salas feels that it also reflects an important part of *mestiza* idiosyncracy: negation of the indigenous component and the failed attempt to identify with a European heritage, minimal as it may be. These elements coexist in a society dominated by prejudices and the desire to maintain appearances. This is a society filled with daily personal tragedies, where people wake up trying to be somebody else, but ultimately must resign themselves to being who they are.

"Mery Yagual (Secretary)" won third place in the first short-story contest "Pablo Palacio" in Quito and was subsequently published in 1991 with other winning entries in *Primera Bienal del Cuento Ecuatoriano "Pablo Palacio" (Obras Premiadas)*.

In 1995 Ortiz Salas graduated with a degree in architecture from the Universidad Central del Ecuador. In addition to writing, Mónica Ortiz Salas has also studied painting and has participated in a number of exhibitions in Quito. Her combined interests in art and literature have led to her current work on an illustrated book of short stories for children. She currently lives in Mississippi, where she continues to write and paint.

MERY YAGUAL (SECRETARY)

Mónica Ortiz Salas

She gets up every day in order to be Mery Yagual (*even though on her identity card it says María de las Mercedes Yagual Pozo*). She would have preferred to put her second surname first, because Mery Pozo sounds less "Indian" to her (*Mercedes Pozo would be ideal*). She gets up every day being María Yagual and she wants to be Mercedes Pozo when she takes her first look in the oval mirror with the gilt frame on her dressing table lined with formica and thinks about that "less Indian" thing, and then she feels guilty about her father's surname (*a merchant from the coast, a shoe store owner, living in a city in the north*). She runs the brush quickly through her long, shoulder-length (*dark brown, but not black*) hair and she stands watching how it becomes electrified. She pulls it into a ponytail with an elastic band so it won't get wet in the shower (*the shower that she takes religiously even though she might freeeeeeeze to death*), a shower with tepid water (*hot water loosens the skin*) and finally a shot of cold water (*to tone*).

To have to get up every morning in order to be Mery Yagual and find out in spite of all of her precautions that her hair got wet, and knowing that she can't use a hair dryer because Mery Yagual (*secretary, dry hair*) would have frizzy hair if she used a hair dryer every day.

For breakfast she drinks a glass of milk and takes a red capsule (*Mery Yagual, pale cheeks—iron deficiency—one capsule daily*). When she swallows the capsule she feels a certain tightness in her throat when she remembers that she once read that the pills should not be taken with any liquid. She remembers, for example, that you can't take sulphur with orange juice and that orange juice should not be drunk from a ceramic cup, but she can't remember anything about milk and an iron pill because when she read the article in the Sunday supplement they hadn't yet diagnosed her iron deficiency. . . . Some day she will have to look it up. Alright, now to brush her teeth (*two minutes in circles*) and wash her face (*Lux soap, delicate like my skin*). Put the uniform on (*suit: "pearl" gray and "melon" blouse on Mondays*) and make-up, put on rouge (*"blush," Mery Yagual, pale cheeks*), pink lipstick (*a e i o u, nothing better than saying the vowels and exaggerating the movement of the lips in order to distribute color uniformly, according to Vanity Fair*). And remove the excess with toilet paper (*buy Kleenex*), mascara (*eyelashes curled with a spoon, complicated procedure*).

She leaves every morning, being Mery Yagual, a half hour early, in order to walk to work (*walking accelerates the metabolism and burns more calories . . . so I can eat more*).

After three blocks she opens her purse and takes out a coin for the beggar in the doorway of the ministry building. She looks at him for only a second, to return his greeting and acknowledge his appreciation, because the sight of his stump makes her stomach churn.

She walks without stepping on the cracks (*cracks in the cement on the sidewalk*) a habit that has remained with her from childhood games. She feels a slight annoyance in her stomach when she misjudges the distance and her foot falls squarely over a crack, or when the cracks lose their regularity and she has to shorten or lengthen her step.

She likes her office and her office likes her (*Mery Yagual, easy smile, courteous and confident, a good advisor*). While she waits for the boss in his office, she wipes dust from his desk with a flannel cloth; she is proud to always be ready a few minutes before the old man arrives (*punctuality, German virtue*). The boss always arrives in a bad mood, but he never has a reason for being angry with Mery Yagual (*impeccable and efficient*). She reads him the daily schedule and he gives her some instructions (*boss, eye glasses: myopia, at least nine in each eye; shiny head*) after which she prepares black coffee for him.

The morning progresses with dictation, the typewriter, and chats with the other secretary (*five feet tall, without heels, bulbous nose*). From time to time the office boy appears with his racy comments and off-color jokes.

At noon, lunch (*dining room on the second floor*). At 1:00, retouch the make-up in the bathroom and listen to Chelita (*cashier, first floor*) tell her secrets (*Chelita, 30 percent overweight, blue eyes, freckles under a layer of make-up*), Chelita telling about her romances (*adventure with client last week*). Chelita asking if it would be alright if she called her (*Chelita, six months ago secretary, sixth floor, romance and break-up with assistant director, today, cashier, first floor*).

The afternoons are always lazy, the food is bad, a lot of fat, cholesterol, then sleep in the afternoon (*stop eating meat, someday*).

At 5:30 she waits with displeasure for John's visit, who says he's a lawyer, although everyone in the office knows (*top secret*) that he has never passed third-year law at the university. John comes every day to court Mery Yagual and she treats it like a joke, answering him with ingenious phrases to disguise the disdain she feels toward him (*stuck-up Indian*). The ritual lasts a quarter of an hour, after which, invariably, Mery Yagual has the urge to urinate. When she goes into the bathroom you can still observe in the mirror the vestiges of the painted-on smile designed especially for John, and she feels something like disgust (*for John? For herself? From the smell of strawberry air freshener mixed with the bathroom odors?*)

From that moment on she can no longer continue to feel the self-satisfaction (*which gives her such comfort as she completes her work*), and every time she presses her finger on a key, she wishes more and more that it were time to go home. The conversation from the other secretary, so pleasant in the morning and the first hour of the afternoon, now seems insufferable to her.

Fortunately, all this will be over when the loudspeaker in a corner of the ceiling will stop playing ballads in order to announce, "It is seven o'clock sharp, seven o'clock sharp." Then her life returns; she arranges her desk in a minute and runs to the bathroom with the other secretary (*the boss for some mysterious reason always has to leave before 6:00*), to comb her hair and touch up her make-up. She rejoices at her own "good taste" when she sees the other secretary (*five feet tall, without heels, bulbous nose*) painting on cat eyes with eye-liner (*so vulgar and out of style according to* Vanity Fair: *the ten unpardonable sins of make-up*). At the building's exit her boyfriend waits for her (*somewhat insipid, but with light skin and a nice person*) and they kiss each other on the cheek, after which, invariably, he gives her a piece of mint candy while he sucks on another (*for their breath, words never spoken but well understood*), while they walk to the parking lot. He takes her home, but she won't let him come in (*decent girl, living alone in a studio apartment*). In the tiny car, twenty years old, they kiss until her boyfriend (*blond, skinny with a large nose*) has to change positions, uncomfortable, feeling that his pants are shrinking up on him. Then she separates herself from him feeling embarrassed, from her own dampness, and looks toward the street (*Mery Yagual, dying to . . . but not daring to . . .*). He, understanding that he must "respect" her. Both of them beginning to talk about anything, laughing nervously. Then they become romantic, talking about "when we get married," "when you are a mother you shouldn't work anymore, right?" "when you come home late don't even think that I'll get up to heat your dinner." When Mauricio marries Mery Yagual, virgin (*Mery Yagual trusting that after two years, her hymen will have miraculously been restored*), properly raised young lady (*or at least her vagina will have closed up enough so that combined with her nervousness and his number of drinks, she'll be able to successfully bleed on her wedding night*). He, promising her eternal love, and she, remembering another promise made two years ago.

They say good night at 8:30 because he has to pick up his sister at the university (*future sister-in-law, classmates during the first year, today about to graduate, Mery Yagual, secretary*).

Mery Yagual heavily climbs the stairs to the fourth floor, wishing it were Friday so she could pick-up her boyfriend's sister at 7:30, along with the sister's boyfriend, so the four of them could go out together, go to the movies and later to eat, or perhaps go dancing . . . then to get up on Saturday with great willpower at 6:00 to catch the bus, where she can sleep during the trip until arriving at the city in the north to visit her father (*merchant, owner of a shoe store*) and be Mery Yagual, model daughter, until Sunday night at 7:00, after mass, to catch the bus again to return to the capital, where she will again become Mery Yagual, secretary. Thinking about all this while opening the door to her studio apartment (*a room with a bath converted into a tiny apartment by the addition of a wood partition: a corner kitchen with a dining area off to one side, a bedroom on the other*). When she first began to work, sometimes a friend or two would visit, but now, with her boyfriend waiting for her after work every night, she no longer has any visitors. When she pushes the door open, for a second she feels afraid that a thief or a maniac has gotten in and is waiting for her, hidden, but she overcomes that feeling quickly, which doesn't keep her from feeling great relief when she sees that the kitchen remains in its place and that during the quick journey to the bedroom to leave her purse, she notes nothing suspicious. She later prepares herself a cup of hot chocolate and throws in little pieces of cheese so they will melt; she takes them out one by one with a teaspoon and eats them with great satisfaction, after which she stirs the hot chocolate-with-a-pinch-of-salt-left-by-the-cheese and immediately washes the cup (*Mery Yagual, never a dirty plate or spoon in the sink*).

Then she goes to her bedroom and looks at herself reflected in the full-length mirror (*Mery Yagual, weighing 112 pounds, measuring 5′6″ tall with heels*). She sits on the edge of the bed and turns on the color television bought a few months ago (*discounted 30 percent from her salary with many months left to pay*) to watch the soap opera and then the police series. Following that there is a news summary, but she doesn't pay much attention to this because at that hour she does her aerobic exercises (*low impact, so the old lady below doesn't complain about the noise*) trusting that someday her stubborn tummy will disappear. She always finishes her exercise routine with a mixture of relief and satisfaction, although, as she repeats to herself every night, it would be better to do her exercises in the morning. Immediately afterwards she washes her face and brushes her teeth (*two minutes, in circles*). She turns off the light and goes to bed, snug inside her two-piece cotton pajamas, the same ones that allowed her great ease of movement during her aerobics. She stays up watching the 11:30 movie until it finishes at 1:30, she turns off the television and prays an Ave María, after which she settles onto the right side to sleep, thinking that that night she will also sleep for six hours and not the required eight, promising herself that someday she will break the bad habit of watching television and will go to bed at 10:00 . . . and will get up at 6:00 . . . and will do her exercises in the morning . . . someday. . . .

One night she fell asleep without seeing the end of the movie: she woke up to the sacred-notes-of-the-national-anthem, but she fell asleep again before thinking about turning off the television. She woke again during the night and made out in front of her a grayish-blue square with little black dots dancing to a buzzing sound; when she realized that it was the television set, she stretched out her hand and took the remote control off the night stand, with her eyes half-open she pointed the apparatus and managed to place her index finger on the red "power" button, but sleep overtook her before she was able to press it.

At 7:00 in the morning she woke up and finished the act begun hours before. But before the television set turned completely dark, she was able to make out the image of a famous model promoting a new brand of lipstick. She rose that morning in order to be Mery Yagual and she couldn't avoid thinking what it would be like to get up every day to be the beautiful model. What would it be like to have the fabulous aerobics instructor waiting on the side of the pool . . . the bath prepared in the jacuzzi . . . a tropical breakfast, to bronze herself all morning beneath the California sun, as in a movie she had seen, instead of the diiiiificult life that destiny had assigned to Mery Yagual. The seeds of dissatisfaction had begun to grow, climbing up her neck and threatening to squeeze her throat, when very opportunely she remembered that famous people were very unhappy (*like on Dynasty*) and that all those women were whores besides, which pulled her out of her ruminations and she threw herself into her routine, full speed. So she was ready, as usual, a half hour early in order to walk to work, with her face radiant beneath the layer of make-up, which was two shades lighter than her skin.

In the doorway of the ministry building, the beggar was also punctual, waiting for Mery Yagual's coin, and she, as she did every day, cast the coin into his hat. She tried to look at him for only a second so she could say good morning, but this time she wasn't able to retract her gaze as quickly, and while she was looking at his stump, she couldn't help but think about how it would be to get up every day knowing that you didn't have a leg, in some park or in some doorway, and feel your stomach growl from hunger until the charity you received amounted to the value of a piece of bread. (*What would it be like to be seated every day from Monday through Friday and be a beggar with an amputated leg, pretext for the generosity of Mery Yagual, who walks hurriedly without stepping on the cracks in the sidewalk?*)

When she arrived at the boss's office he was already there. Inexplicably, Mery Yagual had been delayed. (*Was the route longer today? Or her watch incorrect? No, her watch was fine*). When the boss scolded her, she saw reflected in his shiny head what it would be like to rise every day to be a fat nearsighted boss with a head like a billiard ball and wait everyday for the black coffee that Mery Yagual prepared for him . . . (*to be a dirty old man and be secretly in love with Mery Yagual*).

She spent the morning imagining what it would be like to be a short secretary with a bulbous nose, or a messenger full of morbidness . . . (*a secretary who was envious of Mery Yagual, an Indian office boy dreaming about Mery Yagual . . . or to have "loose underpants"*) like Chelita, fat and freckled, a final thought that kept her occupied until lunch time.

That afternoon Mery Yagual surprised herself by waiting for John's visit, so she could be even more disdainful towards him, imagining what it would be like to get up every day trying to pass yourself off as a lawyer, having no license, knowing deep down that everyone knows you haven't even graduated. But at 5:40 John still hadn't appeared, and since the other secretary had gone out to leave some official letters in the manager's office, having no one to talk to made her even more nervous, so she left the office to go downstairs to buy some chocolate. But barely had she closed the door behind her when she saw a horrifying scene at the end of the hallway: John and the other secretary kissing! She stood there for a moment, paralyzed, but it was 5:45, and invariably at that hour Mery Yagual felt the urge to urinate, so she left running for the bathroom; good thing they hadn't seen her. When she returned to the office, the other secretary had already returned to her place and was applying lipstick. Mery Yagual looked at her pointedly, but when the secretary didn't raise her eyes (*her face was radiant and slightly flushed*), Mery Yagual couldn't help but notice that she was pretty (*in spite of her bulbous nose and her height*). She sat down in front of her typewriter to type, to fill out a form, and it was then that the rupture of the vicious cycle of her neurosis allowed her a moment of lucidity, and she became conscious of her continuous mental masturbation, of her self-justifications, of her eagerness to degrade others so she could feel "better." She felt ashamed for having to constantly repeat to herself that she was good, virtuous, fair, and beautiful, so she could believe it herself, ashamed for having deceived herself at every turn, putting on airs, for being ashamed of being Mery Yagual, daughter of Pedro Yagual Kinga, a-shoe-ma-ker.

But all this lasted only a second, after which she concentrated all her efforts on thinking that John was a stuck-up Indian and the other secretary was an idiot midget with a bulbous nose and that both were deviants. But all her efforts were not enough to counteract the nausea that rose from her stomach and expanded in her chest, fighting to escape through her throat and growing by the minute.

Seven o'clock sharp, seven o'clock sharp! Hearing the nasal voice on the radio and leaving at a run without retouching her make-up, descending by the stairway instead of the elevator, running, seeing Chelita out of the corner of her eye trying to tell her something, run, run, run, as if it were possible to distance herself from that nausea. She exited at a run through the service door so she wouldn't have to encounter her boyfriend, who remained standing in front of the main entrance waiting for her.

Mery Yagual continued to run until the nausea forced her to double over.

She didn't know how many hours she had spent running into the middle of the night, nor how many times she had to stop to vomit, knowing only that each time she bent over, she vomited Mery Yagual.

She awoke in her bed, not knowing how she had gotten there, with a great feeling of well-being, and she knew that today she had awakened to live. She rose and opened the window to let the sun in and stood there a moment enjoying the warmth. She took a long shower with hot water, she shaved her legs, and then smoothed over her entire body an imported lotion that she had purchased a year ago and had never dared to waste. She prepared herself as if she were going to meet a lover. When she was about to leave, when she took a last look in the mirror, she could see that the clock on the dresser showed 9:00 in the morning. She imagined her boss screaming and assigning all the work to the other secretary. Perhaps they would be worried when at noon she had not appeared or telephoned. They might even send a messenger to look for her. No one would imagine that she, so responsible as she had always been, would have decided not to go to work that day, or that perhaps she would never return. She felt strong and exhilarated, she would look for another job, one that would make her feel "fulfilled." Still, for a moment, she doubted, and considered the possibility of continuing to work anyway while she looked for something else, when she saw her uniform hanging neatly in the closet (*blue suit, beige blouse, Fridays*). But she knew that if she didn't take advantage of the impulse she was feeling that day she might later lose her nerve and she didn't want to leave any door open that would return her to her insufferable past life. She had to cross the bridge and then burn it. "It must be today," she thought. "Today is the true beginning of my life." Before leaving she scribbled a note using eyebrow pencil: "Don't bother to look for me, I'm never going back to that fucking office." (*Mery Yagual had never in her life pronounced or, worse, written a vulgarity such as that!*) and she stuck it on the door with a thumbtack. She left the house laughing while she imagined the messenger's face when he read the note and the faces of all the others when he told them about it.

She walked with a new vitality, with her face, for the first time in years, free of the thick cloak of make-up two shades lighter than her skin. She breathed deeply: the air seemed less contaminated and the day more luminous. She remembered painfully, with something like affection, the beggar in the doorway of the ministry building; she thought that if someone were to truly miss her that day, it would be him. He was someone whose daily routine involved watching pass before him, each one for only a few seconds, a mass of unknown people and a few familiar faces, whose daily schedule required them to walk by at a certain hour for a few moments in front of the ministry door. But thinking this, she felt confused; it was better to think about something else.

That day Mery—María—had gotten out of bed to live, to enjoy, to be, to lift her eyes and look at the sky, to walk with that, until today, unfamiliar feeling of freedom, and although she didn't notice because she wasn't paying attention, she was stepping on the cracks in the sidewalk.

She went to have breakfast in an outdoor café, with umbrellas. While she was waiting to be served, she watched the passersby. They all seemed more relaxed than on other days, more willing to enjoy life, they strolled without hurrying, no one seemed to be concerned about getting to work. It even seemed to her that there was less traffic. In a moment she began to think that the change that had occurred within her had not been an isolated one, rather that it was part of a great collective phenomenon, but this didn't seem probable to her, and she deduced rather that her own way of looking at the world had changed and that the saying "Everything looks rosy through rose-colored glasses" was true.

While she drank her orange juice, she noticed that a very attractive mulatto was looking at her from his table and she amused herself wondering if it were true, the reputation that Blacks have when it comes to intimate matters. She decided to flirt a little to see what would happen. The man was reading the newspaper and her gaze suddenly became paralyzed when she was able to make out some text. Her face became pale. The mulatto made a move to speak to her, but he stopped short when he noticed the girl's expression. For a minute she couldn't move, then, very slowly, she stood up, left a bill on the table, and began to walk toward a magazine stand. She thought for a moment about asking someone, but she was afraid they would think she was crazy. Pretending to be interested in the magazines, she looked at all the newspapers out of the corner of her eye, incredulous. Feeling her anxiety mounting by the second, she chose at random a sample of every newspaper, paid mechanically, and headed toward a park. Once there, she selected a solitary bench where she began to examine, one by one, all the pages of each newspaper, trusting still in a printing error. While trying to comprehend how such a detail could escape her, she recalled the useless note stuck on her door. Feeling ridiculous while imagining the smiles of the neighbors when they climbed the stairs, she arrived at this inevitable conclusion: either that day was actually Saturday, or the entire world had conspired against her . . . and from those two possibilities, only the second one seemed admissible to her.

She rose on Monday to be Mery Yagual, and the burden that was herself seemed unbearable.

Translated by Kathy S. Leonard

Fabiola Solís de King

Born in Quito in 1936, Fabiola Solís de King has lived in that highland city most of her life and remembers her childhood there as happy and bright. A rebellious child, she refused to accept the precept that there were things she shouldn't do because she was a girl, and she preferred climbing trees to playing with dolls.

Now a clinical psychologist by trade, Solís de King began to write as a kind of catharsis, a way to release the powerful emotions that the experiences she encountered in her practice evoked inside of her. One day her son discovered several of her writings and was so impressed that he encouraged her to continue. In 1963 she sent four stories to a national short-story contest run by the newspaper *El Tiempo*, winning second place with one story, premier honorable mention with another, and honorable mentions with the other two. From that experience, her first book of short stories, *Al otro lado del muro* (On the Other Side of the Wall), was born.

Solís de King's stories clearly reflect her perspective as a psychologist, and her writing frequently examines the struggle of a psyche caught in the grip of overwhelming social and psychological forces. Her books powerfully denounce the way in which a rigid society can cripple its members, and the psychological damage created by poverty, parental indifference, prejudice, and sexism. She allows her characters to tell their own stories, and one of the most notable characteristics of her writing is the authenticity of the voices she creates. We can see this clearly in "Before It's Time," in which we watch the disintegration of a family due to poverty, alcoholism, and mental instability, through the eyes of the child who narrates the story.

Solís de King is currently working on a third book of short stories, which she has tentatively titled *Cuando el tiempo se precipite en la neblina* (When Time Rushes into the Mist), after one of the stories in the collection in which she explores old age and the process of aging. She lives with her husband of forty years in Quito, where she works as a clinical psychologist at the Central Bank of Ecuador.

I don't find that by virtue of being a woman or of being a man we have to write differently, rather . . . that each human being is different. We're unique, unrepeatable. . . . Masculinity and femininity are, I'd say, alienating identities created by societies, they're not natural. . . . So I don't agree that a woman, by virtue of being a woman writes differently, but rather, because she is a different person she writes like a different person. . . . I don't agree with the idea that there are necessarily masculine tendencies or feminine tendencies in literature.

[To be a feminist] for me . . . means to rebel against all the thicket of society's prejudices which have entangled us, men and women, in stereotypes which have done a lot of damage to us. . . . [It means] trying to break that thicket of prejudices, allowing women, and by the same token, men, to save each other as persons, to respect each other as persons, and that we not respond simply . . . according to gender.

BEFORE IT'S TIME

Fabiola Solís de King

You see, Señorita, I don't remember anything, and what you're telling me makes my skin crawl. Just like when my father's eyes used to bug out when he yelled really loud making the handle on the door shake. That's right, Señorita, I remember the days when Papá didn't love us. Those days were long and frightening. Papá had a face you couldn't look at straight on and a voice that seemed to come from a deep hole. It seemed to me that during those times he wasn't really my father at all but somebody else's, like the policeman on the corner who used to kick my brother because he yelled at him, "*Chapa maricón*, you queer bear, take off your underwear."

My brother did it to make us laugh, but the policeman didn't like it. The same thing happened with my father. We wanted to make him laugh, but he was always in a bad mood. It made my eyes hurt to look at him and tears came out, and Señorita, I had to run as far as I could so my father wouldn't see the fear that made me tremble from head to foot. That I remember. I also remember that when I didn't take care of myself my father would hit me with a belt and say ugly things to me, like, "When will I be rid of you, you're nothing but shit."

It used to feel like hundreds of rats were climbing on my body and they were biting me everywhere and what he was saying to me also hurt. Every few minutes I would start to think about what Papá was saying and I couldn't sleep because I was thinking about why my father thought I was shit and why he always punished me with the belt and I had to keep my eyes wide open when he was in the room. That's why I saw him the night he left so quietly with his clothes and his anger, tiptoeing and feeling around in the dark with his arms stretched out. I think my mother also saw him, but she closed her eyes tight to keep from saying anything. I also remember, Señorita, that my mother no longer had the strength to speak in a loud voice and only spoke softly, as if she were telling secrets. All you could see were my mother's bones from so much crying, from so many scares, and from so many hurts. She had these huge tears that fell and fell from her eyes, eyes which became tiny and wrinkled like a dog's and her face began to taste like pure salt. Mamá ate very little and complained constantly. I kept my face covered with the blankets and I stuck my fingers in my ears to keep from hearing her, because the sound seemed so ugly to me, like a dog that has seen some ghost. I think they did something to Mamá in the hospital because she came back from there like that, skinny and complaining. She had her body all tied up and she didn't allow anyone to see it or to touch it. I think, Señorita, that my father left quietly in the dark without saying anything, not even about where he was going, so that he wouldn't have to see or hear my mother. He must have gone far because he never came back. In spite of the yelling and lashes with the belt, I miss my father. Maybe he went to look for medicine for my mother's pains, so she'll be able to speak in a loud voice like before, like before she came home from the hospital and all those ugly hurts appeared that made her salty tears fall. Maybe, Señorita, my father couldn't find that medicine or he's earning money so he can buy enough. My father was always complaining about money because he had so little and he used to say, "I'm damned with no way out and all of you do nothing but ask for more."

I never asked for anything, Señorita, because of fear and shame, because once when I asked for a pretty skirt that a lady was selling, my father yelled at me and I felt like my face was on fire and it turned red and whenever I saw that lady again I would run and hide. It hurts me that my father doesn't know that my mother no longer wanted to feel those pains and that one night she screamed and screamed and woke up purple and very cold. She hadn't even had time to close her eyes properly and they stayed open, staring at everything as if she were afraid or maybe ashamed. What I also remember, Señorita, is that my mother was ashamed of everything, just like me. For example, she used to say that she was very ashamed that our neighbor Carmen knew that my father had left quietly in the night, and that she knew about the pains my mother had. When my father used to have those ugly days when he would hit us with the belt he used for the rats, he would say softly, "Don't yell, just take it, because it will make the neighbor happy if she hears you and she'll try to send us away from here."

My mother got cured of her tears, Señorita, because so many of them had run down her face that her eyes didn't burn anymore like mine did. It was worse when she stayed calm and didn't move. The neighbor Carmen told me, "Your mother is dead."

I heard her from far away and I didn't answer. It's because I didn't understand very well what she was telling me because I was so tired. It's because that night, the night my mother couldn't close her eyes, I had some ugly nightmares. I saw clearly how a black-colored monkey, the same color as the night, angry and screaming like my father, with four arms on each side that moved like branches in the wind, forced me to drink dirty water filled with cockroaches. I didn't want to drink it and the monkey shook me with all those arms it had. I remember, Señorita, that every so often the monkey looked like my mother, with the same thin yellow face and with the same quiet and hoarse voice that used to yell at me, "Drink it, drink it, because I can't stand it anymore, it's better if we all die."

In the nightmare my brothers saw how scared we were and the monkey also wanted them to drink that black water. But they ran away and only the smallest one remained because he couldn't walk yet. I remember that in the nightmare the monkey that looked like Mamá was squeezing me really hard and it kept growing more hands and it kept yelling, "Drink it, you fool, drink it quickly, there's no point in living."

I was crying and afraid to see that an ugly monkey like the devil could have the same face as Mamá, and that it could keep growing hands. I was also afraid for my youngest brother, the baby, because the monkey wanted to make him drink that black water, and he's terribly afraid of cockroaches. So I defended him, but the monkey kept growing more arms and more hands and it tried to catch all of us, my little brother and me. I had no voice because I was so afraid and I could only scream from inside my belly, but nobody could hear me there. Later, I think the monkey went away, leaving me tired and screaming inside and clutching the baby. When I woke up I found my silent mother, motionless, with her eyes wide open, looking at everyone as if she were afraid, with her cold face and large mouth. Maybe the monkey did something to her and I didn't realize it because I was protecting the baby. Carmen the neighbor said, "You have to notify the police because I think that terrible mother took *diablillos* and I think she tried to make the babies take them too."

Then I remembered, Señorita, that once my father sent my brother to buy those *diablillos* to scare the neighbor on New Year's Eve. I don't know why my mother, instead of scaring the neighbor, tried to scare herself, especially being afraid of everything like she was. I also remember, Señorita, that my brothers were laughing because some men came and they said, "We have to take her away so they can do an autopsy."

I think that strange word made my brothers laugh. My mother, however, no longer said anything, because she would have said something to my brothers for laughing at those men who were so serious. After they took my mother away to do that thing that made my brothers laugh, they told me that we had to go somewhere. Carmen the neighbor said:

"Now what are you going to do with your brothers since even your Papá was going to throw them out?"

I didn't know how to answer since every time she said something to me I got a knot in my throat and felt awfully sick to my stomach, but I took it, just like when my father used to hit me with the belt. I didn't want to leave the room where my mother had been and where my father had also been, although at times they didn't love us, and I didn't want to go, Señorita, because my brothers and I should have stayed there. I also remember, Señorita, when my father did love us and when my mother didn't have those pains. It was right there, in that very room. It was nice because Mamá put a lot of drawings on the walls. There was a lady who looked like you, with long hair, smiling, with a dress as blue as the sky and with her arms wide open as if she wanted to embrace us all. That was the picture I liked best because she looked like a good angel and I would see her every time I felt like crying because of everything that was happening and it even seemed like she was smiling at me and it made me feel beautiful. We also had a red blanket on the bed before my mother went to the hospital and before she had those pains. That blanket was brought by my father when he still loved us sometimes and he would come home smiling and singing. He used to bring us sweet coconut and we were all happy. All of that was right there, in that same room. That's why, Señorita, I wanted to save all the nice things. I remembered the sweet coconut and I thought that I could sell enough pieces of it so that my brothers and I could stay in that room we knew. When I told this to Carmen the neighbor, she said, "I think you are crazier than your mother."

Señorita, I never understood the neighbor very well. Every time she told me something, I would keep thinking about it with that knot in my throat and I wouldn't know why I felt sad. That's when I began to have those thoughts about her that gave me goose bumps, and that's when I started to not remember the things you say I did, Señorita. I remember that Carmen the neighbor left us alone for few days and I was able to sell sweet coconut and other things so that my brothers didn't cry from hunger, especially the baby. It's because I really did love my baby brothers so much and when they cried I didn't know what to do. I would give the littlest one brown sugar, he would eat it and sleep quietly. I would sing him some songs I learned when I used to go to school a long time ago. He would laugh with his little mouth with no teeth; he looked so precious and I would feel so happy that it scared me. It's just that my mother used to say that when poor people are happy, some terrible piece of bad luck will happen to them. And that was true, Señorita, because one day a nun showed up to see us with Carmen the neighbor who told her, "Here they are, Sister, these children with no father or mother, living however they please."

I don't understand why she was saying that either, but I remember, Señorita, that they took my brothers to a really big house, really sad, and really cold. They shaved their heads and they put aprons on them. They left only the littlest one and me and again I started to cry because of the neighbor Carmen. But when they tried to take the baby away, from then on I don't know what happened to me and I don't remember anything, Señorita. Only that the idea came to me suddenly and I couldn't get it out of my head. I went quietly into where Carmen the neighbor was, walking slowly like rats do so no one will see them. My heart was really beating, I had an even bigger knot in my throat, my arms felt long like the arms of that monkey in my nightmare. And just like that monkey it felt like I had a lot of hands and I climbed in the window that was open, because Carmen the neighbor never closed her window so she could hear everything we said and did and so she could talk bad about us like she was always doing. I climbed inside walking along the floor like a rat and I kept getting closer, closer, my arms kept growing and I was as strong as the black monkey. And after that, Señorita, I don't remember anything.

Translated by Kathy S. Leonard

Eugenia Viteri

If there were a *grand dame* of Ecuadorian literature, it would be Eugenia Viteri, who has dedicated a great deal of her life not only to her own writing, but also to the advancement and dissemination of the literature of her country and its authors. Involved in literary circles most of her adult life, she spent thirty-two years teaching literature at the high school level to young women, generally of modest means. It was a labor of love in which she struggled to light a spark in her students, and to inspire them to read and to discover literature—and the world. In 1987 she published *Antología básica del cuento ecuatoriano*, one of the most comprehensive collections of its kind, which includes sixty of the best-known Ecuadorian authors of the past century.

Born in the coastal city of Guayaquil in 1928, Viteri was one of six children of a widowed mother and grew up in a family with little money or emphasis on education. She loved to read, however, and as a child she would rent stories from a man who went door-to-door leasing stories and pages of books. She learned to read rapidly, since keeping a story past the twenty-four-hour rental period meant paying an extra ten cents. She began writing her own stories around the age of fourteen, but she insists they were terrible. Nevertheless, she continued writing through the years, publishing her first book of short stories in 1955 (from which "The Ring" is taken) and her first novel in 1969. Her works have been highly praised, and she has won a number of literary prizes.

Viteri writes in spare, clean prose, and her writing reflects a social realism concerned with the conditions of her people and the social inequalities and extremes of wealth and poverty in Ecuador. Exploitation, the situation of women (particularly from the working and poorer classes), abuse, and poverty and its children are frequent themes she tackles. It is the human condition and the struggles of people, with all of their strengths and weaknesses, which fascinate her and which she paints in her works. She hopes through her writing to be able to reach people, to wake them up to the harsh reality of social problems, to the ability of the human spirit to overcome obstacles, and to the need for human compassion and concern.

"The Ring" clearly represents these tendencies. Its protagonist suffers from grinding poverty and an abusive husband, but the discovery of a ring lost in the sand changes the course of her life. In this story, the ring becomes a metaphor for Teresa herself, something lost, buried in the sand, but which, upon discovery, turns out to be multifaceted, brilliant, shining, and valuable.

Viteri has lived for many years in Quito with her husband, the writer Pedro Jorge Vera. Still very active in literary circles and cultural activities, she continues to work tirelessly to further the cause of literature in her country. She is also at work on a new novel in which she is exploring the theme of infidelity and the way it is viewed differently depending on whether the adulterer is a man or a woman.

> I've been influenced by Hemingway, Victor Hugo, Dostoyevsky, moved by their dramas. All of those themes definitely reflect the life of a human being, which is what a writer must do. I think that if a writer doesn't reflect that, the anguish, the joy, the drama of man with his contradictions, with his greatness, with his limitations, then I don't know what that writer is doing.

THE RING

Eugenia Viteri

Every day of the week, but especially Sunday afternoons, Teresa wandered the broad beach near the town of La Libertad. Her bright, quick eyes moving constantly, she would scrutinize the distant shore, then throw herself into the hunt for a pair of sunglasses, a barrette, a comb: any object left lying forgotten on the beach by the wealthy bathers from the city. Sometimes she found herself waging a furious battle with the angry sea for her prey. If the waves won, she would sit in the damp sand staring sadly out to sea.

She would walk slowly, her head down, her eyes darting about searching the sand. Her emaciated figure reflected little charm and no one noticed her as she wandered by. But she was doing this for Luís. . . .

She was doing this for him, because in her hunt for objects left forgotten in the sand, she hoped she could somehow contribute to their economic survival, to "help him a little," as she would think when she saw that his salary wasn't enough. She would never say it, even to herself, but she also hoped that her efforts would make him change. But no, he never would. Because the abuse that he continuously inflicted on her seemed to provoke in him a kind of secret pleasure until she fell at his knees begging for forgiveness. Still, if she could just have better luck this time. . . . Until now she had only been able to find worthless trinkets tossed in the sand. "Dear God, let me find something good today," she thought.

And at any rate, she was happy helping him, even if it only brought in a few pennies. When he hit her, and it happened almost daily, she suffered terribly, and waited for the compensation of at least some gentle if awkward touch. After all, he was her husband. . . .

Suddenly a bright flash of light caught her eyes like a fleeting streak of lightning. Veteran connoisseur of forgotten objects, she knew when to take notice: there was something very interesting over on a far point of the beach, and she ran quickly toward it. She hurriedly dropped down in the sand next to it, afraid that someone might notice her. "Because this lovely thing, this they would take away from me," she thought.

It was a ring, covered with brilliant stones that seemed to open their shining wings to the sun. Teresa cradled it in her small hands, like a living thing, afraid that the waves or the wind might snatch it from her. Then, hopping about in the sand like a wounded bird, she headed off, murmuring: "It's a real ring, a real ring."

But suddenly her joy was cut short. Because this would be like all the other times: "Let me see. What did you find? Give it to me." And upon seeing the object: "Junk. . . . This isn't worth a thing." And he would get up to give her two or three hard slaps across the face. But then, looking more closely at the ring: "Ah no. Now this, this might be worth something. This one yes, yes. . . ." And then he'd go off to sell it for a few miserable pennies.

No, she wouldn't give it to him just for that. It was so beautiful! She rolled it around in her hands, discovering new facets of the ring each time, as if it were several rings and not just one. . . .

She wouldn't give it to him. No. She would keep it for herself, to gladden her heart in secret. When she was alone, she would put it on her finger, and, she was sure, she would appear wondrously beautiful reflected in the tiny mirror formed by the central stone of the ring.

She wondered about the owner of the ring. Was she beautiful? And her hands, what were they like? Smooth and white from being well-protected, lazy because she didn't have to hurry in her comfortable life, her tranquil life. Ah, Teresa's hands were going to look like that now, adorned with these divine little stones.

Luís sat up sleepily when he saw her come in. "So, did you find anything?" Fearful, she was slow to reply:

"Nothing, nothing. . . . This time, nothing."

"Hmm. That's strange, it being Sunday and all. . . ." He didn't hit her. Perhaps he was too tired, perhaps he noticed a different air about her. He shrugged his shoulders and returned to his nap.

But the next day the violent scenes began again. Except this time it mattered to her less because now she had her triumphant moments when, alone, she flattered her feminine vanity, lighting up the feeble soul of the ugly girl she had been by embellishing her hand with the precious ring. Luís must have noticed something different about her, because after scorning the trinkets she'd gathered and spitting out insults, he stopped suddenly with his hand in mid air, ready to strike her face.

"The way you've fixed your hair," he mumbled. "It looks good on you. . . ."

She had done her hair in homage to the ring, to this sacred ring that was transforming everything. And he had noticed, and had noticed her face shining with a new brilliance that also came from the sacred stones in the ring. And so he kissed her, and stroked her face, without the blows she was so accustomed to.

But the next afternoon he returned home unexpectedly and surprised her in the doorway with her hand held out in silent adoration of the ring.

"And that?" he demanded. "That looks valuable. Did you find it today?" She hid her hand behind her back.

"No. No, I didn't find it," she said hastily.

"Well then, what did you do, steal it?"

"No! No. . . . Someone gave it to me. . . ."

Luís let out a loud laugh. "They-gave-it-to-YOU!" he said mockingly. "Who in the world would be giving you rings?!"

Teresa raised her head. The words fell from her lips, a lie that was a protest of her insulted dignity: "A man. . . . A man. . . ."

Luís frowned. His fingers twitched as he formed a fist, and Teresa closed her eyes, waiting for the blow. But it never fell. Luís was stopped, confused by the unfamiliar brilliance in her face. He spun around and went into their hut, but returned after a few minutes.

"Listen, are you trying to make me mad? Where did you get that ring?"

"A man gave it to me."

"What man?" She could hear the fury rising in his voice.

"A dark man. . . . Tall. . . . With black hair. . . . A man. A man who says he loves me." She no longer thought about what she was saying. The words fell unbidden, rising spontaneously from the dream she was living. "He wants to take me with him. . . . He calls me 'my sweet,' 'my dear'. . . ."

"Bitch! You just wait. . . ." He raised his fists again as if to strike her, but again he stopped in mid air, paralyzed by her face, as calm and serene as a quiet lake. But this other man. . . . "I'll kill him!" he cried. "Oh yes, I'll kill him!" Teresa smiled softly.

"You can't. He's waiting for me far away. I'm going to meet him soon."

Luís changed suddenly, completely. All the anger drained away and he looked at her with agony in his eyes. This time it was he who fell to his knees, begging:

"No, Teresa, you can't leave me. I love you. Give him back his ring, I'll buy you a better one. Just today they raised my salary."

Teresa sweetly stroked his shaggy head with her ringed hand. And the stones of the ring sparkled like stars in an ebony night.

Translated by Susan Benner

Alicia Yánez Cossío

Alicia Yánez Cossío is perhaps Ecuador's most famous woman writer, and she has been a major figure in the country's literary history for decades. In recognition of her contribution, she was awarded the Medal of Cultural Achievement of the First Class by the national government in 1990, and that same year she was unanimously elected a member of the Ecuadorian Academy of the Spanish Language.

Born in Quito in 1928, Yánez Cossío remembers a happy and boisterous childhood. She was a rebellious child, one who was expelled from Catholic school four times, and she has never lost that characteristic. It surfaces frequently in her novels, both in her protagonists and in the themes and issues she chooses to tackle.

Yánez Cossío first began writing at the age of nine or ten. Having no living grandparents, she invented a grandfather who lived in Africa, to whom she wrote numerous letters and invented his responses. Through this correspondence she began to develop her skills in writing and creating stories. After finishing high school, she began to write poetry, but she found her real calling when she wrote her first novel, *Bruna, soroche y los tíos*, published in 1972 and considered a classic of Ecuadorian literature. Later, married, working as a teacher, and with five children, Yánez Cossío would write at night while everyone slept, sometimes falling into bed at four or five in the morning. But she saw her writing then as a challenge that gave her great satisfaction and happiness, and despite the many pressures of those years, they were the ones in which she wrote the most.

Yánez Cossío writes with irony, wit, biting sarcasm—and a touch of tenderness, and her novels are scathing but delightful denunciations of a society's narrow-mindedness, prejudices, and injustices. Her protagonists are often strong, rebellious women who denounce and struggle against the sexism, provincialism, and bigotry of the culture around them, and who usually triumph in some way.

The creative use of language is one of the hallmarks of Yánez Cossío's writing, and her prose exhibits a striking musicality and a keen ear for the sounds and rhythms of language. She makes full use of prosodic elements such as alliteration, assonance, repetition, parallel constructions, and plays on words to create a flowing, lilting narrative that almost hypnotizes the reader with its rhythm and music. Her prose is full of powerful metaphors, allegories, and allusions, which weave a dense texture rich in images.

The work presented here is a chapter from Yánez Cossío's novel *La casa del sano placer,* a novel that examines prostitution and the hypocrisy and exploitation with which society treats this issue. In this chapter, the wife of the mayor in a small Andean town has just become aware of her husband's infidelity, and this narrative describes the firestorm of emotions and inner battles elicited by this knowledge.

Yánez Cossío recently finished writing her first film script, a piece about Manuela Sáenz, Simón Bolivar's lover of many years, as well as a novel about Ecuador's Saint Mariana of Jesús. She has also begun writing children's stories in the last few years, and she is currently working on her memoirs.

> In this country so often women are portrayed as victims in literature, women who put up with everything, and that bothers me, it bothers me terribly. It doesn't lead to anything. We all know that Latin American women have been victims for years and years, but perhaps it's better if a writer presents models of women who are different, in order to inspire something different.

Despite the fact that I've always had to steal the time to write, it has always been a great pleasure. If it wasn't that way, I wouldn't write. Always, in the worst moments and under the worst circumstances, for me it has always been a pleasure to write.

THE MAYOR'S WIFE (Chapter 13 from *La casa del sano placer*)

Alicia Yánez Cossío

When the mayor's wife left Doña Carmen Benavides's house (where Doña Carmen had made it perfectly clear that there was something very shady going on between the mayor and the woman they called the Redhead, who had created such a bad impression among all the curious neighbors) then, in a fraction of a second the whole scaffolding of her life fell apart, shattering into a million pieces.

It was like opening a window and having the tail of a lost tornado break into the house, scattering all the papers on one's desk—similarly she saw her marriage drowning in a whirlpool. Like a storm that topples even the strongest trees, mixing the dust, the dry leaves, and the trash in the streets, so her passions and emotions whirled about inside of her when her earlier nagging suspicions became reality in the guarded conversation she had with Doña Carmen. It was an indifferent earthquake, and she was at the very epicenter trying to maintain an impossible equilibrium in order not to be swallowed alive, watching everything she had once thought of as firm and secure fall apart and turn to dust while she herself was flung from one side to the other.

Nothing would have happened if he had only told the truth from the beginning and had her there to help him free himself from the Redhead's blackmail, because that kind of secrets had a tendency to grow rapidly out of control, and when it blew up, what had been nothing but microbes or bacteria were suddenly transformed into enormous elephants. But what might have been didn't matter anymore. The reality was what she felt at that moment, even if she were acting on an assumption, a mirage.

If she had only noticed the Redhead's withered face and ungainly body.

But that would have been worse. She would have felt the insult more deeply, for she most definitely felt she had been tossed aside.

She felt hot and cold at the same time. The sting of hail and licks of red-blue flames. Burning persistent hatred and diffuse sparks of love. Humiliation that feels like the slap of a hand on your cheek and finds its way into your psyche. Uncontrollable fury that blurs the contours of things and makes you see red and yellow spots. Truth and lies; confusion and hope. All together, turned about and unraveled, jumbled and deformed in a tremendous confusion, swelling up so as to produce some kind of terrible abortion that fed itself with a ravenous hunger on its own blood.

She walked with slow, uncertain steps, feeling as if there were a red-hot nail in the middle of her chest, as if she had an obsidian splinter stabbing her ribs or a large corkscrew screwed in and then removed, taking with it threads of her own worn and withered flesh. Unsteady on her feet and unable to control her mental equilibrium, drunk on the passions that assailed her, she felt an accumulation of uncontrollable sensations. She fled from the presence of others and answered their greetings without knowing who they were or what they were saying.

"The mayor's wife was acting very strangely. She didn't answer my questions. I'd say she wasn't in her right mind."

"She didn't even say good-bye, like she ought to. She left me with my hand in mid air waiting to shake hands."

The vertical walls, the half-opened doors, the closed venetian blinds, the twisting, cobblestone streets, the familiar houses, were all beds in which she saw details of entangled, nude bodies: buttocks, mouths, hands, and torsos, without their usual erotic connotation but, rather, immensely tragic. It wasn't possible, and yet it was. She felt as if she hated and forgave at the same time and with a violent intensity that could shatter anything, including one's life.

Certainty and doubt blended together in one mass, then scattered in different directions, separating and reuniting like the lights of the will o' the wisp. 'Yes' and 'no' jumbled together with the bewilderment that fell like a lightning bolt, point down and vertical, like an unsheathed sword, and the inquisitions that twisted about in her and in her terrible and desolate situation, pursuing her with questions that didn't wait for answers. Blind vengeance and possible pardon splashed together in the same sickening swamp of jealousy. Rage spurred her on with an intensity so unknown to her that she felt the need to reach a level of physical violence, of blood and blows, of tearing skin and flayings, of strikes of a metal-tipped whip and the kind of bites that leave pieces of dripping flesh in your teeth.

At moments she was able to stand back and look at herself, and then she felt a pitiful compassion. She saw herself shrunken, dehumanized, broken, like some worthless old object you throw away when you can replace it with another, newer one for a reduced price. She walked quickly, almost running down the path of hysteria and the torturous trail of a gratuitous insult, not to her vanity, but rather to her feelings.

"What's wrong with the mayor's wife? She wasn't even watching where she was going. She pushed me aside like she owned the street. If she's in such a hurry she should use her car instead of assaulting defenseless citizens."

The tornado continued inside her, jumbling everything: good memories and bad ones, which appeared in illogical sequences, sweet words and bitter ones repeating themselves, leaving a crust of honey and bitter herbs, promises which were made and then, little by little, broken, as if they were made to some other people who had died. Arguments that ended in endearments like the raging waters of a river returning to their banks, although they weren't the same. Long silences that devoured words like a terrifying tunnel without escape, and other times when words were smooth as silk, confidences that one only says, only hears, once.

If it were possible to go back in time to retrieve something forgotten, she would have looked more closely at the woman they called "the Redhead," but it was too late now, and she only concentrated her attention on the signals of her husband's infidelity and the woman's long, clawlike nails. It was all so fast and so senseless, like those misfortunes that approach silently on tip-toe and then suddenly explode with a certainty so real that it remains incomprehensible.

That a woman would destroy herself for a man, patience and more patience until suddenly she explodes, but that the cause should be another woman, was outrageous and repulsive.

Feeling ridiculously crazed and base, she thought of going through his personal mail piled on the table in the front hall. She thought of checking his pockets and the lining of his coat and searching his office. Masochist, as if pain itself had turned against her, she bit her lips until they bled, breathing raggedly in order to quiet the wail struggling to escape her throat. She clenched her fists tightly, digging her nails into the sweaty palms of her hands, leaving marks like blue half-moons in a line. Her face burned as if shame itself had taken possession of all the pigment cells. It wasn't just that they had snatched away from her something that was more or less hers, it was above all else this pain of an irreparable affront, it was this representation of jealousy in its most feminine form.

She at least had the good sense to take the long route home in order not to pass the house with the green eaves and shutters where the Redhead lived. Her heart pounded at a savage rhythm as if death were fluttering nearby. She didn't want to die; before that she wanted to take some kind of horrified delight in the butcher shop of bodies that stubbornly appeared everywhere.

"The mayor's wife went by and didn't even bother to look at me. Her face was all red like she had sunstroke, and it even looked like she'd been crying."

She finally reached her house, but it didn't seem like the place from which she had left just a short while ago. She fell face down on the bed as if collapsing after dragging herself across the burning sands of some absurdly desolate desert, and gave in to the torrent of tears she had been fighting down the entire endless trip from Doña Carmen Benavides's house to her own, a journey in which she could find no oasis, just the mirage of a woman offended and displaced. There was nothing to be done nor anywhere to go nor anything to say, except perhaps to ask herself if it was his fault, as it had been so many times before; if it was the fault of the woman in the house with the green eaves and shutters, who was probably stunningly beautiful, and the poor man succumbed to her charms; or if it was just that she herself was old and hideous. She didn't understand anything anymore.

And she walked over to the mirror and looked at her face and saw that the years were etching dreaded crow's feet there, but you could only see them if you got up close. And she saw two long lines extending up from the corners of her mouth, but they were still faint. And she touched her face and began to examine herself closely, inch by inch. She didn't look at all old for her age. She noted her double chin, swearing softly, but her neck wasn't yet like that of an old woman. And with one stroke she tore off all of her clothes and stood naked in front of the mirror.

She was herself and no one else. She had put on a little weight, and it made her seem shorter, but that wasn't enough to make her ugly. Standing naked like that in front of the mirror, she looked as if she were confessing and intended to absolve herself. Her breasts were no longer firm nor quite in the same position as before. But they had served their mission well with each of her children. If men only knew how to look beyond appearances, they would discover that hidden beauty that you can't see, but that you experience all the same.

And she saw the four or five long stretch marks on her stomach that were neither ugly nor beautiful, but made her remember that a human being had grown inside of her, which was an amazing fact in itself, astounding enough to be sacred. And she examined her back and her sides and she saw that she looked older, but not repulsive. And she thought with a slight chill that if by virtue of fathering children men were to develop some kind of scars, she and all mothers would love those marks and would stroke them over and over again to remember those times and to feel young once more.

There were no two ways about it, she had been young and now she was old, but even as she was, old and getting older, she was herself and she liked that. Her body began to radiate a new light, and if others couldn't see that light, too bad for them. She knew that old age could never be ugly because being old was no one's fault. Poor, pitiful humanity with its wretched ego would still have to struggle forward on crutches for millennia and millennia before learning to love beyond those things that age.

She tired of standing in front of her own body and sat down in order to examine herself inside. She closed her eyes and began to see herself. She was a woman with an irrefutable capacity to love, but she was seeking the impossible if she expected others to react similarly, even just a reflection, an imitation.

She thought about the past that one always remembers in such moments. Together, shoulder to shoulder they formed their family. In the beginning they were poor and poverty united them. He worked as a clerk and she washed his shirts. They hoped they would inherit some day, but their relatives refused to die. As soon as they escaped from poverty, he began to visit the Bronze Ass Sisters. He said he was a lover of Chopin and Beethoven, but she knew he was really a lover of Clarisa. He tired of her in time and got involved with an entertainer from the first circus that came to town. He disappeared for several days. They said the circus company threw him out by the scruff of the neck because the performer swore she didn't know what he was talking about. When he came back, she didn't make a scene as she had often done before because she didn't want the neighbors to talk, and because it broke her heart to see him come back like a beaten dog. And even more, she felt a petty, but very maternal indignation to think that some low-life singer had rebuffed him. And she continued to think of this moment and that moment and all the moments of their life.

In the end there was herself, without resignation, because she saw herself above it all. It was as if she were the mother of all mortal beings, the begetter of life itself and its customs, the one who picked up the pieces when others stumbled and made mistakes; even if she were a sacrificial vestal, with the energy of the slow-dying phoenix, she was who she was, the one who never betrayed herself.

She turned and dressed herself and felt as if she had grown. Her intimacy needed no clothing because none that she had could fit. She grew in size and volume, so much so that the house felt as if it had shrunk, so much so that she could tell all her everyday sorrows to go to hell, so much so that she could gather up all the pieces of herself, one by one, to fit them together again in a complicated puzzle, so much so that she felt as if she had died and then discovered the desire to live once more, so much so that she could stand on top of her own heart and feel that no one in the entire world could make her give in. She was consoling herself in her own way; what kept her together after such a terrible storm was pride.

Whatever happened, it was her pride in being a woman and nothing else.

Translated by Susan Benner

PERU

Gaby Cevasco

Born in 1952, Gaby Cevasco grew up in Ica, Peru, a rural region south of Lima, where she was a child who very much enjoyed her life in the country. After completing high school, Cevasco moved to Lima, an event that eventually influenced her literary work. Disliking the big city, Cevasco began to write to help her reclaim and re-create the part of her life that she had left behind in the country.

Although Cevasco never intended to become a writer, she feels that her family influenced her greatly. She grew up surrounded by people who loved to tell stories, especially at night after dinner, their faces lit only by an oil lamp because electricity had not yet come to her town. At an early age she began to tell her own stories, but not to family members; her audience included the trees, flowers, and birds she encountered as she took many solitary walks, narrating her latest creations out loud. She never wrote her stories down until she moved to the city, motivated by the loss of her "audience." At first, Cevasco felt no desire to publish her work, but in 1990, a friend encouraged her to do so, and by the end of that year, her first book, a collection of short stories titled *Sombras y rumores*, appeared.

Cevasco's story "Between Clouds and Lizards" resulted from her eavesdropping as a child. She often listened behind closed doors to the conversations of landowners and rich farmers, who exploited the land and those who worked for them. Stories of death were always told during family mealtimes, and many of these stories were based on fights between two friends who had been drinking, who grabbed machetes, and later asked each other for forgiveness, horrified at the brutality of their actions. "Between Clouds and Lizards" re-creates this all-too-common show of machista bravado, which is still a commonplace occurrence in certain circles of Peruvian society.

Gaby Cevasco currently resides in Lima, where she works as a journalist at the Centro Peruano de la Mujer "Flora Tristán," specializing in articles dealing with discrimination against women. She is also completing work on her second collection of short stories, titled *Historias de no amor*.

BETWEEN CLOUDS AND LIZARDS

Gaby Cevasco

Don't look at me that way, I'm not crazy. What happens is, when you've lived a full life, you become wise, or perhaps you turn into a witch doctor, which is the same thing. For a few days now I've had the feeling that there's going to be a tragedy. Yes, there's going to be an important death. . . . I say important, not for the number of deaths, but because the one who dies will be a man of power. And the only one who has power around here is Don Augusto Javier de la Piedra, the owner of the town. Look at the clouds; you'll see that they confirm my premonition. When they turn dark, it's because there's going to be a tragedy, or, because it's going to rain. But since the rain in these parts is so scarce, it's more likely that there's going to be a tragedy. But what kind of tragedy could it be if it's not death! . . . Yes sir, someone's going to die and it's going to be someone big. There are reasons for Don Augusto Javier de la Piedra to die. But you know as well as I do that there are many who have reason to wish him dead. It's as if Don Augusto Javier were a scourge; wherever he goes he causes misfortune. He has a lot of money, and a heart of stone. The fortune was made during the lifetime of Don Augusto Javier senior, and his son's heart was formed from the time he was a child. Yes, I remember him well because we grew up together; sure, his father molded him, and my father molded me. No, don't be surprised, it's as if I were seeing him again. I remember when his father used to take him there at the end of each day, to the summit, and pointing to the horizon he would say to him: "When I die, all this will be yours, but take care that it remains that way. And when someone tries to take it from you, don't hesitate to crush him, like this, just like I'm crushing this lizard!" How can I forget it! We were both children and we used to play together, hunting for lizards and climbing rocks so we could spy on women bathing in the river. But no, his quarrelsome nature never left him. And if my father taught me anything, it was to not let the turkey buzzards peck at me, and the De la Piedras are turkey buzzards: wherever they go there's death. And death was their solution when someone dared to oppose them. "Kill him, don't let him do that, kill him!" That's what Don Augusto Javier senior ordered his son to do when we used to knock each other down in unruly brawls. But Don Augusto Javier junior always ended up running home where a whipping by his humiliated father waited for him. And if the old man never laid a hand on me, it was because he had a lot of respect for my father. That's how we grew up then; me working my little plot of land, and he, crushing lizards, which is to say, crushing poor people. The years passed and the old men died, his and mine. Now, sometimes Don Augusto Javier junior comes to the house to have a drink, but you should know that I figure he hasn't forgotten those beatings. One day I found my dog dead and he came by to offer his condolences for my loss. "What happened to your pet, friend?" Yes, he calls me "friend"; he says he has to be the one to take my first-born child to be baptized, and he makes fun of me by saying that I don't look for a wife because he doesn't. But I'm patient with him. Poor wretch; he can't forget my punches and he's looking for an excuse to get rid of his pain. One day we went out drinking, I don't remember the reason. Suddenly, machetes in hand, we stood face to face, but the liquor couldn't rid him of his fear. "You're going to be my friend. There's no reason to insult one another and even less reason to attack each another," he told me, and left for his house. A few weeks later, I found my cattle dead. Poor things, their bellies were all swollen. "It's poison, poison!" the townspeople whispered. He came by again to console me. "Nobody does that to another human being, my friend," he told me, and he offered me a new pair of animals so I could start again. But right then and there I said, "With my little plot of land I have enough." Then, my crops burned. The fire covered the whole countryside. The corn and cotton fields burned. For days and days the whole town smelled burnt. You can still smell it in the air. Yes, it's a windy afternoon. The dark clouds are already retreating. But it's a shame: the clouds were announcing an important death and there you are, my friend, belly-up just like my cows. He came to have a drink with me and it was a tragic toast, friend; like I was telling you, those clouds were announcing either death or rain, but today it hasn't rained.

Translated by Kathy S. Leonard

Pilar Dughi

Born in Peru in 1956, Pilar Dughi completed studies at the Pontificia Universidad Católica and at the Universidad Nacional Mayor de San Marcos, both in Lima. She has also completed postgraduate studies in social sciences at the Sorbonne in Paris. She is currently finishing work on a master's degree in Peruvian and Latin American literature, completing a thesis dealing with the psycho-literary criticism in the works of Mario Vargas Llosa, concentrating on his work *El pez en el agua*.

Dughi's fiction often treats the sociopolitical situation of her native country. Between 1980 and 1993, Peru was plunged into a deep economic crisis, when the most prolonged hyperinflation in world history reached heights of 2,000,000 percent. At the same time, the country also entered into an armed conflict that lasted some fourteen years, causing 25,000 deaths and 5,000 disappeared. The "war" was not a battle that had been declared in the conventional manner, but rather a war waged by subversives. During these horrendous times, the inhabitants of Lima lived in fear and uncertainty, needing to leave their homes to work and carry out the chores of everyday life, but feeling constant fear about what might happen to them in the streets. Dughi says of this time, "My greatest fear was being caught in a bomb attack as I walked near some public building, embassy, or movie theater. My only goal was to survive such attacks and dream about my future escape to some other city or some other country."

Dughi's story "The Days and Hours" reflects this era in Peru's history. She chose one of Lima's dark and sinister streets for the setting of the story, selecting one of the houses on that street as her protagonist's home. The protagonist of the story represents a combination of young girls Dughi saw daily in the poorer neighborhoods of Lima: a clever, discerning, intelligent girl, who knew that her options in life were few. Without money, without opportunities to obtain a university education, without a job, and hating the future awaiting her, the young protagonist is attracted by a promise of change, which she believes can be brought about by subversive activities.

This young and naive woman is impetuous, lacking in life experience, and searching for a rapid change, which she is unable to find. Her desperation is fueled by the tedious routine of her life, reflected in her mother. Her rebellious spirit finds an outlet in the subversive movement, where atrocious acts are perpetrated against innocent people, acts which become almost trivial, which are considered justified by those who commit them.

Dughi's story serves as strong criticism of the numerous subversive groups that sprang up in Peru—criticism of those misguided, proud individuals who felt that the act of being a "terrorist" or "subversive" lifted them out of social anonymity. "Those who participated in terrorist activities wanted more than quick social change, they wanted to inspire terror and admiration in others, to convert themselves into major figures, something that would satisfy their individual narcissism."

Pilar Dughi has published short stories in various journals such as *Caretas*, *Sí*, *La Moneda*, *Comercio*, and *La República*, as well as a collection of short stories, *La premeditación y el azar*, in 1989. In 1995 she was awarded the national prize for the short story by the Asociación Cultural Peruano-Japonesa for her unpublished collection of short stories titled *Palabra errante*, which includes stories dealing with daily life, historical events, and the jungle regions of Peru. Also in 1995, Dughi was named among nineteen finalists out of 3,710 from around the world in the short-story contest Concurso Internacional de Cuento Juan Rulfo, organized by Radio France International in Paris.

THE DAYS AND HOURS

Pilar Dughi

A star freed in the Apocalypse
among the roaring of tigers and tears.
César Moro

She looks out the hallway window, attracted by the strong penetrating light at that time of day, which announces the sun, that persistent crushing sun which drains energy and extinguishes the best intentions. It flashes across the roofs of the houses, announcing the beginning of summer. Between the heat and the suffocating fumes from onions, urine, lemons, and trash, food carts are lined up below in the street, one after another, like a disorganized army of roving street vendors on the corner between Jr. Saloom Street and Buenos Aires Avenue. Back-door suppliers of noodles, boiled potatoes, meat stew, and fish offer their wares by shouting in the middle of the confusion of chicken vendors. People walk by, some alongside others, flowing in a deafening ocean of car horns. Buses crammed with human bundles move forward through the streets and alleys, dodging the masses of men and women who march in an aimless procession.

"Help me sweep the stairs," her mother says from the end of the hallway. "Hurry up, because I'm going to buy the chicken and I want you to start the rice and prepare the noodles," her voice continues with an urgent and commanding tone.

"All right," she responds.

She moves away from the window and walks toward the living-room table. She picks up the small geraniums and magnolias that lie scattered like bodies over the plastic tablecloth. Some are pink, others are whitish and have small reddish spots that look like drops of blood. Just like blood.

"It's important that you arrive on time," Victor had told her the previous afternoon. And he had not been able to disguise that imperceptible quiver in his voice that invariably exposed him, and which had caused her to respond energetically, "Of course."

She places the flowers in a small clay pot on the table.

"In the afternoon go talk to Don Julián to see if he still wants you to help him in the shop," her mother orders while standing at her side. Giving a small snort, the woman drags the mop over the blue floor tiles and looks suddenly and with curiosity at her torn bathrobe. "My pocket is ripped," she exclaims disgustedly. "This fabric has lasted so many years, and look how worn out it is now," she says with great sadness. "Do you see it, honey? Well, now it's about ready for the trash."

"Ready for the trash," she repeats automatically. She heads slowly toward the broom and the dust pan that are waiting for her in the corner by the stairs.

The old woman descends the steps heavily with the huge basket hanging from her arm. "It must be around one o'clock," she mutters from the landing on the first floor. "It's so late!" her mother finishes saying before disappearing through the door leading to the street.

She waits in silence for a few seconds. Now the house is deserted. Just her and that sinister throbbing that she sometimes feels when she's alone. She gestures with her hand, as if dispelling bad thoughts, and heads toward the kitchen.

She takes out a bag of rice. She opens a small hole in it, letting the rice spill out in a narrow but forceful stream into the metal bowl. Then thousands of grains hit the surface of the bowl, mixing together, like little beings with no destiny, but whose force is so intense and so violent that despite their minute volume, they are able to bore through the narrow opening in the plastic bag, making it larger, making it grow until it opens completely and the torrent of rice rushes out with incredible speed, covering the entire bowl. Then comes the purification, she tells herself while she places the bowl under the stream of crystalline water. The grains remain submerged, transforming the transparent liquid until it becomes whitish and thick. She squeezes the mass several times with her hands and checks to see if the water becomes clear and pure again. She remains like this, distracted for a few minutes, with a fixed and empty stare resting on that white mass, when she is surprised again by recent events that appear to her in sudden lights like flashes that deafen and blind everything. She sees herself on that bluish night, standing under the faint glow of the public lighting system at Victor's side, crouched down near him, but also distant and remote. "Because we're alone now," he had told her, "because you'll do your thing and I'll do mine." And that was the first and only moment in her life that she had understood, with horror, that she was shaping a destiny where nothing and no one could accompany her.

She turns on the gas stove and places the blackened frying pan on top of it. A little squirt of oil, some garlic. Wait until they're golden brown to add the rice, she thinks, repeating the old recipe that she had always heard from her mother's mouth during her childhood years, when she used to scatter her notebooks on the kitchen table, the one they used for lunch, for dinner, for crying, studying, for talking with someone, or for being alone, where they would sit and wait for something that would never arrive.

"Here I am!" the voice of the old woman growls from the stairs. Her daughter listens to the clumsy movements, the sound of the heavy basket hitting the corners.

"You have to prepare that lunch. Let's see, here I have the chicken."

And the old woman throws the large bird wrapped in newspaper on the sink.

"Did you wash the lunch pail?" her mother asks.

"Yes, mother."

"You have to take lunch to the workers. Today I'm going to charge them two each," she continues while she lifts the lid on the saucepan. "One piece of chicken for each plate, the rice and noodles, okay? Ah, I ran into Margarita on the corner, dear. That poor old thing is losing all her teeth, you should see her," she exclaims sadly. "She has money, like always. That's the luck of whores, but I still don't understand how she goes around well-dressed and with money."

She helps her mother with the basket. She places it on the old woman's head and some of the carrots, potatoes, tomatoes, one after another, fall, knocking into one another on the table.

"They say there are rats on the ground floor. Jesus, as long as they don't make it up here."

She sticks a sharp knife in the potato. She peels it carefully and watches how the peeling falls off easily, without breaking.

"Make the stew. I'm going to clean the room."

She nods her head.

Someone begins to sing nearby, very close to her. She lifts her face and looks through a hole in the wall above the sink. Facing her, there's a neighboring building where she can see a bedroom with small, open windows. It's the girl who stands in front of her mirror every day at the same time, getting dressed, fastening her pants, taking the rollers out of her hair, putting on red lipstick while she sings, making gestures and faces with a carefully practiced self-confidence. She's the same age and goes to the university. She's seen her leave and meet her boyfriend on the corner. They take the same bus. The girl carries her notebooks with one arm and her purse with the other. Later, she'll look for a job, she thinks. She'll stand in line in some obscure office full of people, she'll wait until she gets bored. She'll wander from one place to another and finally that college girl with her degree will figure out that her only hope is to work as a cashier in Monterrey. People are so stupid, she tells herself.

She finishes peeling the carrots. She throws them into the chicken stew and the red sauce splatters on the white tiles. She adds a little water and turns the fire down. At least she's calm. She knows now that nothing waits for her in those streets out there, in that city she didn't choose to be born in or to live in. There's nothing that she hasn't measured or premeasured before. She sees him again. On that corner of Jr. Canevaro Street, she's nervous, her forehead beaded with sweat. Doesn't he realize? Doubts are no good here. She knows perfectly well that there is no room for words or oversights. Not on those streets, or in those people, or in that future without surprises, except for those who are crazy or for the dreamers who still believe in lottery tickets or the soccer pool.

"Is it ready?" the old woman's gray head appears in the doorway.

She places the lunch pail on the table and puts shredded pieces of chicken on each one of the plates.

"Serve less, girl, or there won't be enough," her mother murmurs somewhat worriedly. "Oh yeah, that miserable rotten father of yours could have sent me money. But no, he never will. If I hadn't started this little business we would have died of hunger."

And the subject seems so normal, she thinks, as if Jr. Canevaro Street were very far away, and as if Victor were being erased like a shadow in the night, and as if the brilliant moon illuminating the sidewalk had become hidden, little by little; but she is running, distancing herself from that stiff body stretched out on the street, with its open eyes and twisted lips.

"Honey, are you going to go to the store?"

"Later."

"I'll be back," her mother grumbles.

She watches the large fat body of the old woman go slowly downstairs.

She listens to the faint huffing coming from that bundle of clumsy humanity, which then loses itself behind the habitual slam of the door to the street.

She walks to her bedroom. She stretches out on the bed waiting for the time to pass. There are exactly two hours left. When was it? It's a story that repeats itself in her dreams. A shy and pale boy who had approached her after school two years ago. His tone of voice was solemn and ceremonious. The first contact. If it hadn't been for that, she never would have dreamed beyond the harsh reality that was closing her doors, and she would still be at the shop, wasting years, destroying her fantasies, exposing her movements to the lascivious glances of Don Julián who, attentive to her slightest oversight, would stand alongside her murmuring words that she was determined not to hear. And she feels peaceful. So much so that she could eat beef kebabs on any street corner, waiting patiently for her time to arrive. She goes slowly back to bed. Her eyelids close, but she should be alert, not give in to sleep. She tries to sit up, but no, it's better to rest. There's no reason to resist, it's justified, she mutters finally, before losing herself in the depths of sleep.

"You're still here?" the voice of the old woman echoes from the end of the hall.

"I'm leaving now," she answers, climbing off the bed, startled.

"It'll get dark this afternoon," exclaims her mother from the kitchen.

She lifts the mattress.

"Are you going to eat something before you go?"

"I don't have time."

She listens to the stream of water, far-off, on the plates, the utensils clinking. She saw him again, standing, a thousand times, lighting a cigarette, the last one he would smoke in his life.

"Tomorrow we'll make the beans that I bought yesterday."

Dressed in the green uniform that was to be his shroud. She approached from the rear and saw nothing but his eyes at the last and sudden instant, in that infinite moment for him, brief for her, because life now was like that, with neither long nor short times, without limits, and that man didn't know it, or if he did, it was too late because he fell so quickly that he didn't realize he was dead.

"Did you know that the workers finish next week?" her mother asks.

And it was only grabbing the weapon and running, running and taking off her sweater, throwing it away, "So they don't recognize us," Victor had said.

She takes out the revolver.

"But later I'm going to talk with the woman at the hardware store. She told me that they want someone to take lunch over there. There's no lack of work, huh?"

She places it inside her pants.

"Are you listening to me?"

She puts one sweater on over the other.

"I don't want you coming back late. If you do, I'll lock the door."

She leaves the room.

"There are a lot of drunks out there. Anything could happen to you, honey."

"I'm leaving, mother."

"Don't be late."

She goes down the stairs. She opens the door. The sky is gray; there aren't any food carts out yet. The bundles destined for market are piled up on the sidewalk, the street vendors are tying up their wares with rope, they're closing up their stands. She hears a scream. It's a miaow, she thinks. It's a cat. The night is just beginning.

Translated by Kathy S. Leonard

Carmen Luz Gorriti

Carmen Luz Gorriti was born in Lima in 1951 to a mother who was a professor of philosophy and literature and to a father who was a book vendor and a political militant. Gorriti was influenced by her father's activities, and when she entered the Universidad Mayor de San Marcos in 1968, she divided her time between the study of sociology and an intense dedication to political militancy. During the 1970s she joined the struggle for human rights, for the formation of unions, and for a radical change in Peru.

In 1975 Gorriti married a *mestizo* who was a union mine organizer, and with her husband she relocated to Morochoca, a mining town in the mountains where she lived for three years, sharing the difficult life of the miners and their families. It was during this time that she began to write seriously, moved by the need to relate what she saw and what she was experiencing. Several of her stories were published under the pseudonym "Marcelina Ríos" by the newspaper *El Diario de Marka*.

Between 1977 and 1979, Peru was rocked by a series of struggles between small mining towns and unions. These problems also affected Morochoca, resulting in a general strike in which Gorriti actively participated as the leader of the Women's Committee. Her political involvement resulted in a period of persecution for Gorriti and her husband, who was eventually fired from his position. They were then both expelled from Morochoca.

Gorriti returned to Lima, where she began graduate work in sociology with the hope of using her knowledge as a tool for improving conditions in her country. Upon completing her studies, she moved to Huancayo, where she worked as a sociologist and struggled to understand the mentality of the *mestizos* who lived in the area. The cultural isolation she experienced during this time led her to begin writing again; however, the work she produced during this period has never been published.

In 1990 Gorriti's story "The Legacy" won the only prize in the contest "Magda Portal" in Lima. The story was subsequently published along with other stories in *Memorias clandestinas*. "The Legacy" was written while Gorriti was working with grassroots women's organizations and reflects the subjugation that women experience at the hands of a patriarchal society. The protagonist, Felícitas, embodies the simplicity and goodness of the Peruvian woman who has dedicated her life to helping others. This self-sacrifice has not benefitted Felícitas during her lifetime, but her kindness is her legacy, for all who knew her remember her, and even in death, her presence has the power to transform the hate and distrust felt by those left behind.

Gorriti currently works as a psychocorporeal therapist, a profession which she feels has allowed her to understand her own body, her emotions, and her individual existence. She is an active member of a writers' group called "Anillo de Moebius," which recently published a volume titled *Historias de miércoles*.

THE LEGACY (A STORY FROM HUANCAYO)

Carmen Luz Gorriti

She was dying, but still she succeeded in finding her dentures, which had fallen. "*Comadre,* my dear friend, sit right here, drink this water." Felícitas grabbed her dentures with all the strength she possessed and thought about Julia, who had taken her to the dentist ("For what, my dear, since I'm old") and who had paid the millions of *soles* that the doctor charged. Too much money for Felícitas, who had always worked in order to pay the bills at her house, a lot of money for the vegetable vendor from Royal Street. But of course, it was no longer too much for Julia, who came to visit her from the United Sates, making everyone call her "Julie."

"Don't throw the water out, *comadre,* drink it, drink it, it's good for you." But nothing stayed inside Felícitas. On the contrary, everything came out: tears, mucous, sweat, and white-foaming vomit. . . . "What will my old man say?" she thought. But the old man didn't say anything when he saw her at Carmen Hospital, with the probes and the tubes and the needles and the immobile face of one who has suffered a stroke.

Justina, on the other hand, did talk. She talked, she begged, she prayed. The talking was what most frightened Felícitas, because her daughter was yelling at her father, "It's your fault, it's your fault." Felícitas would have liked to grab her by the arm and stop her, "Shut up, child, he's going to hit you." But for some hours now, her voice no longer came out and her hand didn't obey, it was simply quiet somewhere. Tears no longer flowed when her daughter spoke softly in her ear: "Don't die, Mamita, don't leave me."

For what, she told herself . . . for a long while, everyone in the house knew that she would have to die soon. Since they had told her in the hospital, when half her body became paralyzed: "Avoid heat and things that upset you." But how? A mother can't do that. What will happen to them now? She remembered her children, one by one, those who were born with their tiny wrinkled faces, those who died before reaching their first birthday, those who had left without saying good-bye, fleeing their paternal home, those who couldn't leave.

Still, it was Manuelito who caused her the most pain, her oldest, the child of the dawn who knew the night's tenderness when she gave him her breast and they slept together, warmed by their bodies that were almost like one; Manuelito, who played with the chickens, with the guinea pigs, with little cardboard boxes. What will he do now, without a mother, that child who never grew up?

"I'm afraid, Mamá," Manuel told her. That was the last word Felícitas heard while she was entering the black hole. Afraid . . . afraid. . . . Felícitas had felt afraid when her mother said good-bye out there in Pampas, handing her toasted maize and cheese for the journey, telling her, "You're going to study." But she didn't study because she was afraid to say to her godmother, "I want to study," and later she was afraid to say to Juan, "I don't want you to touch me like that," and later she was afraid to tell the others that her belly was growing, and she had preferred to run away with Juan, who was now her husband.

"The poor person who is afraid," she thought as she felt herself dissolving. She no longer felt afraid of anything while her thoughts began to wander around the room, trying to alight on some warm body that could receive them.

They fluttered over old Juan, but he had no door open, only an immense rage that sealed his jaws, which clenched the muscles in his stomach, in his throat: "You're abandoning me, old woman, just like you always wanted, that's what you're doing."

Her thoughts flew over Justina and found her fury alive. "My mother has died of exhaustion," she repeated to herself, feeling the weariness of all the years lying ahead of her, working hard to support her father. "It's no use for me to be angry, because I'm going to have to do it anyway. I married for pleasure, I had children for pleasure. Now, I belong to my father anyway, until he dies or I die. It would have been better to run away, like my sisters did, and out there in those places, lose respect for everything."

Felícitas's thoughts searched, but could not enter Manuel, who was sobbing in a corner. He was trembling with the sensation of being nothing more than his weeping. His father's eyes looked at him as always, telling him "coward," and he was once again the child who, from beneath the table, waited to see the threatening whip fall. No longer would his mother's body be there to receive his father's punishment or life's punishment. Manuel remembered his mother's sweet body, which, with the passing of the years, had begun to shrink in stature, hunching at the shoulders, weakening in the legs.

"The poor person who is afraid. . . ." During that afternoon of memories, no one opened their heart for Felícitas's last thoughts, and they remained wandering through the streets of Chilca, flitting through the market, over the heads of the *comadres* and the housewives.

"The old woman has died." The word was passed from person to person and the hem of many an apron was lifted to catch the abundance of tears which were falling. "The dear old woman has died," circulated among the cart drivers and the travelers and the porters and the milkmaids and the food vendors and the abused women who she had nursed and the hungry who had tasted her bread and the rape victims who had confided in her and the drunks who Felícitas would gather from the street and the grieving who had so often opened their hearts to her.

So for three days and three nights they sat with the old woman's body, accompanied by an abundance of sugar-cane liquor, which this time the old man insisted on buying with his own money. The third night, they had to bring a nurse to deflate their mother's body, which had continued to swell after death; they had to bring benches from the church and rent the neighbor's patio to make room for the ranks of pilgrims who still continued to arrive.

No one realized, during the wake, that that night, terrorists had blown off the barracks door and that the army had left to give chase. No one realized, because everyone was talking about the death, though in reality, they were talking about themselves, about the wounds she had helped to heal. "She gave me an herb that helped cure the heaviness in this leg"; "She got rid of the evil darkness that had taken possession of my head"; "She paid me a few cents extra for the food I used to sell her"; "Every day she took soup to the crazy man in the neighborhood."

With all the whispering, they didn't pay attention to the dynamite, to the noise, to the sounds of running. But the soldiers entered: "No one move, everyone here is a terrorist!" And all became silent. The blackened faces blended into the shadows; one couldn't recognize among them the neighbor's son, the cousin, the friend who was taken away last month. Slowly, a collective memory was formed about those relatives from town who had been taken to the barracks and who had never returned.

"The poor person who is afraid," thought Felícitas when she was entering the black hole, while she was ridding herself of her fear; that is how her thoughts continued to wander around the proximity of her body; that is how they resounded clearly in the patio where the wake was taking place, while the soldiers ordered to their knees all the people she loved so much.

"The poor person who is afraid . . . and he who is afraid is only poor," thought Manuel, while he felt tenderness toward all those humble souls who were crying for his mother. That is how he was able to take Justina's hand, who then took her father's hand, who took the hand of the skinny washer woman, who took the drunk's hand, who took the hand of the cafeteria waiter, who took everyone's hands when the circle of strength closed.

No one moved from their place. "There is no more fear, there is no more fear," said the people in a whisper that grew, while the courage of the commanding officer diminished. He had already begun to consider that, since there were more than two hundred mourners gathered and only twenty soldiers, perhaps it was necessary to realize that what he had in front of his eyes was a common, everyday wake, with civilians who possessed civil rights.

When they closed the casket the next day, everyone was able to observe that Doña Felícitas, the old vegetable vendor, was quite beautiful and almost seemed to be smiling inside her coffin.

Translated by Kathy S. Leonard

Bethzabé Guevara

Bethzabé Guevara's career has been guided by her commitment to environmental and feminist issues. Born in Lima in 1957, she studied at the School of Biological Sciences at the Universidad Nacional Mayor de San Marcos. As a biologist and conservation activist, Guevara has participated in a number of campaigns for the conservation of the Manu National Park and has presented papers dealing with marsupials and other wildlife found in the region.

Most of Guevara's creative works are written for children. However, her first published work, the story "The Señorita Didn't Teach Me," is based on stories her mother told her when she was a child. This story is representative in both subject and tone of the work currently being produced by young women in the Andean countries of Latin America. The story is set in Peru, a country with a large, unassimilated indigenous rural population that historically has been singled out for exploitation and barred from education and other opportunities for self-advancement, dooming them to misery and poverty. Few Indian children in Peru attend more than a year or two of school, if that. Many of them may never have the opportunity to attend school at all, for they are often needed by their impoverished families to perform essential chores that ensure the family's survival. Females, however, fare more poorly than do males, and studies show that female adults are more likely to be illiterate than are their male counterparts. Those fortunate enough to attend school often find the institutions ill prepared to provide them with even the most basic education. Teachers may have dubious credentials, often having received no more than a few years of schooling themselves.

This is the reality faced by the young Indian students in "The Señorita Didn't Teach Me," who realize that their only hope for betterment will be found in their own solidarity and action. Urged on by an older and more experienced student who acts as their mentor, leader, and, when necessary, their punisher, the students rebel against the ethnic oppression shown by their white school teacher, and against the farcical attempts by the church and state (represented by the priest and mayor who test them) to show that the system has provided an education for its poor indigenous wards. In a final act of rebellion, the students band together to form a united front against the neglect and denigration heaped upon them by an inequitable system that will continue to marginalize them if they do not act.

"The Señorita Didn't Teach Me" is a story that depicts young Indian women working for change through protest, rebellion, and revolution. Their battle cry of "The Señorita didn't teach me" echoes far beyond the walls of their classroom on their examination day: with those simple words they denounce their own history of neglect and abuse and cry out for change, for themselves, as well as for those who will follow them.

"The Señorita Didn't Teach Me" was selected as one of the winning entries in the short-story contest Primer Concurso de Cuento "Magda Portal" and was subsequently published in *Memorias clandestinas* along with other winning entries in 1990 by Ediciones Flora Tristán.

THE SEÑORITA DIDN'T TEACH ME

Bethzabé Guevara

That's what you should say. Did you hear me? And pity the poor girl who answers her or writes something on the blackboard; if she does, we'll beat her good outside in the dark alley. You had better say, "The Señorita didn't teach me," and nothing more. That devil deserves it. Haven't we already been here for two years? And her? Sewing the whole time. And us? Forever ignorant, getting hit with sticks and having our hair pulled. "The Señorita didn't teach me!" That's our battle cry.

That's how Julia Prickly Pear finished her speech, who at fourteen was one of the oldest girls in the class. She was thin, long, and ugly; and now with her sharp nose shining and her cheeks flushed with anger, she is even uglier. Only her long gold earrings, the envy of the whole class, give her the appearance of a proud and noble Indian.

All of the older girls are convinced that the agreement is fair; the younger of us don't understand the reasoning very well, but we know we must obey or suffer the consequences. Julia Prickly Pear has a hard fist and is afraid of no one, not even the Señorita.

It's enough just remembering that on one of the many days we arrived at school, we found all of our chairs in the middle of a pool of mud on the back playground. We frequently found one or two chairs being "punished" in the middle of the mud puddle used to make adobe, each one with its respective sign: "Here's Abdulia, for laughing"; "Here kneels Lucinda, for hitting"; "This is Imelda, for not loving me." The last time there was no little sign with an explanation, but it was obvious that it had been César or José again, the Señorita's younger brothers. Surely it was in retaliation for the beating that the girls had given them the day before, after school.

There we all were, busy recognizing and pulling our chairs out without getting muddy, when the Señorita arrived. "You little bandits, you wretched girls, you do this to upset me," and grabbing the first chair she found, she lifted it high and started advancing towards us, trying to corner one of us; we all ran from her path, frightened, like doves in front of a nose-diving hawk. We saw that Julia Prickly Pear didn't move; on the contrary, she stopped short and with both hands held high, she received the chair-bashing, and with the same hands, she gave it right back to the Señorita. The

Señorita, who wasn't expecting this, took the chair on the forehead, which then split open; she reacted with a scream, covered her face with both hands and ran to shut herself in her sewing room.

That's the only time I remember that after such an incident, we weren't the ones who turned out to be unlucky; it must be because, like the girls say, Señora Rosa Campujón raises Julia Prickly Pear as if she were her own daughter, and that's why she's so secure and stubborn.

Today it looks like we'll spend the day as we have many others, playing and having a good time. Lastenia has brought her blonde doll, the one that has a face made out of porcelain; Priscilla, on the other hand, has brought her doll made of *dulce de leche,* a kind of sweet caramel. The doll is a bread roll with cheeks that shine from egg whites and a mouth of painted pink dough. But most of us get together to play house, and for that I bring, hidden in my sleeves, tiny little packets of rice, salt, little tubers, baby potatoes, or whatever I can find; other girls gather little oranges or love apples, as some people call them, and they sell them in our "market."

Some play at being mothers and they cook in our little clay pots, and when they use real firewood, we actually eat. Lucila is the funny one who plays "husband": she puts her hands on her hips and walks around us taking long heavy steps, all the while making serious faces and frowning theatrically; then, she stops in the middle of the room and yells, "What—my dinner isn't ready yet?" and puffing up like a turkey, she continues to circle the cooks.

We also play "tag" and that's where Julia ended up with the nickname "Julia Prickly Pear" because she likes to tag with a prickly pear or whatever is at hand.

Anyway, today we'll play, that is, if the older girls don't decide to begin their revolution. Yes, it's been several days since we've seen the teacher. On such occasions they tell us all to yell at the same time and we even beat on the chairs with sticks and on the floor with our feet. That's what we do, just to "bug the old lady," or simply, "to see if she'll come and teach us something."

But that isn't good, because she comes, or her sister comes, and they grab us and thump us, one and all; or else, their specialty, they grab us two at a time when we're seated, and they knock our heads together; "thunk, thunk," the poor things sound like they're empty, and home we go without being taught anything.

This makes me feel sad and disappointed, both things at once. I always wanted to learn to read. My uncle Raúl taught me a few letters and at the same time he tried to convince my grandmother that if she sent me to school I would learn "to write letters to my suitors." Then, when he convinced her to spend the seven *reales* that it cost every month for the nearest school, that time I really believed that I would learn.

But the little school that belonged to the Vigil sisters closed down two months later and my grandmother transferred me to the "state school where they teach you better and they don't charge." What has remained with me from the Señoritas are two songs and the image of a baby elephant after the letter "E" and a nice-looking bunch of grapes hanging from the "G," things that will take me far some day.

The first and only lesson that the Señorita taught me was the first page of the book *Rosita and Pepito*; we repeated it during the whole darned class:

"Rosita and Pepito are brother and sister.
Rosita loves Pepito because he takes care of her
and Pepito loves Rosita because she is tiny and beautiful.
Together they go to school."

When I can, I run my finger along the letters while I recite the verse with great pleasure; maybe this way the letters will stay with me and I might learn to read, and that's why I always bring my book.

Actually, the Señorita is rather devious. Last year she made us take a test and she passed us for being able to make a letter that she never wrote for us or for being able to draw an animal that she never drew for us. She asked me to write the number 2, and luckily I knew it because the older girls, bored from doing nothing, teach us once in awhile. I would be glad if this year they didn't allow the Señorita to steal someone else's job again.

Time to go home! What waits for me today? What "assignment" will my grandmother have received? It could be the two or three large baskets of wool that my aunt always brings for me to spin and that I give back to her in big balls from which she makes saddle blankets that later my uncle sells on the coast. For me that means several days of taking the spindle of wool with me everywhere, even to pee.

It could also be big kettles of corn to make *chochoca*; if that's what it is, it will belong to some neighbor who will have peasants working for them and I will have to wake up early and grind corn until I finish. What bothers me about this is that my grandmother has the idea that I can study while I grind. She places the book in front of me, open to any page, and resting it against the wall, she says to me: "Study, you lazy girl," and on top of that she gives me a rap on the head that makes me see stars, as if with the movement of the grinding stone "tan tan, tan tan," I could understand anything. The only thing I feel is that the sound makes me sleepy and that my back is breaking.

If there are no assignments, for sure they will send me out to get those huge bundles of alfalfa for the guinea pigs or branches for firewood. The bad thing about that is I must return home when it's pitch black and it scares me to pass behind the cemetery. All in all, like my Uncle Alfredo says, I'm only ten years old and I can believe the ghost and goblin stories they tell around here, in Chota, in Celendín, and in other towns farther away.

The story that really scares me is the one about the head that detaches itself at night so it can go and drink water; I can already see it bouncing around out there. What also scare me are those ladies they say walk without touching the ground, who lead you away so you'll fall over the cliff. It's a good thing they only look for men who are returning home drunk. But what I never want to see are those processions that, when it's dark, all you can see are their candles, and all the while you can hear the dragging of chains attached to the souls who have been damned. *Achichín!* No, I hope I never see that; that's why, when I'm out carrying my bundle that reaches to my heels, covering me like a shack, I make myself smaller and I quicken my step.

Luckily for me, yesterday I only had to go to the river with my backpack full of clothing to wash; the bad thing is that when I return, the huge pile weighs more. But anyway, I made it to the big day of the final exam. Today I got up early so I could go to school slowly, looking at how beautifully the cobblestones fit together in the sidewalk and how the water from the most recent rain runs through the central canal in the street. I also like to look at the roofs on top of the houses, but I don't do it often because, according to the teachings of my grandmother and the pinch that goes with them, "Decent girls walk modestly with their eyes cast down," and I'm decent.

The immense door on Don Eriberto Benel's house is suddenly in front of me; you have to enter through the little door to one side and lift your leg and take a long step in order to get in. It seems that my schoolmates have also arrived early.

The moment is approaching. We are all seated and scribbling anything in the notebooks that rest in our laps. How the town authorities make you wait!

There they come, the same mayor and priest from last year; the mayor has on his black three-piece suit, his white shirt and black tie with the gold clasp; the priest is wearing a robe, long and black, the one I always associate with the "pumpkin priest," the one from Lajas whom they used to sing this verse to: "The pumpkin priest, when he hears the bells, runs like a rooster to a feast." He has had that nickname since the day on which (because he's a drunk and falls in love with young girls, old ladies, married and single women) the town made him parade naked through the streets, mounted on a burro with a pumpkin filled with lime and a sack of coconuts hanging from his neck, while on his chest hung the distinctive sign: "This is the pumpkin priest." And that's how the name remained.

Señorita Julia Benel is wearing her best suit and is all smiles; she has made the mayor and priest sit on each side of her and she is showing them who-knows-what on her desk. They are beginning to call us, silence.

"Ester Cieza," calls the mayor in a serious voice.

The silence becomes intense. Ester, with her short hair and white hair-band, leaves her place, pale.

"Let's see, dear, write the number '1' on the blackboard."

Ester takes the chalk and looks at the Señorita.

"Come on young lady, don't be shy," says the Señorita with an affectionate tone of voice that comes from who-knows-where.

Ester looks at Julia Prickly Pear who, from underneath the only portfolio in the room, shows her fist. Ester lowers her eyes and says: "The Señorita didn't teach me."

The priest looks at the mayor and the mayor looks at the priest, both, mute, turn to look at the teacher who is becoming pale in her chair. The mayor turns toward Ester:

"Dear, then draw a duck, go on."

Ester, already appearing to cry, responds: "The Señorita didn't teach me."

The mayor sighs and continues: "All right, that's fine. Adelaida Gasco!"

I look affectionately at Adelaida, my best friend. She is the one who combs my curls, two on each side and two in the back, when my grandmother goes to Hualgalloc and leaves me on my own for months. There goes my little friend.

"Write a 'U,' dear."

"The Señorita didn't teach me," Adelaida immediately responds, now more confident.

The mayor, on the other hand, is annoyed, and his eyes shoot daggers toward the Señorita, who remains silent. The priest intervenes to calm him down.

"That girl, Mr. Mayor, please." The mayor agrees.

"Let's see, let's see, that chubby redhead won't fail me. What is her name?" he asks the Señorita.

"Teófila Gálvez."

From nervousness, I have begun to arrange my white dress with the little purple dots; the bodice fits me nicely and the bow on the back is cute. I like it very much because my Aunt Leonor made it for me from the fabric my Uncle Alfredo sent her from Chepén and. . . .

"Come on young lady, hurry up. Come and write an 'E' on the blackboard," the priest speaks to me, smiling.

All right, I'll go slowly, and I'll stand in front of them and I probably should lower my eyes.

"The Señorita didn't teach me."

"Come on, little girl," the priest says insistently. "EEEE like your big eyes, EEEEEEEE," and he draws an "E" in the air with his finger.

I already know it, but it wasn't her who taught me; I'm going to make an ignorant face, and here goes.

"It's just that the Señorita didn't teach it to me, Señor."

After that they sent me to my seat and they picked on all of us, here and there, searching for anyone who could respond to anything. They told us to do things like: "Draw a duckling," "a rabbit," "a line," or, they drew a burro themselves, without a tail or ears, and they asked us to complete it.

But all of us, all forty-eight without exception, repeated the words: "The Señorita didn't teach me," and nothing more.

During all this, the aforementioned Señorita turned every color and didn't know where to hide. After they finished questioning all of us, the mayor closed his notebook, got up, and without looking at or saying good-bye to anyone, he left. The priest, for his part, still trying to maintain a smile, left with his huge belly swaying, looking behind him every so often as if he thought that someone was going to tug at his robe or harm him.

"Aye!" The Señorita, feeling alone, began with the hysterics: "You shits, stupid half-breeds, stinking sows." But by that time we were already stampeding and we weren't going to stop until we reached home.

The following week, I found out that they had closed the school and cancelled the school year. I suppose this is how I will remain, having completed only the first year of school, since my grandmother has already decided to give me to a distant aunt, because she says that she doesn't have the money to pay even half of what a Faber pencil costs. But of course, if I tell her to take money out of the bag full of gold bricks and coins that she hides under the bed, she's likely to beat me, or hang me again.

So now I must cook with firewood, sweep the house, grind corn, mend at all hours, and wash huge piles of clothes in the river, just like before, but now with the darling "little nephew" loaded on my back.

Someday I will learn to read.

Translated by Kathy S. Leonard

Catalina Lohmann

Catalina Lohmann was born in 1952 in Lima, where she has lived most of her life. She studied literature at the Universidad Católica in Lima and worked for many years as a teacher of language and literature in high schools and institutes of higher learning. She is now a senior editor in the area of language and literature for a major textbook publisher in Lima.

Although Lohmann had previously worked on film scripts for television, she began writing stories only about four or five years ago as her children grew older and more independent, thus giving her more free time to write. The story presented here, "The Red Line," was the first short story she wrote. She entered it in a contest under the auspices of the Flora Tristán Peruvian Women's Center, and was delighted when she won an honorable mention. Several years later, she won first prize in the short-story contest of the Peruvian-Japanese Association with her story "De agua y de tierra" ("Of Water and Earth").

In her stories Lohmann often examines, at times with biting humor and irony, as in this story, various aspects of Peruvian society. It is a terribly divided society, one which suffers great extremes of wealth and poverty, and intense discrimination—thus one which breeds violence. The violence inherent in her country and its social inequality are constant themes in her writing.

"The Red Line" grew out of a disastrous bus ride she took one day on the local bus in Lima, where amongst the crush of people and the ever-increasing tardiness of the bus, she began to imagine this story. Peru at that time was in the middle of a presidential campaign between then-President Alberto Fujimori and the writer Mario Vargas Llosa. Leftist discourse was suddenly the rage, and phrases such as "class struggle," "the masses," and "historical materialism" were bandied about, but little was done to deal with Peru's real problems: economic crisis, extreme poverty, and terrorism. This story satirizes the way in which certain political opinions become fashionable, while the will and commitment to actually live up to such ideals always seem to remain highly unpopular.

From her vantage point in Lima, Lohmann continues to observe Peruvian society with a keen eye. She is currently working on a collection of short stories about Peruvian women from various points in Peru's past. She hopes that through these stories in which she examines the reality of women throughout Peruvian history, she will be able to explain and illuminate many aspects of the situation of women in her country today.

THE RED LINE

Catalina Lohmann

A quarter to six! It was late! I ran as fast as I could to the corner. I still couldn't see it, but I could hear it coming. At that time in the morning it's the only sound you hear in my neighborhood. Did I say sound? "Moan" is a better word. What? Not in your neighborhood? What must it be like where you live then?

I made it, got on, and said "hi" to everyone, since at that time of day the few of us there treat each other quite politely. Later, no. Later it's a different story.

Like I said, it was still empty. And everything was a shabby mess—the seats all broken down and the floor reeking of gasoline. Luckily, at that point on Angamos Avenue you still have the privilege of getting a seat. You have to look for two things: first of all, avoid the broken windows, which are awful. Second, look for a sheltered spot to prevent uncomfortable situations later on: elbows in your face, perverts trying to touch you, people stepping on you, etc.

I still couldn't figure out who the conductor of the bus was. It could be any of us, those of us sitting down. Not knowing who is who always makes me feel uncomfortable, what can I say?

The bus moved slowly, like it was still waking up, you know what I mean, it wasn't in any hurry. The driver, a big, fat guy with a huge mustache, stopped and scanned the scene at every corner, hoping to find more customers arriving late. He waited lazily, greeted everyone politely, and the bus continued on its way, alone on the avenue.

When we reached Arequipa Avenue, the bus filled up and the conductor was finally revealed. He was a big, unkempt, dark *mestizo* in blue jeans, with quick eyes and hands, who obviously thought he was the lord and master of all this chaos. He was plenty bossy, if you know what I mean. What? Of course you know one just like him. They're all the same.

We reached the gully without any problem, but at the Scala Shopping Center the entire neighborhood of Surquillo climbed onto the bus. Despite my strategic location, I started to feel the crush of people, the bumps, the baskets, lunch boxes, briefcases, and above all, the grime. What grime! But at the intersection with Atocongo Street, another mass of people got on. Now we really started to complain: this can't go on. How many more people are you going to let on here? There's no more room!

Those of us who had seats, feeling solidarity despite everything, forgot about our privileges as the first ones on and volunteered to hold other people's packages and children. The bus was one big tangle of legs, heads, arms, and feet. Atrocious. I tell you, it was brutal.

The problem was the time of day. The thing wasn't moving, and the genteel stubbornness of the driver to wait for every latecomer running for the bus was becoming unbearable. Inside we couldn't move an inch, I swear.

Complete immobility. Every time someone wanted to get off, they had to help eight others climb down and then get back on. Can you imagine? And the quick-handed conductor who didn't have to suffer with the rest of us, yelled at those selfish enough to try to keep a little air for themselves. What nerve! "Hey buddy, you in the yellow jacket. Come on, move on in, there's still space back there. Move, move back."

But it was the driver who set off the explosion: for the umpteenth time he stopped at the umpteenth corner looking for the umpteenth straggler. Hell, no! This is an indignity! And then it happened: a woman in a plaid dress began to yell at the driver, saying this was enough and she was going to be late. The conductor, insolent bum, pointed to the little sign in the bus window next to the picture of the naked lady: "If you left late, it's not the driver's fault." That's when the mob, I mean all of us, took a stand, developed a consciousness, saying, "Let's go already. What are you waiting for? Who do you think you are? What insolence! Have a little respect for the customers, you bully."

That's when the Dictatorship split up. Quick-Hands kept yelling at everyone, but the driver shut up and obeyed orders. Now the deed was done. The bus was ours.

We went along in this tense struggle for a good stretch. With the bus ours, the man at the steering wheel didn't dare go against our class interests. He'd lost his prestige, and with all the social pressure that we controlled, he didn't put up a fight. Even the shifty-eyed conductor gave up. He just glared at us bitterly, clinging to the bus as he rode on the running board.

So, panting, we arrived at Chacarilla Bridge. There we stopped to let off the woman in plaid, who left amid bravos and applause. Of course, she left without paying, as a symbol of protest for all the mistreatment she'd received. We all began to look at each other, looking for a new leader who could adequately represent us. But we didn't have time to decide democratically because suddenly we saw a huge mass of people trying to join our little community. Despite our howl of protest, the crush of people, and the numerous kicks, the dictator let loose this mass of people on us, pushing them inside. The situation was precarious. The bus tilted dangerously and continued down the street rocking like a rowboat in a storm.

Taking advantage of all the confusion but, most of all, taking advantage or our orphaned state, the driver gathered his forces and regained control of the bus. Then, the worst happened. You know that speed bump in front of the shopping center? You don't? Of course not, you never go by Monterrico. Okay, anyway, Fatso decided he couldn't get over it with such a load of human cargo, so he swerved into the opposite lane, going against the oncoming traffic, in hopes of avoiding the jolt and the fatal fall. There we got all tangled up with another bus, causing us to lose ten more minutes and all of our hope of ever arriving on time. Desperate, we found our voice again. I don't know how, don't ask me, but I began to hear my own voice rising above the others. By the time I realized it, I had already replaced our previous leader. You know I'm not one for political intrigue, I never have been. I don't have any political ambitions. Besides, my new status as Secretary General meant I had to give up my privileges, you know, because when have you ever seen a leader who rules sitting down? Have you ever seen such a thing? Of course not. So, I had to stand up in order to better hear the complaints from the masses.

My first task was to organize the comrades democratically and regain control of the decrepit bus. I personally insisted that Fatso get back in the right lane and that we have no more of such deviations from that point on. Secondly, we had to solemnly swear to be on guard against any new attempt by the driver to take advantage of the chaos and take over. Our solidarity grew, my friend, and suddenly we all fit together fine in that space, a tiny little space, but it was ours. We had the most important thing: power. But for me, as the leader, it was somewhat difficult; I had to convince Those with Seats to share their privileges. Their power had corrupted them and they thought they were now the dominant social class. They treated the Newcomers as if they were upstart immigrants. But that didn't wash; we were all equals on that bus. Besides, there were also the scabs to deal with, who always threaten a group's unity by complaining about everything without understanding the tremendous advantages of our having taken power. And of course we had to have the drunk guy with bad breath, who, I swear, at that time of the morning is unbearable. I'm sure the poor guy hadn't slept it off yet, and he kept shouting such wild comments that we weren't sure if he was with us or with the Dictatorship. The Newcomers didn't understand a thing about what was going on, so I felt obliged to explain the dialectic of our movement and the struggles which had led us to power. Last but not least, I had to somehow pull in the stuck-up *pituca* woman in high heels who kept looking at us with disgust on her face and who didn't want to participate in this historic task. Don't laugh, it almost killed me.

By this time we were at the golf course, and our democracy was moving along strong and steady toward the bus stop at University Avenue. Excuse me, this is where I get off. How much do I owe you? I'll pay my fare so no one can accuse me later of having taken advantage of the situation. And you know what?—the passengers wouldn't let me get off; they insisted that I was now committed to this movement with them, that I was undermining the government, that they'd never arrive at their stops, that this was treason. Can you believe it? What nerve! I'm not going to be late to my class on Historical Materialism just to lead some bus full of crazies. I'm not going to sacrifice my future defending some useless revolution, much less a pitiful, filthy, miserable bus like this.

Why are you looking at me like that, huh? What?! Permanent revolution, class struggle? I don't give a damn about that stuff, that's history, it's over and done with. Perastroika has arrived and the Berlin Wall has fallen. We're now a country of free enterprise. Everything else is communism. Just a bunch of university theories. . . . What? No, my dear, in this country it's the person who yells the loudest who wins. Yeah, yeah, it's class security, as you say, but you can see that it works great. Besides, politics is a bunch of bull. That's where all the corruption gets in and the mess begins. And if you don't believe me, remember Those with Seats. That's how it always is. What did you say? They weren't my comrades! They were just a bunch of passengers, which is an entirely different thing. Hell no, I haven't betrayed anybody; on the contrary I did them a favor, and they didn't even have the decency to thank me! Don't keep saying that or I'm going to get mad. It's impossible to talk to you. I'm no snotty *pituca*—she was the one with high heels. I'll rub elbows with anyone—it doesn't bother me! You sound like an extremist. Stop it, stop it, don't say any more. Listen Lucy, you're not some kind of terrorist, are you?

Translated by Susan Benner

Laura Riesco

Laura Riesco defines herself not as a writer, but as a woman who writes. "I began to write when I was a child," she explains, "but everything that has piled up in my drawers and files doesn't count. Writers, in general, gain their identity from their writing, so they take care that what they write eventually gets published. I have a lot of energy for life, but little discipline for the task of becoming an author."

Born in 1940 in La Oroya, Peru, Riesco grew up the only child in a liberal household. From an early age she loved reading books, finding in them a world of imagination that was more captivating than that of reality. She read insatiably from her parents' small but diversely stocked library: works by Gorki and Mauriac, Maugham and Cronin, as well as nineteenth- and twentieth-century Spanish novelists introduced to her by her father. At fifteen she discovered Sartre and subsequently developed an interest in French literature and philosophy. For a time she pushed aside Spanish authors, although she reacquainted herself with them later in her studies.

When Riesco turned eighteen, her parents decided that she should spend a year of study abroad in the United States: she never returned to live permanently in Peru. In the years that followed, she married her French instructor, had three daughters, and earned a master's degree in French and a doctorate in Spanish, both from the University of Kentucky. After nearly forty years in the United States, however, she still feels a certain transitoriness here, as if this life is something that she is passing through and her initial year of study abroad is still in the process of being completed. "I have never entirely adapted to this society," she says. "At work I still find myself reacting a bit like an *étranger*. I feel marginal to a system that I cannot or will not understand."

In 1978 she published *El truco de los ojos*, an experimental novel, with a second novel, *Ximena de dos caminos*, eventually appearing in 1994. She explains the long period "in between" as one in which the demands of daily life, as well as her duties and responsibilities as a teacher, allowed her little time for writing. "Besides," she adds, "there are just too many temptations that keep me away from the computer."

In 1995, she was awarded first prize for Latino narrative by the Institute of Latin American Writers of New York for her novel *Ximena de dos caminos,* considered by Peruvian critics to be one of the best novels of 1994. The novel has been compared to *País de Jaula* by Edgardo Rivera Martínez, although the similarity is coincidental. "I did not have a chance to read Martínez's novel until after my own appeared," Riesco notes. Her novel is being translated into English, French, and German.

"The Twins of Olmedo Court," previously unpublished, is a semiautobiographical story in which the narrator recalls the strange and somewhat eerie events that took place in her household when she was young, events which seem to take on multiple significance with respect to human nature when filtered through a child's memory. The narrator continually questions herself and others to determine what they remember and what they have forgotten about the untimely guests at Olmedo Court. The answer is shadowed in doubt: ". . . perhaps they were angels who had fallen from heaven or who had been elevated from hell, since they appeared and disappeared from our lives without leaving a single trace."

Laura Riesco lives in Orono, Maine, where she is an associate professor at the state university. She is also working on an as-yet-untitled novel.

THE TWINS OF OLMEDO COURT

Laura Riesco

My sister and I could never establish if a possible relationship existed between the Solórzanos and the strange occurrences in Olmedo Court. The truth is that every time I try to bring up that episode, Doris shrugs her shoulders and becomes melancholy. "Why do you think about something that doesn't make any sense? It's like trying to find meaning in a dream you had forty years ago," and avoiding my eyes she adds: "Face it, you're not going to figure it out, don't even think about it anymore." Then she looks at me with the same exasperated tenderness as when we were children, and I have no other choice but to stop. She rises with her usual calm and goes into the kitchen to prepare pisco sours for us. While I wait for her, I try not to feel out of place, surrounded by the extreme cleanliness and the perfect decor of her small living room. When she returns with the drinks, I settle as comfortably as I can on the sofa, careful not to put my feet on the pale green of the cushions, and then we touch our glasses together to toast in unison the old maids of the world. We talk for a long while, conscious that our words fluctuate between discomfort and affection.

With my parents it's completely useless to bring up the subject of Olmedo Court. I know that old age has filled their thoughts with cobwebs and that in those fragile moments of lucidity they want to remember only pleasant incidents. But before, when their bodies still held a vitality for the future, they would agree to recall the past with me, although they always obstinately avoided any reference to those weeks that my mind tenaciously refuses to forget. During that time, I insisted on searching for some clue from my parents, some more or less rational answer for the inexplicable forces that caused our eventual move from the courtyard. But no longer. I leave them alone, old and lost in the selection of a perhaps precarious happiness, seated in old wicker rocking chairs and surrounded by the olive trees in their orchard.

I was never able to determine if my parents were expecting the Solórzanos to visit or if they showed up unexpectedly. I am sure, it's true, that they hadn't been personally acquainted. Based on those genealogical coincidences that take place in the provinces, they told my parents that they shared a distant relationship with our family. They arrived, they said, with the intention of settling in Lima, and they needed lodging until they could find an apartment. Our house was situated on a quiet street in the Jesús María district; it was spacious, convenient to various means of transportation, and hospitality toward others from a neighboring province was sacred for my parents during that time. The Solórzanos weren't the first to arrive with their suitcases in tow; however, they were the last to enjoy the open generosity that reigned in our household.

Our life was healthy and carefree, although, no doubt, quite unusual. Today my sister has a different opinion: "We lived in constant chaos," she maintains without nostalgia. To the astonishment of everyone, Papá, who had the reputation of being absentminded, was stupendously successful in business, and about Mamá they used to say, without an ounce of ill will, that she had never reached maturity. Doris has to concede that the atmosphere at home was a happy one. The latch on the street door was always unlocked and friends came and went as the spirit moved them, even when no one was at home except Pancha, the old cook, and during those years, Tregismunda (that was the poor woman's name), a girl who helped with the cleaning. The four of us would meet at the same time just for lunch, and it was served according to the whims of Pancha and the distraction of Tregismunda. At times we began with dessert and finished with soup, and sometimes the necessary utensils were not set on the table, and to keep from bothering Tregismunda, who was very sensitive, we would get up every so often to go and get a glass or a fork. Other times, if the drinks had not been prepared on time, my father, whistling all the while, would mix up a delicious sangría that would knock us into a sweet sleep and make us miss school in the afternoon. Nonetheless, I don't remember any complaints and it's not that my sister and I longed for the set routine found in other families. Mamá would sleep until late morning, and since everyone ate according to the dictates of their hunger, dinner wasn't served in the evenings. In retrospect, I think that there were probably days when we barely bumped into my parents.

In any case, there were always friends and aunts and uncles who went directly into the kitchen to eat something or who used any one of the bedrooms to take a nap. Doris herself has to admit that neither she nor I was frustrated by this domestic disorganization and that, in spite of it all, we did quite well in school. In emergency situations, our parents would gladly help us with our schoolwork, and once in a while they would become so involved in drawing maps or verifying theorems that we would leave them alone and go outside to play.

There were eight houses around the courtyard, two with a door to the street and with exterior gardens with sidewalks running through them. We lived in one of these, number 935, and in the other, number 937, lived a family with money and lineage, judging by their luxurious automobile and by the barely courteous distance that they maintained from the rest of the neighbors. A uniformed chauffeur would take their three children, all blonde and immaculately coiffed, to a prestigious school, and he would bring them home around five o'clock, as impeccable as when they left. We never struck up a friendship with them nor with anyone else in the courtyard. My parents would greet the neighbors politely, but they greeted almost everyone in the same manner, and I don't think they ever knew who they were dealing with. Besides, the interior homes, along with the regular tenants, housed a multitude of boarders or their relatives from the provinces. There were no children in the building, besides the nervous, asthmatic boy in 935B, and a fat, ill-dressed girl in 935C. The girl didn't attend school and was the stoic victim of our teasing, which although sporadic, was nonetheless cruel. The courtyard was quite wide and it had a black-and-white tiled floor. The windows of the interior houses were protected by iron grilles, and through the perennial opaqueness of the glass, we shamelessly spied into the rooms. When the panes were open, we would become more daring and throw fruit peels through the circles in the grilles, congratulating one another if they managed to land in a serving dish or in some empty flower vase. The neighbors had to know that we were the guilty ones, but since they never said anything, we continued desecrating the simple order of their rooms, whose sad and dusty semidarkness couldn't hide the scarcity and shabbiness of their furniture. At the back of the building, in 937C, lived the Gonzálezes, who were newlyweds. An elderly woman lived with them, somber and in mourning, and who, when she passed by, left in her wake a tenuous odor of rose cologne and bleach. The young wife seemed very beautiful to Doris and me. At first she went out frequently, and as soon as we would hear her high heels echoing on the tiles, we would run to see her. She dressed in the latest styles and her thick black hair, knotted in a great topknot, coquettishly accentuated her youthful features. Soon we stopped seeing her. I imagined her at the point of a very painful death because her mother-in-law was evilly mixing drops of bleach with a lot of sugar in her daughter-in-law's daily coffee. My sister, who was more sensible, speculated that she might be pregnant.

We have never been able to agree about her first pregnancy, which was for me a turning point in the unusual events during that time in Olmedo Court. Doris maintains that we lost sight of the woman and that she had the first and second set of twins long before the Solórzanos came to stay with us. I realize that my memory recalls a preposterous sequence, and that good sense contradicts the practical possibility of that memory. But other details that my sister denies, and for years she has refused to remember with me, firmly demonstrate that the impossible did happen in the ordinary and monotonous confines of the courtyard. It's true, as she indicates, that during those weeks we went around too bewildered by what was happening inside our own house to pay much attention to what might be happening in someone else's. Within a few days of the guests' arrival, everything began to change. A monastic discipline was installed and it methodically swept away everything that until that time had been for us a smooth and seamless existence without any worries.

Tregismunda was the first fatality of this assault. Exhausted by Doña Cordelia's incessant orders, she packed up her belongings one morning and left for Muquiyauyo in tears. Pancha, who had served the family since the time of my maternal grandmother, lasted a little longer. We saw her age twenty years in a matter of two weeks. The incense that she burned in various rooms to ward off the evil spirit of the intruders had no other effect than to anger the boarders. This resulted in a humiliating sermon about the dangers and sinfulness of indigenous witchcraft, delivered by Don Remigio in a threatening voice and with an upheld index finger. One Sunday, her sparse possessions bundled up in a shabby multicolored blanket, Pancha departed with a nephew, leaving us more alone and defenseless than ever. The latch on the street door became stuck and the usual visitors gradually began to stay away. Doña Cordelia took charge of the kitchen, and Mamá's clothing and skin became equally faded while she learned the difficult task of keeping the furniture dust-free and everything in its place, no matter how insignificant. At certain times we would all sit down to finish tasteless meals in silence, and paradoxically, Papá began to gain weight. If by some oversight on the part of the Solórzanos we came face to face with our parents, we managed only to confirm their terrible sadness and obtain a weak promise from them that soon the guests would find their own house and would leave ours. To keep from making our parents' desolation even worse, the two of us began at once to obey, without saying a word about the schedule that Don Remigio had set up for us. Little by little we learned to lie, and with ruses more carefully constructed each time, under opportune circumstances, we could evade their strict vigilance. We thus obtained a certain measure of freedom, paltry in comparison with what we had previously enjoyed, but which helped us to survive from day to day.

During the hour designated for exercise, we played on the sidewalk and grass that corresponded to our house, since the Solórzanos completely forbade us from running around in the passageway that divided the courtyard.

With cunning and guile we transgressed this rule and continued, now with less fervor and opportunity, the rhythm of our former escapades. The courtyard seemed more somber to us, the tiles had taken on a uniformly gray color, but the throng of neighbors continued to cross over them to come and go as always. The young Señora González continued to be imprisoned in some bedroom, bewitched, I suspected, and the only novel thing were her four twin girls. We did see the mother-in-law go by carrying the grocery baskets, and the father of the little girls continued to return from work at the same time with the same determined look as before. For a while, the mother-in-law would take the first set of twins out for a walk in a baby buggy made for two, and according to what I remember, in the blink of an eye, she had them seated in a stroller, also for two, while a girl wearing a blue smock would walk alongside pushing a buggy containing the second set of twins. What most surprised us was the fact that the twins were all exactly alike, and that in a very short time, you could barely distinguish among the four of them by their size. My sister and I differ about when it was that this began to intrigue us, although she has no choice but to admit, albeit reluctantly, that the time arrived when each one of the twins was a faithful copy of the other. Plump-cheeked with curly chestnut-brown hair, they would explore their surroundings with their identical enormous brown eyes. It was during that time when we began to notice a woman's distressing screams and cries, which transcended the closed windows and walls of the González house. The ordeal wouldn't last long, and if we tuned our ears, her last few moans would blend with the crying of a newborn, and then a little while later, with more crying, just the same. Then an uneasy stillness would invade the entire length of the courtyard.

One morning, extremely early, Doris and I awoke to the noise of wheelbarrows and stifled voices. I clearly remember that the Solórzanos had taken over the bedroom with the balcony and had banished us to the guest room. That morning, our curiosity was greater than our sleepiness, and we stuck our heads out the window. From there we observed the neighbors in 935C, who, with visible apprehension, were dragging their household belongings toward the street. My sister prefers not to remember what happened next. However, I haven't been able to forget that the next morning, taking advantage of the Solórzanos' providential exit, we moved to the back of the courtyard to jump rope and we stopped next to the window of the unoccupied house. It must have been around the end of March or the beginning of April because we had already eaten dinner and the declining afternoon light was illuminating certain parts of the courtyard. We were standing beneath the shadow that covered the window grille, and illuminated by lamps at both ends of the room they could clearly be seen: there were not only four twins, but ten, perhaps more. Seated or reclining on three spacious sofas placed in a half circle, they were sucking on bottles and looking around engrossed in their surroundings. They were wearing identical pajamas and they all seemed to be the same age. My sister cannot deny that we were witnesses to that first move, and to this day she is unable to hide her anxiety. Turning her face away, she refuses to remember that the next day we also witnessed the invasion of the twins into the empty house.

The Solórzanos were taking a long time to find a place to live, although everyday they marked the ads in the newspaper for apartments that they thought might suit them and they went out more frequently than before. You could see something crestfallen about them even when everything in the house was made suitable according to their orders. Papá continued to be fat and gloomy, and Mamá, whose gait had taken on the severity of those housekeepers in English films, began to show her first wrinkles. Silence was what was most heard in the middle of the austere cleanliness of the rooms, and only my sister and I marred the cemetery-like atmosphere that prevailed. Sometimes our laughter or our galloping up and down the stairs betrayed us, but we accepted with indifference the punishment for each infraction we committed. On the other hand, the Solórzanos didn't have the slightest idea how to punish us. Their penances were futile, because taking away our dinner or closing us in the broom closet, which frightened them, was a blessing for us. The forbidden courtyard, according to Doris, little by little, no longer attracted us. I would say that in spite of our innate daring, the courtyard was the only thing that filled us with terror.

How does my sister manage to avoid certain details that must have been forcefully imbedded in her memory, just as they were in mine? And nevertheless, she repeats that no, that we never noticed that if it was sunny on the street, the space occupied by the courtyard remained in constant shadow; that we had to leave the windows of two of the rooms and the kitchen open because the stale air we breathed between the two ends of the houses was asphyxiating, and that the tiles never completely lost their color and became filthy. She will admit that the moves by the other neighbors who lived in the interior houses continued, but she is determined that they took place during the day and not at dawn or very late at night. How can the fact that after awhile we slept uneasily have been erased from her mind, and that every little thing would wake us up and that we would jump out of bed, despite the unhealthy atmosphere of that place, so we could spy on the anguished exodus of those who were leaving? In less than a month we both witnessed the flight of the family with the asthmatic son, the large brood of Chinese from Lurín, the nurses who worked at the Loayza Hospital, and the family from Huancayo in 937A. They carried or pushed their furniture with the anxious movements of those who were fleeing. Besides the Gonzálezes and the rich neighbors, we were the only ones who remained, and only the walls of those two apartments had not become stained by a greenish and foul-smelling slime.

It's no use, either, to insist that during those days, we had both noticed that the nanny, who now went out alone to take the twins for a walk, returned to the house in a second just to go right back out, and that it wasn't the same woman, but that everything possible had been done so that she *appeared* to be the same one. They had chosen them in such a way that they were all similar in their demeanor, their braids, their features, and their skin color. Amazed, we arrived at the unprecedented conclusion that there wasn't just one nanny, but many nannies, and that there must have been dozens of twins, all exactly alike, surreptitiously occupying the apartments that were believed to be vacant. My sister despairs if I mention this discovery and she gets worse if I add that Papá and Mamá pretended to take it as a joke when we told them. I do remember their awkward laughter, which saddened us so much that we didn't bring up the subject with them again. However, Doris concedes that it's true that they refused to approach the door or windows that faced the courtyard, and if Señora González's shrieks, which seemed to come nearer and nearer, were violating the apparent calm of the room we were occupying, neither of the two, strangely enough, made any comment. They remained quiet and in that way betrayed their terror and their suspicions. Ironically, it was they, unable to hide their uneasiness, who called us one morning so that together we could see the commotion on the sidewalk, caused by the rich neighbors. Apprehensive and less dapper than usual, they were moving during daylight hours, looking askance at the stains that had already covered the walls surrounding the main entrance of their house and ours.

That same afternoon, the Solórzanos, who by then were walking around confused with their heads down, told us that they had found an apartment. With the same pained expression as the neighbors, they gave us the news while stammering and throwing out cryptic phrases of imprecise excuses. Their departure was so unexpected that the four of us stood there without knowing what to do with our sudden freedom, surrounded by the rigorous spotlessness of the living room and by the bloodcurdling screams echoing from the passageway and bouncing off the closed doors. Without a single word being uttered among us, we understood that the time for our own move had also arrived. Days later, when the unbreathable air in the courtyard extended out to the street and the few geraniums still growing in the garden had wilted, we left for the highlands and once there, took refuge in the complicity of oblivion. During those years we never mentioned Olmedo Court and only when absolutely necessary did we travel to Lima a few times.

It was I, much later, when I returned to the capital after having lived a good deal of my life abroad, who began to delve into the buried memories of our childhood. I returned to Jesús María and searched for our block, but I was unable to recognize it. The lawns had been sacrificed in order to build a two-level highway that overflowed with cars, people, and trash. Where the courtyard should have been, I found two gray structures, which, because of their many symmetrical windows, looked like a honeycomb. I also searched for the Solórzanos, but I was never able to discover their whereabouts. The relatives I turned to for help would scratch their heads in thought and assure me, with evident sincerity, that they didn't know them and that they couldn't connect the name with any branch of our numerous family. Perhaps they were angels who had fallen from heaven or who had been elevated from hell, since they appeared and disappeared from our lives without leaving a single trace.

I didn't try to find the Gonzálezes. Their surname is much too common and I would not have known where to begin. And even though my sister now denies it, and my parents take refuge in their silence, I have a feeling that in the neighborhoods, the plazas, churches, and even more in the courtyards that still remain in Lima, undaunted with their identical enormous brown eyes, the twins are exploring new territory, and they are walking and advancing through the city.

Gladys Rossel Huicí

Born in Lima in 1946 into a family of writers (both her father and grandfather were well-known and accomplished authors) Gladys Rossel created her first poems and short stories at the age of eight. She began writing professionally at an early age also, working as a reporter and editor for various newspapers and journals while studying journalism and philosophy at the Universidad de San Marcos in Lima.

Rossel published her first book of creative writing, a book of poems, in 1982, but her career as a writer really took off in 1990 when she published her first book of short stories, which met with great critical and commercial success. She has won a number of literary prizes and distinctions, including mentions in the literary contest of the Centro Peruano de la Mujer "Flora Tristán" in 1990 and 1992.

Rossel is a woman with a burning need to learn, explore, and create, which has pushed her to study art and culture, and various religions and philosophies, as well as to paint and write. She believes in living an intense and very full life, a choice which has led at times to pain and struggle, as well as joy, but which she feels has enriched her life, and her writing, beyond measure. She has traveled widely and has spent many years living outside of Peru, including years in Italy, Venezuela, Chile, and, at present, Costa Rica.

Writing for Rossel is a compulsion through which she finds a way to express the depths of her emotions and the range of experiences she has lived. She believes the carefully crafted use of language to be an indispensable part of good writing and obsesses over finding the perfect word, phrase, or form for creating exactly her desired effect, worrying about everything including the correct placement of a comma. She is constantly making changes in her works, and is the bane of her editors for her tendency to make last-minute corrections up to the moment the work goes to press. But the result is impressive: Rossel's stories are meticulously written pieces in which every word, every phrase, every paragraph is carefully thought out and precisely formed.

Yet it is impossible to define Rossel's style or name recurrent themes in her work. Her stories range from comments on the afterlife of flies to a chilling tale of a rape told from the rapist's point of view. Many of her stories and commentaries reveal a delightful ability to laugh at the absurdity of everyday life and to celebrate the significance of an insignificant moment or event, as well as wry insights into relations between the sexes. Other stories, such as "Light and Shadow," the story presented here, carry the reader into a world of the magical and fantastic, and Rossel is a master at creating a mood, an atmosphere where the reader becomes lost between reality and fantasy. She is also a master of the surprise ending, the sudden twist in the final paragraph or the last sentence that leaves her startled readers laughing, realizing they have been very skillfully manipulated.

Rossel now lives in San José, Costa Rica, with her two daughters. She works as a consultant on style and technique for other authors and leads numerous writing workshops. She has recently published a new book of stories, *Entre calles y sueños*, about incarcerated children, the proceeds of which will go to help street children, and she writes regularly as a correspondent for a French literary journal. She is at work on a new novel and on a guide for writers in which she hopes to share some of what she has learned from her own broad experiences as a writer.

> I think that in writing I've been lucky because I don't have inhibitions, as I do in painting and drawing. In writing I'm not afraid to make jokes, to talk about the fantastic, to delve into something or unburden myself, it's my literary catharsis; I can wreak vengeance or delve as deeply as I want into something, so I'm not afraid of words and I enjoy them very much but with terrible pain as well, because it always hurts to write, it hurts a lot.

LIGHT AND SHADOW

Gladys Rossel Huicí

"Where the devil did you go, you idiot?" I reprimanded her severely, irate, the first time she disappeared from my side without asking me permission and without giving any valid reason to justify such behavior. But she didn't respond, nor show any sign of repentance, or shame, or even annoyance. She sat there quiet, defenseless, or better yet, she lost all autonomy, maintaining an attitude of impassivity that made me even more angry, leading me to attack her with insults.

Yes, I was cruel. I yelled at her with great contempt, pointing out her wretched state of subordination. I repeated over and over: "You are nobody, nobody, nobody, just an unfortunate shadow, tied to me without any right to a life of your own." And I finished the rebuke adding: "You depend entirely on my existence. If I want, then you appear, if not, you disappear." She continued sitting there impassively, although I could feel her pain, a deep, dark, shimmering pain flooding out from her.

I can't deny that I felt sorry for her, but I didn't have any alternative. What else could I do in such a situation? At first our relationship was normal. What can I say, our relationship was always normal until the evening of my sixtieth birthday—well soaked in drink and saturated with emotions—in short, nothing strange: some healthy sexual release and a celebration fitting for the occasion and my new status as a retiree. After the party, I returned to the house just as the clock struck three and headed for the library to cool off with the air conditioning and a glass of good whisky on the rocks. The armchair where I was seated, as well as the wall next to me, were brilliantly lit by the light from the floor lamp. Somewhat aimlessly I took a long sip, and, sprawling leisurely in the chair, I watched the shadows projected on the wall. Or, to be precise, I watched the shadows of a hand (my hand) holding a glass, the other hand grasping a cigarette between its fingers, and the graceful spiral of smoke that played in the air, sketching rings and surrealistic figures. Suddenly, the shadow of my fingers let go of the glass and stretched, rose up, calmly and stealthily, until it reached the edge of the closed window. The shadow of the other hand did the same, but the shadows of the glass and the cigarette stayed firmly attached to the wall as if both objects were suspended freely in space.

Alcohol and strong emotions can produce visual disturbances, I rationalized in my drunken state, and I continued contemplating with growing stupor the unusual spectacle of my shadow prying with long and trembling fingers at the gaps between the thick oak lathes that sealed the window. I don't remember precisely how long I amused myself watching my strange hallucinations, but I was aware the whole time of their unreality. Then the light of the approaching dawn dissolved all contrasts, and I fell into a deep sleep, forgetting everything.

It couldn't have been more than fifteen days after this bizarre incident, which at times I remembered with a smile, when something similar occurred again. This time I found myself visiting in the home of friends, and my shadow, cast sharp and clear on the white lacquered wall while I conversed with my hosts, abruptly gave a start and bent over, energetic, trying to escape through the wide cracks of the poorly shut door. Her dark black figure stretched compulsively, despite the fact that I remained immobile, disheartened, without knowing what attitude to adopt faced with a reality which, if realized by others, would turn me into the object of the most horrendous commentaries. Out of the corner of my right eye I saw her writhing with desperation, attempting to wrench loose the thin line that kept her firmly tied to the end of my feet, but she wasn't able to free herself, despite all of her efforts. I said good-bye, almost rudely, giving some poorly improvised excuse, and left running.

For many weeks I shut myself up in the house, waiting for the arrival of gray days that would put an end to the intense vitality of the strong sunlight. During that time I kept the rooms in my house literally in darkness, closing the curtains during the day, and at night turning on only very low lights, the kind that produce only hazy, dim shadows, practically imperceptible. Meanwhile, mine followed my movements with pallid docility, without making any other attempt to escape.

During those days I made it a habit to monitor her presence, keeping an eye on her, though with much pretense, to assure that her size, her form, and her movements followed mine exactly.

That is, until that damned sunny day appeared, vibrating with optimism, which made me assume that my torment was nothing more than the fruit of my own uncontrolled imagination, a kind of temporary insanity, typical of any mature bachelor who has recently entered a stage of inactivity. I drew wide the curtains, flung open the windows, and let the sun enter in torrents.

She appeared perfectly, my carbon copy. She seemed normal, serene, cast at my feet in the correct spot, following every one of my movements as docilely as you would expect of any old shadow.

"She never did anything on her own," I thought, as I leaned on the window sill in my bedroom on the second floor, facing the sun and all the beauty of life I had been denying myself. Suddenly everything went dark. I lost sight of the street and the buildings in front of me. I couldn't believe what was happening: my eyes refused to accept the sight of the agile, illusive figure of my shadow dancing happily before me. The wretch contorted, did somersaults, and then contracted, vibrating happily, before hurling herself into space, simulating a rain of black sparks which then united once again.

I realized it was in many ways a beautiful sight, almost touching, to see her frolicking in complete freedom. I watched her games attentively. The light outlined her profile while she danced about in space, imitating a circus tumbler made of rubber. She took on a human shape, solid, compact, and immediately afterwards disappeared abruptly, only to later materialize in another spot, transformed into a line. I doubt she took me into account at all; intoxicated by her freedom, she was completely unaware of her surroundings.

For a long time she amused herself, continuing her capers, dancing crazily, transforming herself into numerous whimsical silhouettes, from that of a human, young and feminine (with no resemblance whatsoever to this narrator), to animals, flowers, plants, and even sophisticated geometrical forms. I kept still, watching her as a rhombus, a tarantula, a dancer, a waterfall, a cloud, a gladiola, a bit of sheer netting, a panther, rain . . . until panic seized me and I cried out, "Come back, damn it! Come back immediately before it's too late!"

Her immediate reaction warned me that she had no intention of returning to my side. She pulled away rapidly, mimicking an arrow, and punctured the horizon to become just a point, which lost itself in infinity. My consternation knew no bounds. I spun around, and, leaving the window open, I returned to the library to wait until something would make her reconsider and return to the place where she belonged.

And indeed, as the first signs of night began to appear, I saw her slip timidly in through the open window, a sorry sight trickling back in. Wrapped in meekness, she placed herself against the wall and immediately began to copy each of my movements with synchronized precision. She didn't say a word, she didn't do a thing; she assumed her role, immune to my reproach, imitating perfectly the useless servile attitude of other shadows. But I could feel her silent pain, which lay there thickly in the darkness while she listened to my insults.

For several days I ignored her presence completely. I resumed my routine as if nothing had happened. She behaved as she should, although perhaps just a bit slowly, as if she were distracted. I didn't say a word about such suspicious signs, although something inside of me suspected that she was planning her final escape. Now she had had a taste of what it was like to be her own master.

I saw her leave one uneventful afternoon. I was in the library when she began to stretch voluptuously, slithering across the floor with certainty and skill, turning herself into a thin thread of a spider's web. Then she rolled into a ball, succeeding, thanks to an energetic jerk, in freeing herself completely from my feet, the last point at which we remained joined. Having obtained her objective, she unrolled leisurely, and headed toward the closed window. She climbed up agilely, and began to filter through to the outside, using the tiny crack in one of the windows as her escape route. Appearing as a line drawn in India ink, she showed no haste and no fear. She subtly glided away, emboldened, sketching some ethereal outline, and without wavering or stumbling, she put into play her obviously well-calculated plan. She knew that I was watching her.

I watched her hurl herself greedily toward the sun, like the shadow of a hawk with its claws drawn up, without glancing in my direction nor giving any sign of farewell. She simply took off into nothingness, freed from the slavery of my actions. I don't know if she hoped I would protest or plead with her, or if she sought some dialogue between us. I didn't say a word. I let her leave.

I know that she'll never return, that I am orphaned now from her useless, and absolutely necessary, presence.

I keep my glasses put away in a box; I don't want to be reminded of her absence, nor do I want anyone to notice my absurdly solitary figure.

Several months have gone by since her departure, and now the only thing left for me to do is to use my time contemplating the memory of my shadow, trying to guess what could have created such a phenomenon, what strange force gave her life, thoughts, and a longing for freedom. I would like to know where she is; but then, thinking it over, that isn't really important as long as I know that sometimes she feels a little nostalgia for returning to my side.

I'm alone.

The window is open.

Translated by Susan Benner

Virginia Ayllón Soria

WORKS BY

Short Story Collections

Búsquedas: Cuatro relatos y algunos versos. La Paz: Artes Gráficas Potosí, 1996.

Short Stories

"Verena." *Sopocachi* (June–July 1991): 20–22.

Other

Gritos sin eco: Violencia contra la mujer en la prensa nacional. With Fernando Machicado. La Paz: Centro de Información y Desarrollo de la Mujer (CIDEM), 1989.

De tanto haber andado yo ya soy otra: Bibliografía selecta de la mujer boliviana, 1986–1991. With Fernando Machicado. La Paz: CIDEM, 1991.

La memoria de las ciudades: Bibliografía urbana de Bolivia, 1952–1991. With Godofredo Sandoval. La Paz: ILDIS; CEP, 1992.

Las campeonas: Mujer y deporte en la prensa nacional, 1991. With Fernando Machicado. La Paz: Centro de Información y Desarrollo de la Mujer, 1992.

Volar entre sonidos, colores, y palabras: Mujer y actividad cultural en la prensa nacional. With Fernando Machicado. La Paz: CIDEM, 1992.

"La mujer delincuente y privada de libertad ante el sistema de administración de justicia." *Sobre patriarcas, jerarcas, patrones, y otros varones: Una mirada género sensitiva del derecho.* Ed. Alda Facio and Rosalía Camacho. San José: ILANUD, 1993. 159–71.

"Mujer y elecciones." *Mujer y democracia.* Ed. Denise Aviles. La Paz: ILDIS, 1993.

"Reflexiones acerca de la prevención de la violencia doméstica: un acercamiento de género." *Memorias del seminario taller mujer y violencia.* La Paz: Fundación San Gabriel, 1993.

"Mujer, derechos, legislación, y violencia." *Situación de la mujer en Bolivia: 1976–1994. Informe de las ONGs bolivianas al foro alternativo de Beijing 1995.* La Paz: n.p., 1994.

WORKS ABOUT

Quiroga, María Soledad. "Escritura y dualidad." *Presencia Literaria* [La Paz] 11 Feb. 1996.

Yolanda Bedregal

WORKS BY

Novels

Bajo el oscuro sol. La Paz: Editorial Los Amigos del Libro, 1971. (Winner of the Premio Nacional de Novela "Erich Guttentag.")

Short Story Collections

Naufragio. 2d ed. La Paz: Librería Editorial Juventud, 1977.

Escrito. Quito: Printer Graphic, 1994. (Poetry and short stories)

Poetry

Nadir. La Paz: Empresa Editora "Universo," 1950.

Del mar y la ceniza. Alegatos. Antología. La Paz: Biblioteca Paceña, 1957.

Antología mínima. La Paz: Editorial El Siglo, 1968.

Almadía. 2d ed. La Paz: Librería Editorial Juventud, 1977.

Ecos. 2d ed. La Paz: Librería Editorial Juventud, 1977.

Poemar. 2d ed. La Paz: Librería Editorial Juventud, 1977.

El cántaro del angelito. La Paz: n.p., 1979. (Poetry for children)

Convocatorias. Ecuador: Artes Gráficas Señal Impreseñal, 1994.

Escrito. Quito: Printer Graphic, 1994. (Poetry and short stories)

Works Anthologized

"Peregrina." *Cuentistas paceños*. Ed. Raúl Botelho Gosálvez. La Paz: Ediciones Casa de la Cultura, 1988. 175–80.

"De como Milinco huyó de la escuela." *Antología del cuento boliviano*. Ed. Armando Soriano Badani. La Paz: Editorial Los Amigos del Libro, 1991. 119–22.

Works Translated into English

"Good Evening, Agatha." *Landscapes of a New Land: Short Fiction by Latin American Women*. Ed. Marjorie Agosín. Fredonia: White Pine Press, 1989. 27–30.

Other

Calendario folklórico del Departamento de La Paz. With Antonio González Bravo. La Paz: Dirección General de Cultura, 1956.

Poesía de Bolivia, de la época precolombina al modernismo. Selected and presented by Yolanda Bedregal. Buenos Aires: Editorial Universitaria de Buenos Aires, 1964. (This work includes more than three hundred authors)

Antología de la poesía boliviana. La Paz: Editorial Los Amigos del Libro, 1977. (Encyclopedia of Bolivian poetry from pre-republican and pre-colonial times)

Ayllú: El altiplano boliviano. Text by Yolanda Bedregal, photographs by Peter McFarren. La Paz: Museo Nacional de Etnografía y Folklore and Editorial Los Amigos del Libro, 1984.

WORKS ABOUT

Agosín, Marjorie. "Para un retrato de Yolanda Bedregal." *Revista Iberoamericana* 134 (Jan.–Mar. 1986): 267–70.

Weldon, Alice. "History, Ethnicity, and Gender in Bolivia: Emerging Feminist Novels by Contemporary Women." Ph.D. diss., University of Maryland, 1996.

Mónica Bravo

WORKS BY

Works Anthologized

"Dos alas para Dominga." *Cuentos premiados, segunda bienal del cuento ecuatoriano "Pablo Palacio."* Quito: CEDIC/Abrapalabra Editores, 1993. 77–85. (Awarded mention in the Segunda Bienal del Cuento Ecuatoriano "Pablo Palacio")

"De azul y púrpura." *Fruta mordida: Cuentos.* Ed. Chely Lima and León Alberto Serret. Quito: Ediciones Aché, 1994. 25–28.

"Dos alas para Dominga." *Fruta mordida.* 19–24.

"Por una vez luna." *Fruta mordida.* 28–34.

Erika Bruzonic

WORKS BY

Novels

El color de la memoria. La Paz: Editorial Don Bosco, 1989.

Short Story Collections

Ecos de guerra: Cuentos. La Paz: Editorial Don Bosco, 1987.

Cegados por la luz. La Paz: Editorial Don Bosco, 1992.

Historias inofensivas. Cochabamba: Ediciones Centro Simón I. Patiño, 1995. (Awarded first prize in the XXIV Concurso de Literatura "Franz Tamayo" in Bolivia)

WORKS ABOUT

Vila, Carlos Coello. "*El color de la memoria* de Erika Bruzonic en la línea de la narrativa universal contemporánea." *Presencia Literaria* [La Paz] 23 July 1989.

———. "*Cegados por la luz* de Erika Bruzonic." *Primera Plana* [La Paz] 13 Sept. 1992.

"Ericka [*sic*] Bruzonic: Reseña de *Historias inofensivas.*" *Los Tiempos* [La Paz] 19 Nov. 1995.

Aminta Buenaño

WORKS BY

Short Story Collections

La mansión de los sueños. Guayaquil: Editorial de la Universidad de Guayaquil, 1985.

La otra piel. Quito: Abrapalabra Editores, 1992.

Poetry

Cantos de amor y juventud. Guayaquil: Editorial Arquidiocesana Justicia y Paz, 1976.

Works Anthologized

"Mamá Isaura." *Antología veinte años Premio Jauja.* Valladolid, Spain: Editorial Caja España, 1980.

"Abuelo, ¿por esto no querías que sea flor?" *Antología básica del cuento ecuatoriano.* Ed. Eugenia Viteri. Quito: Editorial Voluntad, 1987. 559–62.

"Mamá Isaura." *Mujeres ecuatorianas en el relato.* (Colección mujer del Ecuador No. 16) Ed. Matilde Mora. Guayaquil: Editorial de la Universidad de Guayaquil, 1988.

"Alguien se escondió por ahí." *Primera bienal del cuento ecuatoriano "Pablo Palacio."* Quito: Editorial CEDIC, 1991. 27–49. (Awarded second prize in the Primera bienal del cuento ecuatoriano "Pablo Palacio" in Ecuador)

"El caballero del sol murió frente al mar una tarde cualquiera." *Antología de cuentos de escritores latinoamericanos.* Ed. Nouvelles D'ailleurs. Paris: Amiot-Lenganey, 1993.

"Abuelo, ¿por esto no querías que sea flor?" *I'Immaginazione, Revista Cultural Italiana* (Nov. 1993).

Gaby Cevasco

WORKS BY

Short Story Collections

Sombras y rumores. Lima: Casa Editora: F & F Artes Gráficas, 1990.

Historias de no amor. Forthcoming.

WORKS ABOUT

Núñez, Charo. "Pequeña muestra de literatura peruana actual escrita por mujeres." *Feminaria Literaria* 4 (1994): 12–21.

Giancarla de Quiroga

WORKS BY

Novels

La flor de "La Candelaria." Cochabamba: Los Amigos del Libro, 1990. (Awarded honorable mention in the XI Concurso de novela "Erich Guttentag" in Bolivia)

Short Story Collections

De angustias e ilusiones: Cuentos. Cochabamba: Editorial Serrano, 1989. (Awarded first prize in the 1989 Literature Competition of the Municipality of Cochabamba, Bolivia)

Short Stories

"Celebración." *Presencia Literaria* [La Paz] 15 June 1993. (Awarded first prize in the National Literary Competition of *Presencia* Newspaper)

Other

Los mundos de Los Deshabitados: Estudio de la novela de Marcelo Quiroga Santa Cruz. La Paz: Piedra Libre, 1980.

La discriminación de la mujer en los textos escolares de lectura. La Paz: UNICEF, 1995.

Elsa Dorado de Revilla Valenzuela

WORKS BY

Short Story Collections

Filón de ensueño. La Paz: Litografías e Imprentas Unidas, S.A., 1977.

Las bacterias no hacen huelgas. Oruro: Offset "Alea" Ltd., 1994.

Works Anthologized

"La lora." *Cuentistas bolivianos.* Oruro: Universidad Técnica de Oruro, 1968. 39–46.

"La vida prestada." *Narrativa minera boliviana.* Ed. René Pastor Poppe. La Paz: Ediciones Populares Camarlinghi, 1983. 118–23.

Other

La libertadora, Juana Azurduy de Padilla: Guerrillera de la independencia americana. La Paz: Impresa Gráfica Alianza, 1980.

Pilar Dughi

WORKS BY

Short Story Collections

Ave de la noche. Lima: Asociación Peruano Japonesa del Perú, Promoción Editorial Inca S.A., 1996.

La premeditación y el azar. Lima: Editorial Colmillo Blanco, 1989.

Works Anthologized

"Los días y las horas." *Nueva crónica: Cuento social peruano 1950–1990.* Ed. Roberto Reyes Tarazono. Lima: Colmillo Blanco, 1991. 211–19.

"La escena incompleta." *Antología Caretas, trece años de los mejores cuentos de las 1000 palabras.* Lima: Editorial Jaime Campodónico, 1995. 191–94.

Short Stories in Journals

"La imagen soñada." *Viva* (Feb.–Mar. 1987): 34–36.

"Uno de los trece." *Lienzo* (May 1987): 37–38.

"La escena incompleta." *Caretas* (Feb. 1988): 47–48.

"Londres." *El Comercio* [Lima] 22 Oct. 1989, Sunday supplement: 15.

"Uno de los trece." *La Moneda* 3.3 (1991): 57.

"Hambre." *Imaginario del Arte* 9 (1995): 52–54.

"Muerte de palomas." *Debate* 17.86 (1996): 63–67.

Other

Mujeres y salud, encuentro nacional. Lima: Centro de la Mujer "Flora Tristán," 1987.

María del Carmen Garcés

WORKS BY

Short Story Collections

Mírame a los ojos. Quito: Abrapalabra Editores, 1995.

Works Anthologized

"Un adiós inesperado." *Fruta mordida: Cuentos*. Ed. Chely Lima and León Alberto Serret. Quito: Ediciones Aché, 1994. 61–64.

"La lupa." *Fruta mordida*. 64–66.

"Premio de lotería." *Fruta mordida*. 66–70.

"Sé mis ojos." *Fruta mordida*. 71–76.

"Final de cuento." *Cuentos premiados, tercera bienal del cuento ecuatoriano "Pablo Palacio."* Quito: Centro de Difusión Cultural CEDIC, 1995. 89–105. (Awarded mention in the Tercera Bienal del Cuento Ecuatoriano "Pablo Palacio")

Other

Materiales sobre la guerrilla de Ñancahuazú: Diario de Pomba. Quito: Editorial El Mañana, 1986.

La campaña del Che en Bolivia (1967) a través de la prensa. Quito: Editorial El Mañana, 1987.

Antecedentes, preparativos y principales acciones de la guerrilla del Che en Bolivia: Diarios de Pombo, Rolando, Che, Baulio y Pacho. Quito: Editorial El Mañana, 1987.

WORKS ABOUT

"La utopía de publicar libros." *La Hora Cultural* [Quito] 8 Dec. 1990: 4–5.

Serret, León Alberto. "Algo sobre *Mírame a los ojos*." *La Hora Cultural* [Quito] 23 July 1995: 12.

"Dos libros con mirada de mujer." *Hoy* [Quito] 15 Aug. 1995: 5B.

"Una autora ecuatoriana trajo relatos verídicos." *El Sur* [Concepción, Argentina] 9 May 1996.

Carmen Luz Gorriti

WORKS BY

Works Anthologized

"El legado." *Memorias clandestinas: Cuentos*. Lima: Ediciones Flora Tristán, 1990. 77–81.

"Estirpe de mujer." *Historias de miércoles. Anillo de moebius, taller 1992–1994*. Lima: Editorial Fekigraph S.A., 1994.

Works Translated into English

"The Legacy." Trans. Kathy S. Leonard. *The Antigonish Review* 101 (1995): 113–16.

Other

Apuntes para una interpretación del movimiento de mujeres: Los comedores comunales y los comités del vaso de leche en Lima. Lima: Documento de Trabajo (Servicios Urbanos y Mujeres de Bajos Ingresos), 1989.

WORKS ABOUT

Herzog, Kristin. Finding Their Voice: Peruvian Women's Testimonies About War. Valley Forge: Trinity Press International, 1993. 36–43.

Bethzabé Guevara

WORKS BY

Short Story Collections

Cuéntame un cuentito. Lima: Derrana Magisterial, 1992.

Works Anthologized

"No me enseñó la señorita." Memorias clandestinas: Cuentos. Lima: Ediciones Flora Tristán, 1990. 127–36.

Works Translated into English

"'The Señorita Didn't Teach Me.'" With an introduction, notes, and bibliography. Trans. Kathy S. Leonard. Critical Matrix: The Princeton Journal of Women, Gender, and Culture 9.1 (1995): 107–20.

Marcela Gutiérrez

WORKS BY

Short Story Collections

Diario de campaña: Cuentos eróticos. La Paz: Ediciones del Ventarrón, 1994.

Poetry

Para matarte mejor. La Paz: Casa de la Cultura de La Paz, 1993.

Beatriz Kuramoto

WORKS BY

Short Story Collections

Juego de tiempos. With Amalia Estela Bringas Cruz. Santa Cruz: Editorial Pynda, 1992.

Works Anthologized

"La estrella." *Taller del cuento nuevo.* Ed. Jorge Suárez. Santa Cruz: Casa de la Cultura de Santa Cruz, 1986. 51–53.

"Escrúpulos." *Cuentario: Selección del cuento breve de Santa Cruz.* Ed. Gustavo Cárdenas et al. Santa Cruz: Fondo de Publicaciones Gilberto Molina Barbery, 1991. 48–49.

Beatriz Loayza Millán

WORKS BY

Short Stories

"El espejo." *Puerta Abierta* (literary supplement of the newspaper *Presencia*) 15 Sept. 1990. (Awarded the Premio "Givré" by the Fundación Givré in Buenos Aires, Argentina, 1990)

"La hija de la portera." *Puerta Abierta* [La Paz] 17 Oct. 1991: 3.

"Amazona." *Pegatina de aquí y de allá* 18.3 (1993): 3.

"Cantata a dos voces." *Pegatina de aquí y de allá* 18.3 (1993): 3.

"Viernes de soltera." *Pegatina de aquí y de allá* 20.3 (1993): 7.

Other

"Soledad, miedo, y muerte en la poesía de Oscar Cerruto." *El Adjetivo y las Arrugas* [La Paz] Oct. 1990, *Puerta Abierta*, literary supplement of *Presencia*: 8.

"El camino ha comenzado, terminó el viaje. A propósito de 'El príncipe idiota' de Dostoievsky." *El Adjetivo y las Arrugas* [La Paz] April 1991: 8.

"Panta Rhei." *El Adjetivo y las Arrugas* [La Paz] 24 Jan. 1991: 8.

"Gonzalo de Berceo: Vidas de Santos." *El Adjetivo y las Arrugas* [La Paz] 14 Feb. 1991: 8.

"Sobre 'Otoño' un cuento de Walter Montenegro." *El Adjetivo y las Arrugas* [La Paz] 23 May 1991: 8.

Catalina Lohmann

WORKS BY

Short Stories

"Línea roja." *Memorias clandestinas: Cuentos.* Lima: Ediciones Flora Tristán, 1990. 41–47. (Awarded honorable mention in the Primer Concurso de Cuentos "Magda Portal" in Peru)

"De agua y de tierra." *Concurso de Creación Literaria. Premio Asociación Peruano-Japonesa. I Concurso de Cuento 1991 "Catalina Lohmann De agua y de tierra y los cuentos finalistas del Primer Concurso de Cuento 1991."* Lima: Centro Cultural Peruano-Japonés, 1993. 11–22. (Awarded first prize in the I Concurso de Cuento 1991 de la Asociación Peruano-Japonesa in Peru)

"Al fin de la batalla." *Quehacer* [Lima] 86, 1993.

"En pos de aventurado sueño." *ABC* [Madrid, Spain] 1 Dec. 1994.

Other

"Dos mujeres, muchos caminos." *Quehacer* [Lima] 94, 1995.

WORKS ABOUT

Núñez, Charo. "Pequeña muestra de literatura peruana actual escrita por mujeres." *Feminaria Literaria* [Lima] 4, 1994. 12–21.

Nela Martínez

Nela Martínez has written an overwhelming number of articles, essays, poems, and stories throughout her life. However, many of these have been written for occasional publications or small, political journals with very limited circulation, and which have now disappeared. Furthermore, many of her works have been written under pseudonyms, since her writing has often been banned. Thus, much of Martínez's work has been lost, and she herself has never taken the time to organize or catalogue the works she has written and published. The bibliography presented here, therefore, is only a very limited list of her published work.

WORKS BY

Novels

Los guandos. Begun by Joaquín Gallegos Lara and finished after his death by Nela Martínez. Quito: Editorial el Conejo, 1982.

Short Stories

"La Machorra." *Altiplano: Revista de la Casa de la Cultura Ecuatoriana, Núcleo de Bolívar 8* (1967): 93–100.

Works Anthologized

"Cuentos de tortura No. 2." *Cuento contigo: Antología del cuento ecuatoriano*. Ed. Cecilia Ansaldo Briones. Guayaquil: Universidad Católica de Santiago de Guayaquil/Universidad Andina Simón Bolívar, Subsede Quito, 1993. 131–36.

Other

Cifuentes, Hugo. *Sendas del Ecuador*. Presentación, Nela Martínez. México: Fondo de Cultura Económica, 1988.

Works Translated into English

"La Machorra." "New Voices: Linguistic Aspects of Translation Theory and Application to the Works of Three Ecuadorian Women Writers." Susan E. Benner. Master's thesis, Iowa State University, 1994. 109–16.

Mónica Ortiz Salas

WORKS BY

Works Anthologized

"Mery Yagual (Secretaria)." *Primera Bienal del Cuento Ecuatoriano "Pablo Palacio" (Obras Premiadas)* Quito: Centro de Difusión Cultural, 1991. 53–73. (Awarded third prize in the short-story contest Segunda Bienal del Cuento Ecuatoriano "Pablo Palacio")

Works Translated into English

"Mery Yagual (Secretary)." Trans. Kathy S. Leonard. *Feminist Studies* 21.1 (spring 1995): 103–13.

Blanca Elena Paz

WORKS BY

Short Story Collections

Teorema: Cuentos. Santa Cruz: Editorial Litera Viva, 1995.

Works Anthologized

"Adela y Alberto." *Literatura desde la universidad*. Ed. Jorge Suárez. Santa Cruz: Editorial Universitario, n.d.

"La luz." *Taller del cuento nuevo*. Ed. Jorge Suárez. Santa Cruz: Editorial Casa de la Cultura, 1986. 175–76.

"Las tres lluvias." *Taller del cuento nuevo*. 179–80.

"Mi abuela." *Taller del cuento nuevo*. 189–92.

"Penelope." *Taller del cuento nuevo*. 177–178.

"Premonición." *Taller del cuento nuevo*. 181–84.

"Proyección." *Taller del cuento nuevo*. 193–95.

"Simetría." *Taller del cuento nuevo*. 185–88

Poetry

Poems in *Breve Poesía Cruceña. Tomo I*. Santa Cruz de la Sierra: n.p., 1990.

Laura Riesco

WORKS BY

Novels

El truco de los ojos. Lima: Editorial Milla Batres, 1978.

Ximena de dos caminos. Lima: Peisa, 1994. (Winner of the first prize for Latino narrative awarded by the Institute of Latin American Writers of New York, 1995)

Short Stories

"La feria de Jimena." *Extramares* 1.1 (1989): 131–43.

Works Translated into English

"Jimena's Fair." *Landscapes of a New Land.* Ed. Marjorie Agosín. Fredonia: White Pine Press, 1992. 135–48.

Other

"62: A Model Kit." *Masterplots II.* California: Salem Press, n.d. 1433–39.
"César Vallejo: Periodismo y lenguaje poético." *Hispanic Literatures: XI Annual Conference (1986), Periodismo y Literatura.* Ed. Juan Cruz Mendizábal. Bloomington: University of Indiana, 1986. 321–32.
"*La amortajada*: Experiencia y conocimiento." *Homenaje a María Luisa Bombal.* Ed. Marjorie Agosín, Elena Gascón Vera, and Joy Rengilian-Burge. New York: Bilingual Press, 1987. 212–22.
"La función del *genitivo* en *Poemas humanos* de César Vallejo." *Discurso literario* 4.2 (1987): 497–507.
"Testimonio." *Análisis: Cuadernos de investigación* 14 (1990): 115–19.
Prólogo to Alfredo Villanueva Collado's *La mujer que llevo dentro.* New York: Editorial Arcas, 1990. 9–12.
"Los músicos de Cahuachi: Crónica y delirio." *Socialismo y participación* (March 1992): 113–18.
"*El viudo Román* y *El secreto de Romelia*: Two Voyages in Time." *Mexico: The Artist is a Woman, Occasional Paper #19.* Providence, R.I.: Brown University, Watson Institute on International Studies, 1995. 55–63.

WORKS ABOUT

Arévalo, Javier. "Recuento literario del 94: Los que ocuparán un espacio en nuestro recuerdo." *El Comercio* [Lima] 8 Jan. 1995, Sunday supplement: 8.
Batalla, Carlos Z. "La mirada de Ximena." *La República* [Lima] 5 Mar. 1995, Sunday literary supplement: 27.
González Vigil, Ricardo. "Acontecimientos literarios de 1994." *El Comercio* [Lima] 6 Jan. 1995, Sunday supplement: A3.
———. "¿Boom de la novela peruana?" *El Comercio* [Lima] 2 Apr. 1995, Sunday supplement: 16.
———. "La gran novela de Laura Riesco." *La República* [Lima] 22 Jan. 1995, Sunday literary supplement: 11.
———. "1994: Las mejores publicaciones." *El Comercio* [Lima] 1 Jan. 1995, Sunday supplement: 7.
Lohmann, Catalina. "Dos mujeres, muchos caminos." *Quehacer* (Mar.–Apr. 1995): 96–99.
Martos, Marco. "El camino de Laura Riesco." *El Peruano, Book Section* [Lima] 3 Apr. 1995: 5.
Mendoza Echevarría, Diana. "Laura Riesco Malpartida, escritora." *Cosas* 22 May 1995: 78–79.

Pollarolo, Giovanna. "Una escritora que no se siente escritora." *Debate* Mar.–Apr. 1995: 72–75.
Rivera Martínez, Edgardo. "Un mundo de ternura, crueldad y poesía." *La República* [Lima] 14 Jan. 1995, Sunday literary supplement: 5.

Gladys Rossel Huicí

WORKS BY

Short Story Collections

Al ladrón se le olvidó la luna en la ventana: Cuentos y relatos. Lima: n.p., 1989.
¡Mala cosecha! ¡Mala cosecha!: Cuentos y relatos. Lima: Editora-Impresora Amarilis, 1992.
Entre calles y sueños: Relatos. San José, Costa Rica: Comisión Costarricense de Cooperación con la UNESCO, 1995.

Poetry

A través de mis ojos. Santo Domingo, Dominican Republic: n.p., 1992.

Works Anthologized

"Desde el balcón." *Memorias clandestinas: Cuentos*. Lima: Ediciones Flora Tristán, 1990. 119–23. (Awarded honorable mention in the Primer Concurso de Cuentos "Magda Portal" in Peru)
"El espejo." *La tentación de escribir*. Lima: Ediciones Flora Tristán, 1993. 44–48. (Awarded honorable mention in the II Concurso de Cuento "Magda Portal" in Peru)

WORKS ABOUT

Artavia, María Elena. "Cambia espinas por rosas: Gladys Rossel con su nuevo libro retrata la cruda realidad de los niños de la calle." *Perfil* [San José, Costa Rica] 289 (1995): 84.
Gamboa, Emilia Mora. "Cuatro niños entre calles y sueños." *La República* [San José, Costa Rica] 10 Mar. 1995.
Rossel, Karen. "Entre calles y sueños." *El Heraldo* (Aula Joven) [San José, Costa Rica] 20 Oct. 1995.

Fabiola Solís de King

WORKS BY

Short Story Collections

Al otro lado del muro. Quito: Publitécnica, 1978.
Mundo aparte y otros mundos. Quito: Editorial Publitécnica, 1983.
Cuando el tiempo se precipite en la neblina. Quito: Abrapalabra Editores, forthcoming.

Works Anthologized

"La condecoración." *Diez escritoras ecuatorianas y sus cuentos.* Ed. Michael Handelsman. Guayaquil: Casa de la Cultura Ecuatoriana, Núcleo del Guayas, 1982. 139–45.

"Todo un acontecimiento." *Diez escritoras ecuatorianas y sus cuentos.* Ed. Michael Handelsman. Guayaquil: Casa de la Cultura Ecuatoriana, Núcleo del Guayas, 1982. 131–38.

"El cajón del armario de la abuela." *Antología básica del cuento ecuatoriano.* Ed. Eugenia Viteri. Quito: Editorial Voluntad, 1987. 27–34.

"Castigo de Dios." *Cuento contigo: Antología del cuento ecuatoriano.* Ed. Cecilia Ansaldo Briones. Quito: Universidad Católica de Santiago de Guayaquil/Universidad Andina Simón Bolívar, Subsede Quito, 1993. 210–15.

Other

La sexualidad femenina en el Ecuador. With Gladys Moscoso. Quito: Editorial El Conejo, 1987.

Eugenia Viteri

WORKS BY

Novels

A noventa millas, solamente. Quito: Casa de la Cultura Ecuatoriana, 1969.

Las alcobas negras. Quito: Universidad del Ecuador, 1984.

Short Story Collections

El anillo y otros cuentos. Quito: Casa de la Cultura Ecuatoriana, 1955.

Doce cuentos. Quito: Casa de la Cultura Ecuatoriana, 1962.

Los zapatos y los sueños. Guayaquil: Casa de la Cultura Ecuatoriana, Núcleo del Guayas, 1977.

Cuentos escogidos. Quito: Casa dc la Cultura Ecuatoriana, 1988.

Theatre

"El mar trajo la flor." *Teatro ecuatoriano: Cuatro piezas en un acto.* Quito: Ministerio de Educación y Cultura, 1962.

Anthologies Edited

Antología básica del cuento ecuatoriano. Quito: Editorial Voluntad, 1987.

Works Anthologized

"Departamento de arriendo." *Diez escritoras ecuatorianas y sus cuentos.* Ed. Michael Handelsman. Guayaquil: Casa de la Cultura Ecuatoriana, Núcleo del Guayas, 1982. 149–53.

"Los hombres no mienten." *Diez escritoras ecuatorianas y sus cuentos.* Ed. Michael Handelsman. Guayaquil: Casa de la Cultura Ecuatoriana, Núcleo del Guayas, 1982. 154–57.

"Nuevas Lilianas." *Así en la tierra como en los sueños.* Ed. Mario Campaña Avilés. Quito: Editorial El Conejo, 1991. 77–79.

"El heredero." *Cuento contigo: Antología del cuento ecuatoriano.* Ed. Cecilia Ansaldo Briones. Guayaquil: Universidad Católica Santiago de Guayaquil/Universidad Andina Simón Bolívar, Subsede Quito, 1993. 176–80.

Works Translated into English

"The Ring." "New Voices: Linguistic Aspects of Translation Theory and Application to the Works of Three Ecuadorian Women Writers." Susan E. Benner. Master's thesis, Iowa State University, 1994. 96–100.

WORKS ABOUT

Engel, Paul. "Reseña de *A noventa millas, solamente* de Eugenia Viteri." *Letras del Ecuador* 155 (1973): 24.

Granda, Euler. "Reseña de *A noventa millas, solamente* de Eugenia Viteri." *Cuadernos del Guayas* 14 (1969): 33.

Handelsman, Michael. *Amazonas y artistas: Un estudio de la prosa de la mujer ecuatoriana.* Guayaquil: Casa de la Cultura Ecuatoriana Núcleo del Guayas, 1978.

"Reseña de *El anillo y otros cuentos* de Eugenia Viteri." *Letras del Ecuador* 103 (1955): 34.

Alicia Yánez Cossío

WORKS BY

Novels

Bruna, soroche y los tíos. Quito: Casa de la Cultura Ecuatoriana, 1972.

Yo vendo unos ojos negros. Quito: Casa de la Cultura Ecuatoriana, 1979.

Más allá de las islas. Quito: Editorial Don Bosco, 1980.

La cofradía del mullo del vestido de la virgen pipona. Quito: Editorial Planeta, 1985.

La casa del sano placer. Quito: Editorial Planeta, 1989.

El cristo feo. Quito: Abrapalabra Editores, 1995.

Short Story Collections

El beso y otras fricciones. Bogotá: Ediciones Paulinas, 1974.

Poetry

Luciolas. Quito: Imprenta Fray Jodoco Ricke, 1949.

De la sangre y el tiempo. Quito: Imprenta Fernández, 1964.

Poesía. Quito: Casa de la Cultura Ecuatoriana, 1974.

Children's Books

El viaje de la abuela. Bogotá: Editorial Colina, 1995.

Works Anthologized

"La iwm mil." *Diez escritoras ecuatorianas y sus cuentos*. Ed. Michael Handelsman. Guayaquil: Casa de la Cultura Ecuatoriana, Núcleo del Guayas, 1982. 166–71.

"Hansel y Gretel." *Diez escritoras ecuatorianas*. 161–65.

"Uno menos." *Antología básica del cuento ecuatoriano*. Ed. Eugenia Viteri. Quito: Editorial Voluntad, 1987. 294–300.

"Hansel y Gretal." *Mujeres ecuatorianas en el relato*. Ed. Matilde Mora. Guayaquil: Universidad de Guayaquil, 1988. 161–65.

"La niña fea." *Antología autores ecuatorianos*. Ed. Pedro Jorge Vera. Quito: Ediciones Indoamericanas, n.d.

"El beso." *Así en la tierra como en los sueños: Cuentos escogidos*. Ed. Mario Campaña Avila. Quito: Editorial El Conejo, 1991. 117–20.

Theatre

Hacía el Quito de ayer. Unpublished. Presented in Quito in 1951.

Works Translated into English

"Sabotage." *Contemporary Women Authors of Latin America: New Translations*. Ed. Doris Meyer and Margarite Fernández Olmos. Brooklyn: Brooklyn College Press, 1983. 250–53.

"The IWM 1000." *Short Stories by Latin American Women: The Magic and the Real*. Ed. Celia Correas de Zapata. Houston: Arte Público Press, 1990. 208–12.

"Sabotage." *Latin American Writers: Thirty Stories*. Ed. Gabriella Ibieta. New York: St. Martin's Press, 1993. 288–92.

"The Mayor's Wife." In "New Voices: Linguistic Aspects of Translation Theory and Application to the Works of Three Ecuadorian Women Writers," by Susan E. Benner. Master's thesis, Iowa State University, 1994. 101–8.

WORKS ABOUT

Angulo, María-Elena. "Ideologeme of 'mestizaje' and Search for Cultural Identity in *Bruna, soroche y los tíos* by Alicia Yánez Cossío." *Translating Latin America: Culture as Text*. Ed. William Luis and Julio Rodríguez-Luis. Binghamton: State University of New York at Binghamton, 1991. 205–13.

———. "'Realismo maravilloso' and Social Context in Five Modern Latin American Novels." *DAI* 50:10 (1990): 3243A.

Carrión de Fierro, Fanny. "La mujer ecuatoriana contemporánea en la realidad y en la ficcion." *Revista de la Universidad Católica* 9 (1975): 49.

Corrales, Manuel. "*Bruna, soroche y los tíos*: Un vértigo ancestral." *Mensajero* [Quito] June 1973: 17–18.

Engel, Paul. "Reseña de *Bruna, soroche y los tíos* de Alicia Yánez Cossío." *Letras del Ecuador* 155 (1973): 23.

García Toledo, Betty, and Myriam Arroyo Rodríguez. "Análisis literario sociológico costumbrista de la novela *La cofradía del mullo del vestido del la virgen pipona* de Alicia Yánez Cossío. Thesis, Universidad Central del Ecuador, 1995.

Gerdes, Dick. "An Embattled Society: Orality Versus Writing in Alicia Yánez Cossío's *La cofradía del mullo del vestido de la Virgen pipona*." *Latin American Literary Review* 18.36 (1990): 50–58.

Guevara, Darío. "Criollismo y folklore de *Bruna, soroche y los tíos*." *Letras del Ecuador* 155 (1973): 19.

Handelsman, Michael. *Amazonas y artistas: Un estudio de la mujer ecuatoriana*. Guayaquil: Casa de la Cultura Ecuatoriana, Núcleo del Guayas, 1978.

———. "*Bruna, soroche y los tíos*: An Ecuadorian Woman Writer's Contribution to Contemporary Feminist Fiction." *Revista de Estudios Hispánicos* 15.1 (1988): 144–45.

———. "En busca de una mujer nueva: Rebelión y resistencia en *Yo vendo unos ojos negros* de Alicia Yánez Cossío." *Incursiones en el mundo literario del Ecuador*. Guayaquil: Editorial Universidad de Guayaquil, 1987. 63–78.

Scott, Nina. "Alicia Yánez Cossío: Una perspectiva femenina sobre el pasado del Ecuador." *Discurso Literario: Revistas de Temas Hispánicos* 4 (1987): 623–30.

Vásquez, Martha J. "Las novelas de Alicia Yánez Cossío: La deconstrucción creadora y el discurso de resistencia." Ph.D. diss., Ohio State University, 1994.

Wolffsohn, Elisabeth. "Algunos aspectos del relato de Alicia Yánez Cossío." *Situación del relato ecuatoriano. Tomo II: Nueve Estudios*. Ed. Manuel Corrales Pascual. Quito: Edición de la Universidad Católica, 1977. 333–80.

Yépez Pazos, Felix. "Alicia Yánez Cossío. *Bruna, soroche y los tíos*." *Escritores contempóraneos del Ecuador*. Ed. Felix Yépez Pazos. Quito: Casa de la Cultura Ecuatoriana, 1975. 109–12.

Bibliography of Short Story Collections by or Including Women Authors from Bolivia, Ecuador, and Peru

Bolivia

Alancoa Fernández, Filomena. *Tiwulampin Wank'umpin Sarnaq'awipa (El zorro y el conejo).* La Paz: Biblioteca del Pueblo Aymara/IRPA, 1989. (Story #10, Bilingual Edition Aymara-Spanish)

Alemán de Uribe, Sonia. *El baúl de los recuerdos.* La Paz: Editorial Don Bosco, 1990.

Amelunge de Lavayén, Paquita. *Hilvando recuerdos.* Santa Cruz: Sociedad Cruceña de Autores, 1994.

Anaya de Urquidi, Mercedes. *Evocaciones de mi vida y de mi tierra.* Cochabamba: Editorial Canelas, 1965.

Andrade Salmón, Lupe. *La tía Eduviges y otras historias.* La Paz: La Vaca Sagrada, 1993.

Antelo Aguilar, Peggy. *Como veo La Paz, mi ciudad.* La Paz: Casa de la Cultura, 1982.

Aparicio y Aparicio, Luz. *Los duendes azules: Cuentos infantiles.* La Paz: Offset Millán Ltda., 1977. (Children's literature)

Aranzaes V. de Butrón, Emma. *Narraciones verídicas.* La Paz: Imprenta y Librería "Renovación," Ltda., 1986.

Arias Molina, Flora. *Aymar Warmin Ch'ama Tukuwipa (El sacrificio de la mujer ayamara).* La Paz: Biblioteca del Pueblo Aymara, IRPA, 1989. (Story #12, Bilingual Edition Aymara-Spanish)

Arnal Franck, Ximena. *Visiones de un espacio.* La Paz: Ediciones Piedra Libre, 1994.

Avendaño Siles, Dilma. *Pedrito.* Potosí: Universidad Boliviana "Tomás Frías," 1976. (Children's literature)

Ayllón, Virginia. *Búsquedas: Cuatro relatos y algunos versos.* La Paz: Artes Gráficos Potosí, 1996.

Barrios Castro, Arnaldo, et al., eds. *Cuentistas bolivianos: IV Concurso Nacional de Cuento, 1968.* Oruro: Editorial Universitaria, Universidad Técnica de Oruro, 1982.

Bass Werner de Ruiz, Zulema. *El lago de la equidadad.* Tarija: Ediciones Codetar-Unicef, 1989. (Children's literature)

———. *La mulita Clementina.* Tarija: Codetar, n.d. (Children's literature)

———. *Por los rastros del hombre.* Tarija: Ediciones Codetar-Unicef, 1982.

———. *Renacer de la tierra.* Tarija: Ediciones Codetar-Unicef, n.d. (Children's literature)

Bedregal, Yolanda. *Escrito.* Quito: Printer Graphic, 1994.

———. *Naufragio.* La Paz: Librería Editorial "Juventud," 1977.

Botelho Gosálvez, Raúl, ed. *Cuentistas paceños.* La Paz: Ediciones Casa de la Cultura, 1988.

Bringas Cruz, Amalia Estela, and Beatriz Kuramoto Medina. *Juego de tiempos.* Santa Cruz: Editorial Pynda, 1992.

Bruzonic, Erika D. *Cegados por la luz.* La Paz: Editorial "Don Bosco," 1992.

———. *Ecos de guerra.* La Paz: Editorial "Don Bosco," 1987.

———. *Historias inofensivas.* Cochabamba: Ediciones Centro Simón I Patiño, 1995.

Bruzzone de Bloch, Olga. *Tras la cortina de incienzo.* La Paz: Imp. Unidas, 1974.

Cáceres Romero, Adolfo, et al., eds. *Cuentistas bolivianos: III Concurso Nacional del Cuento, 1967.* Oruro: Editorial Universitaria, Universidad Técnica de Oruro, 1982.

Calvimontes de Rodríguez, Velia. *Abre la tapa y destapa un cuento.* Cochabamba: Honorable Municipalidad de Cochabamba Talleres Gráficos H & P, 1991. (Children's literature)

———. *Amigo de papel (diario de un adolescente).* Cochabamba: Colorgraf, 1995. (Children's literature)

———. *Babirusa te cuento de cómo . . . ?* Cochabamba: Colorgraf, 1995. (Children's literature)

———. *Babirusa y sus cuentos del Tawantinsuyu.* Cochabamba: Editora H & P, 1993. (Children's literature)

———. *El uniforme.* Cochabamba: Editores: Editora H & P, 1993.

———. *En la piel morena de Babirusa.* Cochabamba: Colorgraf, 1995. (Children's literature)

———. *Lágrimas y risas.* Cochabamba: Color Graf Rodríguez, 1995.

———. *La ronda de los niños.* Cochabamba: Editorial Vendilusiones, 1991. (Children's literature)

———. *Rinconcuentos.* Cochabamba: Talleres Gráficos Poligraf, 1988. (Children's literature)

———. *Y el mundo sigue girando. . . .* La Paz: Editora Talleres Gráficos Rocabado, 1975.

Cárdenas, Gustavo, et al., eds. *Cuentario: Selección del cuento breve de Santa Cruz:* Fondo de Publicaciones Gilberto Molina Barbery, 1991.

Cárdenas, Ruth. *Habla Francisco.* Florence: INTI, 1992. (Children's literature, bilingual Spanish-Italian)

Cardona Torrico, Alcira. *De paso por la tierra.* La Paz: Ediciones IPRA, 1971. (Children's literature)

———. *Tormenta en el Ande.* La Paz: Cuatro Cantos, 1967.

Casazola Mendoza, Matilde. *Estampas, meditaciones, cánticos: Prosa poética (1984–1989).* La Paz: Universidad Mayor de San Andrés, 1990.

Castellanos de Ríos, Ada, and René Benjamín Arrueta Suárez. *Cuentos.* Potosí: Universidad Boliviana Tomás Frías, Publicaciones de la División de Extensión Universitaria, 1976.

———. *Un viernes de Miguelito.* Potosí: Universidad Boliviana Tomás Frías, Publicaciones de la División de Extensión Universitaria, 1976.

Centro Cultural "Edmundo Camargo." *Antología de cuentos.* II Concurso Nacional. La Paz: Los Amigos del Libro, 1968.
Claros Claros, Gaby. *Kachi (Sal).* Cochabamba: Centro Pedagógico y Cultural Portales, 1982. (Children's literature)
Collazos Bascopé, Patricia. *Con la venda en los ojos.* La Paz: Alcaldía Municipal, 1992. (Pedagogical stories)
Charbonneau de Villagómez, Nicole. *Antología de autores cruceños desde el siglo XVII hasta nuestros días.* Santa Cruz: Casa de la Cultura, 1988.
Chávez Cuellar, Elba. *Patricia: La niña que se extravió.* La Paz: Los Amigos del Libro, 1980. (Children's literature)
Dávalos Arze, Gladys. *El gnomo del espejo.* La Paz: n.p., forthcoming. (Children's literature)
———. *La muela del diablo.* La Paz: n.p., 1989. (Children's literature)
de Quiroga, Giancarla. *De angustias e ilusiones.* Cochabamba: Alcaldía Municipal, Editorial Serrano, 1990.
Dorado de Revilla, Elsa. *Filón de ensueño.* La Paz: Litografías e Imprentas Unidas, S.A., 1977.
———. *Las bacterias no hacen huelgas.* Oruro: OFFSET "Alea" Ltda., 1994.
Estenssoro, María Virginia. *Cuentos y otras páginas: Obras completas IV.* La Paz: Editorial Los Amigos del Libro, 1988.
———. *El occiso.* La Paz: Editorial Los Amigos del Libro, 1976.
———. *Memorias de Villa Rosa.* La Paz: Editorial Los Amigos del Libro, 1976.
Fernández de Carrasco, Rosa. *Caracol.* La Paz: Impresora Editores CLIP, SRL, 1991. (Children's literature)
———. *Malvalushka: Cuentos para niños.* Bolivia: n.p., 1983. (Children's literature)
———. *Ticotín: Cuentos para niños.* Bolivia: n.p., 1983. (Children's literature)
Fernandois de Ballón. *Cartas a la vida.* La Paz: Editorial Los Amigos del Libro, 1992.
Flores, Mario, et al., eds. *Cuentistas cruceños.* Santa Cruz: Sociedad de Escritores y Artistas de Santa Cruz, 1974.
Forgnone, Ana María. *Entre el nido y el mar.* La Paz: Paulinas, 1990.
Garnica, Blanca, and Velia Calvimontes. *De la tierra y las preguntas.* Cochabamba: Colorgraf, Rodríguez, 1992.
Guevara Arze, Walter, et al., eds. *Antología de cuentos: Segundo Concurso Nacional.* Cochabamba: Los Amigos del Libro, 1968.
Gutiérrez Peñaloza, Marcela. *Diario de campaña: Cuentos eróticos.* La Paz: Ediciones del Ventarrón, 1994.
Gúzman Soriano, Rosalba, and Mary Fernández de Oquendo. *Cuentos de luciérnaga.* Cochabamba, 1982. (Children's literature)
———. *Los intrusos.* Cochabamba: Luciérnaga/UNICEF, 1982.
Juegos Florales Universitarios. *Concurso Nacional de Literatura Poemario, Poesía, Cuento.* La Paz: FUL-UMSA, 1985.

Justiniano de Egüez, Angela María. *Lo que el tiempo no se lleva*. Santa Cruz: Casa de la Cultura, 1991.

Lazzo, Consuelo. *Los jóvenes de 60 años y otros cuentos*. Lima: Dugrafis, 1985.

Lijerón Alberdi, Hugo, and Ricardo Pastor Poppe, eds. *Cuentos bolivianos contemporáneos: Antología*. La Paz: Editorial Camarlinghi, 1975.

Limpias Chávez, Viviana. *La espera: Oliendo a jasmín*. Santa Cruz: Editora El País, 1987.

Maldonado, Clara Isabel. *Arcoiris de sueños (Retazos de una vida): Rainbow of Dreams (Patchwork of a Life)*. Sydney: Cervantes Publishing, 1993.

Melgar de Ipiña, Rosa. *Lo sabía: 26 cuentos*. La Paz: Editorial Educacional, 1989.

———. *Micaela Villegas Virreina de Amat*. Sucre: Onda, 1977.

Monte Vega, Patricia B. *Cantando sobre el . . . agua*. La Paz: Papiro, 1987. (Children's literature)

Mundy, Hilda. *Cosa de fondo: Impresiones de la guerra del Chaco y otros escritos*. La Paz: Ediciones Huayna Potosí, 1989.

Murillo, Maru, Graziella de Nogales, Liliana Pellegrini, and Lupe Tejada. *Vértice y matices*. Santa Cruz de la Sierra: Editorial CUIMBAE, 1990.

Núñez de Durán, Olga, and Guillermina Jofre de Flores. *Ronda. Rondín. Rondón el libro más juguetón*. Cochabamba: Ediciones Puente, 1992. (Children's literature)

Oblitas Fernández, Edgar, ed. *El cuento en el oriente boliviano*. La Paz: Ediciones Populares Camarlinghi, 1980.

O'hara, Maricarmen. *Cuentos favoritos/Favorite Tales*. Ventura: Alegría Hispana Publications, 1987.

———. *Cuentos para todos/Tales for Everybody*. Ventura: Alegría Hispana Publications, 1994.

———. *Fantasía bilingüe/Bilingual Fantasy*. Ventura: Alegría Hispana Publications, 1987.

Parada de Brown, Lydia. *Pasajes nocturnos*. Cochabamba: Talleres Gráficos "Rocabado," 1979.

———. *Veintidós y un juez*. La Paz: Papiro, 1989.

Paredes Candia, Antonio, ed. *Las mejores tradiciones y leyendas de Bolivia*. La Paz: Ediciones Puerta del Sol, 1973.

Pastor Poppe, René, ed. *Narrativa minera boliviana*. La Paz: Ediciones Populares Camarlinghi, 1983.

Paz, Blanca Elena. *Teorema: Cuentos*. Santa Cruz: Editorial Litera Viva, 1995.

Peña de Rodríguez, Martha. *Hoy, mañana . . . y siempre*. Santa Cruz: Sociedad Cruceña de Escritores, 1994.

———. *Tengo prisa*. Santa Cruz: Casa de la Cultura, 1989.

Phoenix Finardi, María. *La cebra cuadriculada*. La Paz: Camarlinghi, 1976. (Children's literature)

Quiroga de Urquieta, Rosario. *De la palabra a las alas*. Cochabamba: Ediciones Vialva, 1993. (Children's literature)

———. *En el tapial*. Cochabamba: Ediciones Vialva, 1994. (Children's literature)

———. *Gira sol azul*. Cochabamba: Ediciones Vialva, 1994. (Children's literature)

Quiroga Saavedra, María Celia. *Mis primeras fantasías*. La Paz: Los Amigos del Libro, 1979.

———. *Sigamos soñando*. La Paz: Los Amigos del Libro, 1979. (Children's literature)

Rodrigo, Saturnino, ed. *Antología de cuentistas bolivianos contemporáneos*. Buenos Aires: Editorial Sopena, 1942.

Rúa Heredia, Cecilia. *El árbol quemado*. Santa Cruz: Editora El País, 1987. (Children's literature)

Sánchez de Hoss, Bertha, et al. *Estos cuatro*. Cochabamba: Vientos Nuevos, 1976.

Schulze Arana, Beatriz. *Luces mágicas*. La Paz: Juventud, 1987. (Children's literature)

———, ed. *Semillero de luces: Antología boliviana: Verso y prosa para niños*. La Paz: Producciones Cima, 1981. (Children's literature)

Sefchovich, Sara, ed. *Mujeres en espejo I: Narradoras latinoamericanas, siglo XX*. Mexico: Folios Ediciones, S.A., 1983.

Selum Yabeta, Roxana. *D-efectos especiales: Cuentos eróticos*. La Paz: Editorial Acción, 1994.

Soriano Badani, Armando, ed. *Antología del cuento boliviano*. La Paz: Editorial Los Amigos del Libro, 1975.

———. *El cuento boliviano, 1900–1937*. Buenos Aires: Editorial Universitaria de Buenos Aires, 1964.

———. *El cuento boliviano, 1938–1967*. La Paz: Universidad Mayor de San Andrés, Facultad de Filosofía y Letras, Centro de Estudiantes, 1969.

Suárez, Jorge, ed. *Taller del cuento nuevo*. Santa Cruz: Casa de la Cultura, 1986.

Talarico, Gigia. *Comiendo estrellas*. Santa Cruz: Punto y Coma Producciones, 1987. (Children's literature)

———. *El caracol gigante y otros cuentos*. Santiago de Chile: n.p., 1990. (Children's literature)

———. *Los tres deseos*. La Paz: Alcaldía Municipal, 1993. (Children's literature)

Teixidó, Raúl, et al. *Antología de cuentos: Primer Concurso Nacional auspiciado por el Centro Cultural Edmundo Camargo, 1965*. Cochabamba: Imprenta Universitaria, 1966.

Torrico, Alayza Consuelo. *Kitula*. La Paz: Comité de Literatura Infantil, Juvenil, Filial La Paz, 1979. (Children's literature)

Unión Nacional de Poetas y Escritores de Cochabamba. *Primera antología: Prosa*. Cochabamba: Unión Nacional de Poetas y Escritores, 1994.

Universidad Autónoma "Gabriel René Moreno." *Literatura desde la universidad*. Bolivia: Editorial Universitaria, n.d.

Universidad Boliviana "Tomás Frías." *Cuentos*. Potosí: Publicaciones de la División de Extensión Universitaria, 1976.

———. *Cuentos premiados*. Potosí: Universidad Boliviana "Tomás Frías," 1978.

Universidad Técnica de Oruro. *Cuentistas bolivianos*. Oruro: Departamento de Prensa y Difusión de la Universidad Técnica de Oruro, 1968.

———. *Poetas y cuentistas bolivianos*. Oruro: Editorial Universitaria, 1984.

Urquidi de Miranda, María Teresa. *Cuentos de la abuela.* Oruro: Lilial, 1980. (Children's literature)

Vallejo de Bolívar, Gaby, and Ximema Claure. *Detrás de los sueños.* Cochabamba: Ediciones Puente, 1990. (Children's literature)

Vargas, Manuel. *Antología del cuento boliviano moderno.* La Paz: Editorial Acción, 1995.

Von Borries, Edith. *En un atardecer violeta: Poemas y cuentos.* La Paz: Editorial e Imprenta Gramma Impresión, 1988.

Zamora, Raquel. *Zoo historias: Premio único en el género de cuento para niños del XIX Concurso Anual de Literatura "Franz Tamayo" de 1989.* La Paz: Alcaldía Municipal, 1991. (Children's literature)

Zamora de Chalup, Elena, Bertha Hoss de Sánchez, and Virginia Samos de Molina. *Ecos de Chuquisaca.* Sucre: Proyecto Ciudad Universitaria, 1988.

Zamudio, Adela. *Cuentos breves.* Oruro: Ediciones Camarlinghi, 1971.

———. *Noche de fiesta.* La Paz: Ediciones ISLA, 1983.

———. *Rendón y Rondín: Cuento.* La Paz: Ediciones ISLA, 1970.

Ecuador

Acevedo Vega, Carmen. *Perfiles humanos: Relatos magros.* Quito: Editorial Casa de la Cultura Ecuatoriana, 1987.

Aguilar, Manuel et al., eds. *Cuentos de América Latina.* Quito: Ministerio de Educación y Cultura, 1986.

Almeida V., Mónica Agusta. *Contando cuentos.* Quito: Ministerio de la Educación, Subsecretaria de Cultura, 1980.

Alvarez Dávila, Nadya. *En un jardín encantado: Cuentos y poemas infantiles.* Quito: Casa de la Cultura Ecuatoriana, 1982. (Children's literature)

Andrade, Carolina, ed. *El libro de los abuelos.* Guayaquil: Casa de la Cultura Ecuatoriana, Núcleo de Guayas, 1990.

Ansaldo Briones, Cecilia. *Cuento contigo: Antología del cuento ecuatoriano.* Guayaquil: Universidad Católica de Santiago de Guayaquil/Universidad Andina Simón Bolívar, Subsede Quito, 1993.

Arizaga Andrade, Jorge, ed. *Palabra viviente: Libro del Taller de Literatura de Esperpentos del Departamento de Difusión Cultural del Banco Central en Cuenca.* Cuenca: Banco Central del Ecuador, 1989.

Bahamonde, Ana María. *Alicia y otros espejos.* Quito: Casa de la Cultura Ecuatoriana, 1989.

Barrera, Eulalia, and Inés Barrera, eds. *Los mejores cuentos ecuatorianos.* Quito: Empresa Editora "El Comercio," 1948.

———. *Tradiciones y leyendas del Ecuador.* Biblioteca Ecuatoriana de Ultimas Noticias. Quito: Empresa Editora "El Comercio," 1947.

Borja, Luz Elisa. *Páginas escogidas.* Ríobamba: Editorial Pedagógica "Freire," n.d.
Buenaño Rugel, Aminta. *La mansión de los sueños: Cuentos.* Quito: Abrapalabra Editores, 1985.
———. *La otra piel: Cuentos.* Quito: Abrapalabra Editores, 1992.
Calderón Chico, Carlos, ed. *Nuevos cuentistas del Ecuador.* Guayaquil: Casa de la Cultura Ecuatoriana, Núcleo del Guayas, 1975.
Campana Aviles, Mario, ed. *Así en la tierra como en los sueños.* Quito: Editorial El Conejo, 1991.
Carrión, Benjamín, ed. *El nuevo relato ecuatoriano: Crítica y antología.* Quito: Editorial Casa de la Cultura Ecuatoriana, 1958.
Castro, Zoila María. *En el norte está "El Dorado."* Guayaquil: Editorial Casa de la Cultura Ecuatoriana, Núcleo de Guayas, 1981.
———. *Urbe.* Guayaquil: Publicaciones del Grupo Madrugada, 1949.
Comité Ecuatoriano de Cooperación con la Comisión Interamericana de Mujeres. *Antología de la literatura femenina: Doce escritoras ecuatorianas.* Quito: CECIM, 1988.
Coryle, Mary. *Gleba.* Cuenca: Editorial Amazonas, 1955.
———. *Mundo pequeño.* Cuenca: Núcleo de Azuay de la Casa de la Cultura Ecuatoriana, 1978.
Centro de Difusión Cultural (CEDIC). *Cuentos premiados: Segunda bienal del cuento ecuatoriano "Pablo Palacio."* Quito: Abrapalabra Editores, 1993.
———. *Cuentos premiados: Tercerca bienal del cuento ecuatoriano "Pablo Palacio."* Quito: Centro de Difusión CEDIC, 1995.
———. *Primera bienal del cuento ecuatoriano "Pablo Palacio": Obras premiadas.* Quito: Editorial "Voluntad," 1991.
Crespo de Pozo, María Rosa, ed. *Selección del cuento cuencano.* Cuenca: Casa de la Cultura Ecuatoriana, Núcleo de Azuay, 1979.
Crespo de Salvador, Teresa. *Baúl de tesoros: Nueva antología de literatura infantil.* Quito: Corporación Editora Nacional, Casa de la Cultura Ecuatoriana: Editorial El Conejo, 1991. (Children's literature)
———. *Pepe Golondrina y otros cuentos.* Cuenca: Ediciones del Departamento de Extensión Cultural, 1969.
Chávez, Alfredo, ed. *Antología de cuentos esmeraldeños.* Quito: Editorial Casa de la Cultura Ecuatoriana, 1960.
D'ailleurs, Nouvelles, ed. *Antología de cuentos de escritores latinoamericanos.* Paris: Amiot-Lenganey, 1993.
Donoso Pareja, Miguel, ed. *Libro de posta: La narrativa actual en el Ecuador.* Quito: Editorial El Conejo, 1983.
Estupiñán Bass, Nelson, ed. *Antología de cuentos esmeraldeños.* Quito: Editorial Casa de la Cultura Ecuatoriana, 1960.
Galarza Zavala, Aída. *Cuatro cuentos.* Cuenca: Municipalidad de Cuenca, 1982.
Garcés, María del Carmen. *Mírame a los ojos.* Quito: Abrapalabra Editores, 1995.

Gutiérrez, Teresa, et al. *Paralelo cero: Narrativa joven del Ecuador.* Mexico D.F.: Ediciones de la Revista *Punto de Partida*, 1983.

Handelsman, Michael H., ed. *Diez escritoras ecuatorianas y sus cuentos.* Quito: Casa de la Cultura Ecuatoriana, 1982.

Holst, Gilda. *Más sin nombre que nunca.* Quito: Casa de la Cultura Ecuatoriana, Núcleo del Guayas, 1989.

———. *Turba de signos.* Quito: Abrapalabra Editores, 1995.

Iza, Ana María. *La casa de Tía Berta.* Quito: Editorial Casa de la Cultura Ecuatoriana, 1974. (Novella)

Izquierdo, Isabel. *Confesiones de un pie y otros cuentos.* Quito: Editorial Técnica Moderna, 1983.

———. *Vivos, muertos, marcianos y otros cuentos.* Quito: Editorial Técnica Moderna, 1986.

Larrea Borja, Piedad. *Oníricos y cuentostorias.* Quito: Editorial Casa de la Cultura Ecuatoriana, 1990.

Lima, Chely, and León Alberto Serret, eds. *Fruta mordida: Cuentos.* Quito: Ediciones Aché, 1994.

López, Flavio, et al. *El café literario.* Quito: Casa de la Cultura Ecuatoriana "Benjamín Carrión," Núcleo de Tungurahua, 1980.

Luna, Violeta. *El pañolón de la abuela: Testimonio.* Quito: Editorial Casa de la Cultura Ecuatoriana "Benjamín Carrión," 1995.

———. *Los pasos amarillos.* Quito: Casa de la Cultura Ecuatoriana, 1969.

Maldonado, Lucrecia. *No es el amor quien muere.* Quito: Abrapalabra Editores, 1994.

Miraglia, Liliana. *La vida que parece.* Guayaquil: Casa de la Cultura Ecuatoriana, Núcleo del Guayas, Banco Central del Ecuador, 1989.

Miranda de Stornaiolo, Anna. *Risas y lágrimas: Prosa y poesías.* Quito: Editorial Cultura de la UNP, 1982.

Mora, Matilde, ed. *Mujeres ecuatorianas en el relato.* Guayaquil: Departamento de Publicaciones, Facultad de Ciencias Económicas, Universidad de Guayaquil, 1988.

Mora Ortega, Jorge, and Arturo Armijos Ayala, eds. *Selección de cuentistas lojanos.* Loja: Casa de la Cultura Ecuatoriana, 1979.

Mujica, Elisa. *Angela y el diablo: Cuentos.* Madrid: Aguilar, 1953.

Muñoz, Gladys. *Ritual del medio pelo.* Quito: Abrapalabra Editores, 1995.

Ortega, Julio, ed. *El muro y el intemperie: El nuevo cuento latinoamericano.* Hanover: Ediciones del Norte, 1989.

Paz y Miño Cepeda, María Eugenia. *El uso de la nada.* Quito: Abrapalabra Editores, 1992.

———. *Golpe a golpe: Cuentos.* Quito: Editorial Universitaria, 1986.

———. *Siempre nunca: Cuentos.* Quito: E. P. Ediciones, 1980.

Peñaherrera, Ruth. *Detrás de una silueta oscura.* Quito: Abrapalabra Editores, 1995.

Pérez de Oleas Zambrano, Laura. *Historias, leyendas, y tradiciones ecuatorianas.* Quito: Editorial Casa de la Cultura Ecuatoriana, 1962.

Rodríguez, Ruth Patricia. *Al filo de Clepsidra*. Quito: Buho Editor, 1995.

———. *Algo más que un sueño*. Loja: Universidad Nacional de Loja, 1980. (Children's literature)

———. *Desde el barro azul*. Loja: Casa de la Cultura Ecuatoriana Benjamín Carrión, Núcleo de Loja, 1988. (Children's literature)

Rodríguez Castelo, Hernán, ed. *Cuento ecuatoriano contemporáneo*. Clásicos Ariel, 45–46. Guayaquil: Publicaciones Educativas Ariel, 1971.

Rumazo, Lupe. *Sílabas de la tierra*. Madrid: Ediciones Edime, 1968.

Santa Cruz, Adriana, and Viviana Erazo, eds. *Antología Fempress: El cuento feminista latinoamericano*. Santiago: Fempress, 1988.

Santillán Flor, Elsy. *De mariposas, espejos, y sueños*. Quito: Editorial GRAFICSA S.A., 1987.

Santos, Livina. *Una noche frente al espejo*. Guayaquil: Casa de la Cultura Ecuatoriana, Núcleo del Guayas, Banco Central del Ecuador, 1989.

Sefchovich, Sara, ed. *Mujeres en espejo I: Narradoras latinoamericanas, siglo XX*. Mexico: Folios Ediciones, S.A., 1983.

Selección del nuevo cuento cuencano. Cuenca: Núcleo de Azuay de la Casa de la Cultura Ecuatoriana, 1979.

Solís de King, Fabiola. *Al otro lado del muro*. Quito: Publitécnica, 1978.

———. *Cuando el tiempo se precipite en la neblina*. Quito: Abrapalabra Editores, forthcoming.

———. *Mundo aparte y otros mundos*. Quito: Editorial Publitécnica, 1983.

Taller Literario del Colegio Alemán Humboldt de Guayaquil. *Palabra de joven*. Guayaquil: Colegio Alemán Humboldt, 1986.

Tinajero Martínez de Allen, Eugenia. *Leyendas indígenas*. Ambato: Imprenta de Educación, 1954.

Vanegas Cobeña, Sara. *Luciérnaga y otros textos*. Cuenca: Universidad de Cuenca, 1982.

Vela de Manzano, Carmen. *El río que suena*. Guayaquil: Editorial Manzano de Oro, 1988.

Vera, Pedro Jorge, ed. *Antología autores ecuatorianos*. Quito: Ediciones Indoamericanas, n.d.

Vintimilla, Marcela. *Cualquier cosa me invento para ver*. Guayaquil: Casa de la Cultura Ecuatoriana, Núcleo del Guayas, Banco Central del Ecuador, 1989.

Viteri, Eugenia, ed. *Antología básica del cuento ecuatoriano*. Quito: Editorial Voluntad, 1987.

Viteri, Eugenia. *Cuentos escogidos*. Quito: Editorial Casa de la Cultura Ecuatoriana, 1983.

———. *Doce cuentos*. Quito: Editorial Casa de la Cultura Ecuatoriana, 1962.

———. *El anillo y otros cuentos*. Quito: Casa de la Cultura Ecuatoriana, 1955.

———. *Los zapatos y los sueños*. Guayaquil: Casa de la Cultura Ecuatoriana, Núcleo del Guayas, 1977.

Yáñez Cossío, Alicia. *El beso y otras fricciones*. Bogotá: Ediciones Paulinas, 1975.

Yépez Pazos, Felix, ed. *Escritores contemporáneos del Ecuador*. Quito: Casa de la Cultura Ecuatoriana, 1977.

Peru

Adolph, José B., ed. *Cuentistas peruanos de hoy*. Lima: Instituto Goethe, 1985.

Balta, Aída. *Tiempo de ópera*. Lima: Signo Tres/Editores de Julio Arévalo Piedra, 1996.

Barrenechea Vinatea, Ramón, ed. *Crónicas sabrosas de la vieja Lima*. Lima: Ediciones Peisa, 1969–70.

Bazán, Armando, ed. *Antología del cuento peruano*. Santiago: Zig-Zag, 1942.

Beleván, Harry, ed. *Antología del cuento fantástico peruano*. Lima: Universidad Nacional Mayor de San Marco, Dirección Universitaria de Biblioteca y Publicaciones, 1977.

Bolívar Vélez, Ricardo, ed. *Clamor de justicia: Concurso internacional de cuento breve en castellano sobre derechos humanos*. Paris: Ediciones Ricardo Bolívar Vélez, 1988.

Caretas. "Trece años de los mejores cuentos de las 1000 palabras." Lima: Editorial Jaime Campodónico, 1995.

Carillo, Francisco, ed. *Cuento peruano* (1904–1966) Lima: Ediciones de la Biblioteca Universitaria, 1966.

Carvallo de Núñez, Carlota. *Cuentos de Navidad*. Lima: Ediciones Peisa, 1970. (Children's literature)

———. *Cuentos fantásticos*. Lima: Editorial Universo, 1969.

———. *El arbolito y otros cuentos*. Lima: Biblioteca de la Literatura Infantil, 1961. (Children's literature)

———. *El pájaro niño y otros cuentos*. Lima: J. Mejía Baca, Editorial Nuevos Rumbos, 1958. (Children's literature)

———. *Rutsi: El pequeño alucinado*. Lima: Ediciones de la Dirección de Educación Artística y Extensión Cultural, 1947. (Children's literature)

Casa de la Cultura de Arequipa. *Cuentos*. Arequipa: Ediciones de la Casa de la Cultura, 1964.

Castillo, Rocío, et al. *Cuentan las mujeres*. Lima: Instituto Goethe, 1986.

Cevasco, Gaby. *Sombras y rumores*. Lima: Casa Editora F & F Gráficas, 1990.

Collao Talavera, Jaime, et al. *Cuentos*. Arequipa: Ediciones de la Casa de la Cultura, 1964.

Colmenares de Fiocco, Delia. *Cuentos peruanos*. Lima: n.p., n.d.

Costa, Liliana. *Primer acto*. Lima: Colección del Sol Blanco, 1993.

Departamento de Relaciones Públicas de Petroperú, S.A. *María Nieves y los cuentos ganadores del premio Copé de cuento 1992*. Lima: Ediciones Copé, 1992.

Dughi, Pilar. *Ave de la Noche*. Lima: Asociación Peruano Japonesa del Perú, Promoción Editorial Inca S.A., 1996.

———. *La premeditación y el azar*. Lima: Editorial Colmillo Blanco, 1989.

Embajada Cultural Peruano. *Cuentos peruanos: Antología completa y actualizada del cuento en el Peru*. Argentina: Embajada Cultural Peruana, 1957.

Escobar, Alberto, ed. *La narración en el Perú*. Lima: Librería-Editorial Juan Mejía Baca, 1960.

Flora Tristán, Centro de la Mujer Peruana. *La tentación de escribir: Segundo concurso de cuento "Magda Portal."* Lima: Ediciones Magda Portal, 1993.

———. *Memorias clandestinas: Primer concurso de cuento "Magda Portal."* Lima: Ediciones Flora Tristán, 1990.

Flores, Angel, ed. *Narrativa hispanoamericana, 1816–1981, historia y antología 4: La generación de 1940–1969.* Mexico D.F.: Siglo Veintiuno Editores, 1981.

Flores Scaramutti de Naveda, Carlota. *Algún día: Algún lugar.* Ayacucho: Universidad San Cristóbal de Huamanga, 1980. (Children's literature)

———. *Decires: Relatos populares para niños.* Ayacucho: Universidad San Cristóbal de Huamanga, 1980. (Children's literature)

———. *Esta tierra que gira entre cometas.* Ayacucho: Universidad de Haumanga, 1980. (Children's literature)

Fox, Lucía. *Constelación: Cuentos.* East Lansing, Mich.: Shamballa Publications, 1978.

———. *Un cierto lagar . . . cuentos.* Lima: Editorial Incorporada al Colegio Salesiano, 1980.

Frisancho, Samuel, ed. *Antología del cuento puneño.* Puno: Editorial "Los Andes," 1978.

Gálvez, Lola. *Once cuentos de amor y fantasía.* Lima: Imprenta del Ministerio de guerra, 1972.

Ganoza, Ana María. *De sapos y otras historias.* Trujillo: Editorial Libertad E. I. R. L., 1995.

González Vigil, Ricardo, ed. *El cuento peruano, 1920–1941.* Lima: Ediciones COPE, 1991.

———. *El cuento peruano, 1942–1958.* Lima: Ediciones COPE, 1991.

———. *El cuento peruano, 1959–1967.* Lima: Ediciones COPE, 1984.

———. *El cuento peruano, 1968–1974.* Lima: Ediciones COPE, 1984.

Guevara Gálvez, Bethsabé Nancy. *Cuéntame un cuentito.* Lima: Derrana Magisterial, 1992.

Gutarra Sinchitullo, Isabelita. *Ayacuchanitas de letritas juguetonas y bailarinas.* Huancayo: CONCYTEC, 1988. (Children's literature)

———. *Cuentos de alegría.* Huancayo: CONCTYEC, 1986. (Children's literature)

Halle, Rita. *Diez perlas del collar de la coya.* Lima: Empresa Editora Peruana, n.d.

Helfgott, Sarina, ed. *Cuento.* Lima: Ediciones Tierra Nueva, 1959.

Izquierdo Ríos, Francisco, ed. *La literatura infantil en el Perú.* Lima: Casa de la Cultura del Perú, 1969.

Jaramillo, Ana Lucía V. *Veinte cuentos (para la enseñanza del español en una clase de adultos).* Miami: Ediciones Universal, 1988.

Larrabue, Sara María. *La escoba en el escotillón.* Lima: Los Talleres Gráficos P.L. Villanueva S.A., 1957.

Mellet, Viviana. *La mujer alada.* Lima: Peisa, 1994.

Meneses L., Porfirio, ed. *Cuentos peruanos: Antología de medio siglo.* Lima: Gran Unidad Escolar Bartolomé Herrera, 1954.

Nieri de Dammert, Graciela. *Cuentos infantiles del Perú.* Lima: P.L. Villanueva, 1964. (Children's literature)

Niño de Guzmán, Guillermo, ed. *En el camino: Nuevos cuentistas peruanos.* Lima: Instituto Nacional de Cultura, 1986.

Núñez, Estuardo, ed. *Cuentos*. Biblioteca de Cultura Peruana Contempóranea, 10–11. Lima: Ediciones del Sol, 1963.

Ollé, Carmen. *Todo orgullo humea la noche*. Perú: Lluvia Editores, 1988.

Orrillo, Winston, ed. *Perú en el cuento: Antología de ayer y hoy*. 2da ed. Buenos Aires: Editorial Convergencia, 1976.

Ortega, Julio, ed. *El muro y el intemperie: El nuevo cuento latinoamericano*. Hanover: Ediciones del Norte, 1989.

Osterling, Yolanda H., *Aristillas: Cuentos y textos*. Lima: n.p., 1993.

Palma, Ricardo, et al., eds. *Cuentos peruanos: Antología completa actualizada del cuento en el Perú*. Buenos Aires: Embajada Cultural Peruana/Talleres Gráficos del Atlántico, 1957.

Pollarolo, Giovanna. *Entre mujeres solas*. Lima Ediciones El Santo Oficio, 1992.

Portugal Catacora, José, ed. *El cuento puñeno*. Puno: Tipografía e Imprenta Comercial, 1955.

Primer Concurso Nacional de Cuentos de AEBU: Catorce cuentos por nueve autores. Montevideo: Arca Editorial, S.R.C., 1989.

Puga de Losada, Amalia. *El jabón de hiel: Cuentos*. Lima: Impr. Santa María, 1949.

———. *Tragedia inédita*. Lima: Impr. Santa María, 1948.

Ramos, Angela. *Una vida sin tregua*. Lima: Consejo Nacional de Ciencia y Tecnología, Partido Comunista y Centro de la Mujer Peruana Flora Tristán, 1990.

Rey de Castro, Luís, Rosa Cerna Guardia, and Felipe Buendía. *El túnel, 42, Una rosa blanca, Viaje a Francia*. Lima: Cámara Peruana del Libro, 1973.

Reyes Tarazona, Roberto, ed. *Nueva crónica: Cuento social peruano, 1950–1990*. Lima: Editorial Colmillo Blanco, 1990.

Robles Viera, María Jesús. *Cuentos*. Lima: Marbella, 1990.

Rossel Huicí, Gladys. *Al ladrón se le olvidó la luna en la ventana*. Lima: Asociación Gráfica Educativa, Tarea, 1989.

———. *Entre calles y sueños: Relatos*. San José: n.p., 1990.

———. *¡Mala Cosecha! ¡Mala Cosecha!: Cuentos y relatos*. Lima: Editora Impresora Amarilis, 1992.

Ruíz Rosas, María Teresa. *El desván*. Arequipa: Colección la Campana Catalina, 1989.

Saito, Sergio, ed. *Concurso de Creación Literaria: Premio Asociación Peruano Japonesa: I Concurso de Cuento 1991 "Catalina Lohmann 'De agua y de tierra' y los cuentos finalistas del Primer Concurso de Cuento 1991."* Lima: Centro Cultural Peruano Japonés, 1992.

Sala, Mariella. *Desde el exilio*. Lima: Ediciones Muñeca Rota, 1988.

Sagástegui Heredia, Carla. *La vida íntima de Madeleine Monroe*. Lima: Prometeo Editores, 1994.

Santa Cruz, Adriana, and Viviana Erazo, eds. *Antología Fempress: El cuento feminista latinoamericano*. Santiago: Fempress, 1988.

Silva-Santisteban, Rocío. *Me perturbas*. Lima: Ediciones El Santo Oficio, 1994.

Silva Velásquez, Caridad, and Nora Erro-Orthman, eds. *Puerta abierta: La nueva escritora latinoamericana*. Mexico D.F: J. Moritz, 1986.

Sueldo Guevara, Rubén, ed. *Narradores cusqueños*. Cuzco: Primer Festival del Libro Sur-Peruano, 1958.

———. *Narradores cusqueños*. 3da ed. Lima: Imprenta Avanzada, 1984.

Taxa Cuadraz, Elías, ed. *Cuentos peruanos para niños*. Lima: Editorial Universo, 1968.

———. *La costa en la narración peruana: Antología del cuento*. Lima: Editorial Continental, 1968.

———. *La sierra en la narración peruana: Antología del cuento*. Lima: Editorial Continental, 1967.

Tellería Solari, María. *Mi amiga Paquina*. Lima: Impresiones y Publicidad S.S., 1966. (Children's literature)

———. *Mi amiga Paquina, Cristóbal y Luís Rodomiro*. Lima: CONCYTEC, 1988. (Children's literature)

Torres Morales, Emperatriz. *Conoce mis cuentos de tierra y cosmos*. Lima: Estudio de Relaciones Periodísticas Profesionales, 1984.

Vásquez Pereyra, Elsa. *Cuentos de mi tierra y apuntes para el folklore cajamarquino*. Cajamarca: Instituto Nacional de Cultura Departamental Cajamarca, 1987.

Compiled by Kathy S. Leonard

General Bibliographies for Bolivia, Ecuador, and Peru

Bolivia

Guttentag Tichauer, Werner. *Bio-bibliografía boliviana, 1962–1994.* La Paz: Editorial Los Amigos del Libro, 1962–1997.

Gúzman, Augusto. *Biografías de la literatura boliviana: Biografía, evaluación, bibliografía.* Cochabamba: Editorial Los Amigos del Libro, 1982.

———. *Poetas y escritores de Bolivia.* La Paz: Editorial Los Amigos del Libro, 1975.

Pastor Poppe, Ricardo. *Escritores bolivianos contemporáneos.* La Paz: Editorial Los Amigos del Libro, 1980.

Ecuador

Barriga López, Franklin, and Leonardo Barriga López. *Diccionario de la literatura ecuatoriana.* Guayaquil: Casa de la Cultura Ecuatoriana, 1980.

Jaramillo Buendía, Gladys, Raúl Pérez Torres, and Simón Zavala Guzmán, eds. *Indice de la narrativa ecuatoriana.* Quito: Editora Nacional, 1992.

Welch, Thomas L., and René Gutiérrez. *Bibliografía de la literatura ecuatoriana.* Washington, D.C.: Biblioteca Colón Organización de los Estados Americanos, 1989.

Peru

Foster, David William. *Peruvian Literature: A Bibliography of Secondary Sources.* Westport, Conn.: Greenwood Press, 1981.

Rodríguez Rea, Miguel Angel. *El Perú y su literatura: Guía bibliográfica.* Lima: Fondo Editorial de la Pontífica Universidad Católica del Perú, 1992.

Compiled by Kathy S. Leonard

About the Editors

Susan Benner is an instructor of English and Linguistics at Iowa State University and an Iowa Arts Fellow in the M. F. A. in translation program at the University of Iowa. She has lived in Quito, Ecuador and San José, Costa Rica and travels frequently to Latin America. She is currently working on translating several works by Ecuadorian and Uruguayan authors.

Kathy Leonard is an associate professor of Spanish and Hispanic Linguistics at Iowa State University. She has lived in Spain, Mexico, Argentina, and Bolivia. Two of her works are *Cruel Fictions, Cruel Realities: Short Stories by Latin American Women Writers* (Latin American Literary Review Press, 1997) and *Index to Translated Short Fiction by Latin American Women* (Greenwood Press, 1997).

Professor Leonard was a 1998 Fulbright-Hays Scholar in Bolivia.